W9-CIM-915

As one warrior's life ends, another begins.

A longship had pulled into view around the headland of the fjord. Its mast was bare; a sail would have been useless in the still air. The oars raised and lowered rhythmically, beating the surface of the water, dragging the ship forward.

People began running from the longhouse and outbuildings down to where Gunhild stood anxiously watching the ship, the switch in her hand now forgotten. Ubbe, the foreman of the estate, whose leg was crippled from an old wound, arrived at a halting run. He carried his sheathed sword in his hand.

"It's a warship, my lady," he announced, though that was plain for all to see, even at that distance, for the ship was long and narrow, with many oars. "They could be raiders. I'll have your horse saddled so you can ride to safety if need be. We have scarcely enough men left, even if we send for help to the village, to put up much of a fight."

Turning finally to face Gunhild, my mother spoke, a strange, triumphant look on her face. "There is no need to fear," she said, in a low voice that was little more than a whisper. "Yon ship does not bear raiders. It is his ship. The *Red Eagle*. All day I have felt it coming. They are bringing Hrorik home to die."

THE STRONGBOW SAGA,
BOOK ONE

VIKING
WARRIOR

DENMARK
A.D. 845

JUDSON ROBERTS

HARPER TEEN
AN IMPRINT OF HARPERCOLLINSPUBLISHERS

To my sisters,
Shelley and Trish,
who have always been there for me.

To Nick, Dennis, Laura, and Connor—
always dare to dream.

And most of all,
to Jeanette,
for everything.

HARPERTEEN IS AN IMPRINT OF HARPERCOLLINS PUBLISHERS.

THE STRONGBOW SAGA, BOOK ONE:
VIKING WARRIOR
TEXT COPYRIGHT © 2006 BY JUDSON ROBERTS
ALL RIGHTS RESERVED.
PRINTED IN THE UNITED STATES OF AMERICA.
NO PART OF THIS BOOK MAY BE USED OR REPRODUCED
IN ANY MANNER WHATSOEVER WITHOUT WRITTEN
PERMISSION EXCEPT IN THE CASE OF BRIEF QUOTATIONS
EMBODIED IN CRITICAL ARTICLES AND REVIEWS.
FOR INFORMATION ADDRESS HARPERCOLLINS CHILDREN'S BOOKS,
A DIVISION OF HARPERCOLLINS PUBLISHERS,
1350 AVENUE OF THE AMERICAS, NEW YORK, NY 10019.
WWW.HARPERTEEN.COM

LIBRARY OF CONGRESS CATALOGING-IN-PUBLICATION DATA
ROBERTS, JUDSON.
  VIKING WARRIOR / BY JUDSON ROBERTS.— 1ST ED.
    P. CM.— (THE STRONGBOW SAGA ; BK. 1)
  SUMMARY: DESPITE BEING THE SON OF A CHIEFTAIN AND A PRINCESS,
FOURTEEN-YEAR-OLD HALFDAN LIVES AS A SLAVE IN DENMARK IN A.D. 845
BUT THROUGH A TRAGIC BARGAIN HE GAINS HIS FREEDOM AND SETS OUT
TO CLAIM HIS BIRTHRIGHT.
  ISBN-10: 0-06-079999-4 — ISBN-13: 978-0-06-079999-1
  [1. SLAVES—FICTION. 2. FAMILY LIFE—FICTION. 3. DENMARK—FICTION.]
I. TITLE. II. SERIES.
PZ7.R54324VI 2006   2005028485
[FIC]—DC22   CIP
                                                            AC

TYPOGRAPHY BY ALISON DONALTY
❖
FIRST HARPERTEEN EDITION, 2007

CONTENTS

1

A SHIP

In one moment the Norns changed the pattern they were weaving in the fabric of my fate. It was a late afternoon, and I was working down by the shore beside the boathouses. All that day I'd been squaring logs into timbers, and my back and shoulders were weary from swinging the heavy broadaxe. I didn't mind the labor itself, for though I was but fourteen, I was as tall and strong as many grown men. And I enjoyed working with wood—since I was very young, my hands had possessed an unusual skill to create with both wood and metal, a gift that had saved me from much harder work in the fields. I minded, though, that always my efforts were for someone else. I minded that I lived only to serve the needs and obey the orders of others because they were the masters and I was a slave.

As it often did, my mind wandered as I worked and I dreamed I was free—and a warrior. I had no right to harbor such dreams, for I had lived my whole life as a slave and by rights was doomed to die as one. Yet dream I did, for my dreams allowed me to escape the reality of my life. With each stroke of the broadaxe, I imagined I fought against the English, standing shoulder to shoulder in a shield-wall with other warriors, other free men. Hrorik, the chieftain who owned me, and the man who had sired me, was in England raiding even now. Most of the free men of his estate and of the nearby village were there with him. If I was free, I told myself, I could be there, too.

My mother came down to the shore and sat, wordless, on the slope above where I worked. When her duties permitted, which was not often, she liked to come and quietly sit and observe me at my labors. It embarrassed me for her to watch me so. It made me feel like a child, and once I spoke angrily to her over it.

"I am sorry, Halfdan," she'd said. "It gives me pleasure to watch my son at work. But if it distresses you, I will stop." After that I said nothing more to her about it, for there's little enough that's pleasing in a thrall's life. I loved my mother, and would not take from her what scraps of pleasure she could find.

After a time, Gunhild, the wife of Hrorik, my father, stormed down from the longhouse and chided Mother.

"You have chores waiting," she snapped. "What are you doing here? Get back to the long-house."

My mother did not speak to Gunhild, or even acknowledge that she'd heard. I looked up from my work and saw Gunhild's face turning red with anger. Gunhild was an ill-tempered woman at the best of times. She hated my mother because of the lust that Hrorik felt for her, a mere thrall. Her bit-terness grew greater each night that her bed was cold and empty because Hrorik left her to lie with my mother. I do not believe Gunhild ever felt love for Hrorik. Theirs was a marriage built on position and wealth rather than feelings of the heart. But Gunhild was a proud woman. No doubt she felt humiliated that all who lived in Hrorik's great longhouse knew how often he fled her bed for that of a slave.

Gunhild stomped back up to the longhouse. I feared her wrath, especially since Hrorik, who sometimes would restrain her, was gone. I wished Mother would return to her chores and not pro-voke Gunhild so. But Mother sat silently on the

3

hillside, staring out toward the open sea.

A strange silence hung in the air; even the gulls had temporarily ceased their cries. Every breath of breeze died and the water in the fjord turned as flat and slick as the blade of a fine sword.

A short time later, Gunhild returned, hurrying with long strides, carrying in her hand a long thin branch that she'd trimmed as a switch. As she neared my mother, she raised it high above her head, but before she could strike, Mother stood and pointed out across the water.

"They come," she said.

A longship had pulled into view around the headland of the fjord. Its mast was bare; a sail would have been useless in the still air. The oars raised and lowered rhythmically, beating the surface of the water, dragging the ship forward.

People began running from the longhouse and outbuildings down to where Gunhild stood anxiously watching the ship, the switch in her hand now forgotten. Ubbe, the foreman of the estate, whose leg was crippled from an old wound, arrived at a halting run. He carried his sheathed sword in his hand.

"It's a warship, my lady," he announced, though that was plain for all to see, even at that distance, for the ship was long and narrow, with many oars. "They could be raiders. I'll have your horse saddled so you can ride to safety if need be. We have scarcely enough men left, even if we send for help to the village, to put up much of a fight."

Turning finally to face Gunhild, my mother spoke, a strange, triumphant look on her face. "There is no need to fear," she said, in a low voice that was little more than a whisper. "Yon ship does not bear raiders. It is his ship. The *Red Eagle*. All day I have felt it coming. They are bringing Hrorik home to die."

HRORIK'S DOOM

W hen she'd sailed boldly away from our shore only a few weeks earlier, the deck of the *Red Eagle* had been crowded with a crew of more than fifty warriors. Half were housecarls from Hrorik's estate, the rest men from the nearby village. All eagerly hoped to find fortune at the expense of the English. They'd laughed and boasted as they'd dipped their oars into the blue-green sea and backed the ship away from shore. How I had envied those who'd sailed away, and had longed to be a part of the *Red Eagle*'s crew.

The longship we watched struggling back home this day, though, did not cut a proud figure. Only nine of her sixteen pairs of oars were manned, and as the ship neared land, I could see many men sitting or lying on the deck, wrapped with blood-stained strips of cloth that declared their wounds like scarlet banners.

In the stern, Harald, Hrorik's son born of his first wife, Helge, manned the steering oar. As the *Red Eagle* neared the shoreline, he swung her sharply, so she slid sideways in the water the last few feet and bumped gently against the narrow wharf jutting out from the shore. It was well done. Normally the onlookers gathered on the shore would have cheered his skill. Today they stood silent, the fear in their hearts muting their voices.

A jumbled mound of capes and furs lay in front of the small, raised deck in the stern where Harald stood. As the mooring lines were tied off, the heap of covers parted briefly and I saw Hrorik's face, looking pale and haggard, peering from under a cloak. He stared listlessly toward the shore for a moment, then sank back into his coverings.

From the time of the *Red Eagle*'s first sighting until she made land, a crowd had gathered along the shore. Nearly everyone, free or slave, who lived on Hrorik's estate was there, and many had run from the farms of the nearby village. All wore concerned expressions, for word had spread quickly. The *Red Eagle* was not only back early, she was limping home.

Many on the shore had hailed anxious queries to the ship as she'd approached land and moored. None of the crew responded. Some questions, though, needed no answer. For those who searched excitedly to find their loved ones among the crew, the absence of looked-for faces spoke volumes. I watched as a number of the women standing near me in the crowd began quietly weeping. Grette Ormsdotter, the wife of a carl who owned the small farm closest down the road to Hrorik's lands, pushed past me and raised herself up on tiptoe, trying to peer into the ship. Only a few weeks ago she'd stood on this same shore watching her husband, Krok, and her two oldest sons, Bram and Grim, eagerly sail away. I'd noticed them then, as they'd called their happy farewells to her, boasting of the bounty they'd bring her by summer's end. Grim was only a year older than I. Now, as she stood beside me at the water's edge and searched the faces of the crew, of all her menfolk, only Bram could be seen.

"Bram!" she cried out, her voice trembling. "Where is your father? Where is your brother, Grim?"

Her son Bram, a tall young man with long reddish-gold hair, hung his head and turned his face away, saying nothing.

Harald, Hrorik's son, stepped from the ship

onto the narrow planks of the wharf and held his hands aloft, signaling for silence.

"We have had misfortune," he said. His voice was low but strong, and it carried across the shore so all could hear. "That is plain for all to see. But our tale deserves a proper telling. Only thus may we give the honor due to those who did not return. For now, ask no more. Our journey home has wearied us, and our losses lie heavy on our hearts. Let us rest briefly. Tend to the wounds of those who are injured. After darkness falls, come to the great hall of Hrorik's longhouse. There will be food and drink for all. Come, and then I will tell you of the doom the Norns spun for us when we sailed from this shore on our ill-fated voyage."

Harald stepped back onto the ship and gave an order. Those of the crew who were still able-bodied began stowing the long oars on the raised rack running along the center of the deck.

Ubbe, the foreman, hooked the straps of his sword's scabbard over his belt, then turned to one of the other men standing near him on the shore. "What are you waiting for? What are we all waiting for? These are our comrades," he said and stepped onto the planks of the wharf. Several men followed him. I did, too. We spaced ourselves in a line stretching back onto dry land, and the men on the ship began passing us their sea chests and shields.

After the men's gear and weapons had been offloaded, four members of the crew lifted two long, cloth-wrapped bundles from the deck—clearly the bodies of two men, shrouded in their cloaks—and heaved them up onto their shoulders.

"These two died yesterday," Harald explained. "They almost made it home. One other died from his wounds on the voyage from England, but we had too many days still to travel to bring his body with us. We buried him at first landfall after crossing the sea."

When the rest of the crew had disembarked, Harald and three others, all warriors from Hrorik's household, pried loose two of the long planks from the center of the deck from the area over the ballast stones where they were just fitted in place rather than nailed down. After wrapping the planks tightly with a cloak to hold them together, they laid them down beside Hrorik and eased his limp body onto them. Then they raised the makeshift litter to their shoulders and carried Hrorik up to the longhouse. I trailed behind them, my chores forgotten.

I was filled with curiosity to discover what had befallen the *Red Eagle* and her crew. Unlike most of those around me, my heart was not filled with sorrow. Men I knew had died; that much was already clear. And Hrorik, my father, was gravely wounded, perhaps near death himself, as my mother had asserted when the ship first came into view. At times she had the gift, or curse, of the second sight and could see that which had not yet come to pass. But none of the dead or dying men had been my comrades. Free men are not comrades with thralls. My heart was not touched by their misfortunes. I knew that not a man who'd sailed on the *Red Eagle* would have shed a tear for me if it were I who lay dying instead of Hrorik. I was only a slave, even to Hrorik. To me, my father was just the man who'd forced himself upon my mother. He was just the man who owned me. I had no reason this day to grieve for those dead or dying. I had no reason to grieve yet.

After they entered the longhouse with their burden, Harald and the other men who carried Hrorik did not take him to the small sleeping chamber in one corner of the longhouse that held his and Gunhild's bed. Instead they bore him to one of the raised platforms of stone and packed earth, topped with smoothed planks covered with furs and blankets, that stretched most of the length of the long side walls of the main hall of the long-house. They laid him down on the platform bench in the center of the hall, where he'd be close to the warmth from the fires of the main cooking hearth out in the center of the room. As the men eased the deck planks from under him, Hrorik groaned and his body twisted in a fit of sudden coughing. The force of the deep, shuddering coughs shook loose his covers and revealed the terrible extent of his injuries.

Hrorik's right arm—as big around as my leg, and probably stronger—was gone, cut cleanly off above the elbow. Only a thick stub remained, its end wrapped in bloody cloths, looking almost like the stump of a thick branch jutting from the trunk of a great oak. Hrorik's great barrel of a chest was bare, or would have been had it not been swathed with bandages. A dark stain of blood, as large as a man's head, had soaked the wrappings through on the right side of his chest. Most of the stain was dark, and looked stiff and dry, but I could see fresh, wet blood shining in its center. A bright red splash of blood, brought up by his coughing, trickled out of one side of Hrorik's mouth and into his beard, dyeing the gray hair red.

I heard a quiet gasp behind me and turned to see my mother standing there, staring at Hrorik's wounds, her hand over her mouth. If the second sight had warned her of his coming death, it apparently had not told her of its cause.

Harald spoke quietly to Gunhild, who stood pale and silent gazing at Hrorik's ravaged body.

"Anyone but Hrorik would have died long

before now," he told her. "I doubted even he could survive the voyage, but his will to return home has kept him alive, though barely. It cannot keep him in this world much longer, though. His lung is pierced and will not stop bleeding."

I watched Gunhild closely to see what she would do. She and Hrorik had argued violently shortly before the *Red Eagle* had left our shore. The argument had been, as usual, about Derdriu, my mother. I wondered if the sight of Hrorik, helpless and dying, caused her heart to feel sorrow or if her anger burned still.

Gunhild stepped forward and gave Hrorik's face one brief touch and said simply, "Husband." Her voice was calm, and no tears fell from her eyes. I could not read her feelings from her face. She looked at Harald and said, "Since you have invited the entire village to sup with us this night, I suppose I must get to work. I'm sure *you* will not prepare the meal to feed them." Thus, even in the moment of learning her husband was soon to die did Gunhild's thoughts run to herself.

Gunhild turned to where I'd been standing hidden by the shadows, or so I thought, since I'd followed Harald and Hrorik into the longhouse.

"And you, thrall, stop standing there like a witless fool. If there was time, I would send you into the forest to help find more food for our table. But

13

we have no time. Go to Ubbe and have him slaughter a yearling calf. Skin it out and cut it up for me. And be careful to save the blood for sausage; I'll have no waste. I want the meat cut into chunks no bigger than that," she said, holding her hand up and making a circle with her thumb and finger to show me the size she wanted. "We've cabbage and carrots and barley, and with as many as I have to feed, and as little time as I have to prepare, it will have to be a quick stew that I fix. But there will be food for all."

By dusk, the longhouse was filled with guests. At Gunhild's direction, my mother and the other serving women had set up the feast tables and benches out in the center of the floor. Down the entire length of the hall, oil lamps had been lit and hung from the posts that supported the roof. The shields, helms, and weapons of those warriors in the *Red Eagle*'s crew who were housecarls and lived on Hrorik's estate had been hung along the walls of the longhouse above their sleeping positions on the platforms. Their hacked and battered condition gave mute testimony to the fierce struggle we were to hear of.

Hrorik was too weak to sit at table. He remained lying on the platform opposite the main hearth. Hrorik's daughter, Harald's sister-twin

Sigrid, sat at his side, periodically holding a cup of ale to his lips.

My mother and the other serving women scurried between the hearth and the tables with bowls of food, supervised by Gunhild. The remainder of the slaves, who, like me, for the moment had no work to do, sat wherever they could find space on the far ends of the seating platforms along the walls or on the floor. While Gunhild wasn't watching, Mother handed me a heaping bowl of the stew that the guests were being served.

After I gulped it down, I edged as close as I could to the head table where Harald sat, and eagerly waited for him to begin his story of the *Red Eagle*'s ill-fated voyage. For me, such tales of adventures and battles in distant lands were food for dreams. With the heartlessness of the young who have not yet suffered themselves, I cared not that for many it would be a tale of sorrow.

After every guest had been served, Harald stood. He cut a fine figure, tall, strong, and straight, with a natural beauty to his features. He and his twin sister, Sigrid, were accounted by all to be the finest looking man and woman in the district. They must have inherited their looks from their mother, Helge, for where they were slender and graceful, Hrorik looked like one of his ancestors could have been a bear. Harald smiled easily and laughed often, and was the kind of man other men hope to count as their friend. Young women were more likely to dream of capturing his heart or warming his bed.

Since coming ashore, Harald had bathed and changed his clothing. His long hair and closely trimmed beard, freshly washed and combed, gleamed in the flickering light from the fires and the oil lamps like fine yellow gold. He was wearing a crimson tunic over dark trousers. I thought he surely must look as fine as any jarl or son of a king—not that I'd ever seen such, but I'd heard them sung of by visiting skalds. The room quieted and Harald began to speak.

"Usually when all of us from this estate and the village gather together here in Hrorik's hall, it is for the occasion of a feast day, to welcome the change of season or thank the gods for their bounty," he began in a solemn voice. "We have known each other all of our lives, and we have joined together many times to celebrate. We must join together now to mourn our losses and to give each other comfort. We come together this night to grieve for and honor those who are gone."

As he spoke, Harald turned this way and that, looking into the faces of the people gathered in the long hall. He did not speak in the formal style a skald uses to recite a tale or song. Instead, he spoke with an easy, natural voice, as one would use in conversation to tell a comrade of what he'd seen or heard.

"Normally at a gathering such as this," he continued, "I would not be the one to address you. Normally it would be our chieftain, Hrorik Strong-Axe. But these are not normal times. Hrorik, our chieftain, lies gravely wounded, and many more are dead. Earlier today, down at the shore, I promised that this night—in this longhouse—I would tell you what befell our ship and crew. The time for that telling has come.

"As you all know, we set out to go raiding early this year. The winter was a mild one, far warmer than usual. Because of the weather, we had an opportunity to cross the sea and surprise the English in the last weeks of the winter, rather than waiting for the spring when they would be watching the sea for raiders. A gift of fate, we thought it was. It was a great raid we were joining, more than forty longships filled with Danish warriors, and other Vikings from Ireland were to join us after we reached England.

"We had favorable winds after we cut across Jutland on the Limfjord and struck out across the sea," Harald continued. "No ships were lost in the crossing. After reaching England, we sailed west across the southern edge of its shores, harrying the coastline as we passed. We did not tarry anywhere long, though, for we had a rendezvous to keep with the ships joining us from Ireland. We had planned to meet on the west coast of England in a great bay that opens there from the mouth of a river the English call the Severn.

"We reached the great Severn Bay several days before the full moon, the date set for our meeting with the Vikings from Dublin. We stopped and camped on the bank of a small river near the mouth of the bay, and thought to rest there until the ships from Ireland arrived. But the Norns planned a different fate for us.

"Early on the second morning after we'd made land, one of our sentries came running into camp, calling for the chieftains. He'd been approached by a leader of the English who wished to enter our camp in peace and parley with our leaders.

"Some of our chieftains suggested we should allow the Englishman to enter our camp, then kill him. Others countered that to do so would be foolish and wasteful, and argued we should take the English leader captive, then try to ransom him to the West Saxon king in whose lands we were camped. In the end, though, it was Hrorik's counsel that prevailed.

"'Think what you are saying,' he told us. 'If this Englishman enters our camp, will he not be doing so only because we give him our oath that he may enter in safety? Is there a man among you who would choose to be known as an oath breaker? Is there any man here who would trade his honor for silver?'"

Harald paused and took a long drink of ale from the silver cup that stood in front of him on the table. No one spoke; all eyes were on him. He wiped his mustache with the back of his hand, then continued.

"Though he was our enemy, the Englishman impressed us all when he rode into our camp. He wore no helm and his pale, yellow hair and beard gleamed like fine gold in the morning sunlight. His mail brynie was long, almost down to his knees, and its iron links must just recently have been polished, for they sparkled like silver in the sun. A shield, covered in hide that had been painted white, was slung across his back. A sword hung from his belt in a richly decorated scabbard, and in his right hand he held a spear, its butt braced against his stirrup.

"'I am Eanwulf, appointed by King Ethelwulf of the West Saxons to be Ealdorman of Somersetshire,' he told us. 'I have come to propose an agreement.'

"It was Hrorik who stood and answered him. 'I am Hrorik Strong-Axe, a chieftain of the Danes.

I am not the leader of these many chieftains who are here before you, for we are each our own men, but I have been chosen to speak for all. You say you have come to propose an agreement. What do you want of us—and what are you willing to offer?'

"'What I want from you is your lives,' the Englishman answered, 'and what I offer you is the edge of my sword, and the point of my spear. I and my people have had the misfortune to learn the ways of you Danes in recent years. You are pirates, murderers, and thieves.'

"The Englishman proposed battle," Harald explained. "'My army is not far,' he told us. 'They can be here by noon. Let us come together on the shore in a place where we can join in proper battle. There we will fight, and may the victory go to the warriors whose deeds earn it. If you seek to plunder our land, prove your right by force of arms.'

"As the Englishman mounted his horse and turned to ride away, his parting words were, 'Enjoy the morning. It promises to be a fine day. It is the last that most of you will see.'"

As Harald continued with his tale, I closed my eyes and tried to picture the scene he described to us. Harald was skilled at spinning tales, and as he recounted how our warriors had prepared for battle—sharpening their weapons and donning their armor, marching in ship's companies down to the beach where they formed a shield-wall—I felt almost as though I was there with them, waiting for the English army to arrive. I wondered if any had felt fear or had worried that they would not live to see the night. I knew that if I had been there I would have.

"The Saxon army marched out of the forest and onto the beach and formed into a shield-wall," Harald told us. "They formed their line down the beach from us, farther away than a long bow shot. It appeared our numbers were roughly equal. Their leader, the Saxon nobleman Eanwulf who'd ridden into our camp and challenged us, rode back and forth in front of them as they formed their line. Whenever he raised his spear overhead and called out to them they roared out his name, chanting 'Eanwulf, Eanwulf!'

"The battle began slowly. A group of lightly armed Saxons—poor men they must have been, for most were armed just with slings, with only a few bows among them—ran out from the English line and began launching their missiles at us. We laughed at so weak a show. While our front rank stood firm, shoulder to shoulder, our shields over-lapping, our second and third ranks closed in right behind and raised their shields overhead, creating a roof. The Saxon slingers' stones bounced harm-lessly off the shield-fort we'd created, and their arrows thudded into its walls. Meanwhile, those of our men who carried bows stepped back behind the line of our shield-fort and sent their arrows arcing over our line toward the Saxon skirmishers, who had no wall of shields nor armor to protect them. Soon the beach between the battle lines was littered with the bodies of fallen Saxons, and those not felled by our fire retreated behind the English shield-wall."

Harald paused here and shook his head. "I have fought in seven pitched battles, raiding against the Franks and Irish and Saxons," he told us, "and in many smaller fights besides, but never have I known a battle to begin like this one did. Long our two armies stood facing each other, shouting challenges and jeers. We pounded our spear shafts on our shields till the beach itself seemed to shake with the sound, like a forest trembles with thunder that heralds an approaching storm. Hrorik held us back, though our men were eager to fight—perhaps he sensed some unseen danger the rest of us did not perceive. The English army waited long, hoping that we would come to them, but when we did not, the Saxons finally began advancing toward our line.

"Even then, though, the English did not rush against us, trying to break through our battle line by the force of their attack. Instead, they edged up to us slowly, until we stood, shield-wall facing shield-wall, little more than an arm's reach in between. Still they did not attack. We stood thus for what seemed a long time, staring into each others' eyes, shouting challenges and battle cries, while on each side warriors stabbed out at each other in quick jabs with their spears, much as swordsmen do at the start of a duel to test their opponents' skill.

"A tall Saxon thegn, with long arms that gave him a dangerous reach, stood in the English line across from Hrorik. He must have been one of their wealthier warriors, for he wore a mail shirt, though most of the English were armored with only helm and shield. His spear flicked out and back like a serpent's tongue, jabbing high at Hrorik's face, or darting low toward his legs, but each time Hrorik was equally quick, deflecting the spear's blade with his shield.

"This Englishman was unable to harm Hrorik, but his attacks angered him, like a yapping dog angers a bear by snapping at its heels. When the Saxon jabbed his spear forward again, Hrorik released his shield's handle, letting it hang from his neck and shoulder by its strap, and darted his hand out toward the spear like a falcon strikes at a bird in flight. He caught the spear shaft just behind its metal head, and, with a grunt, jerked the spear forward with all his might, pulling the Saxon out of the English line. Then did Hrorik show why he is called Strong-Axe, for the steel blade of his great axe flashed brightly in the sun as it arced down, cleaving through the Saxon's helm and splitting his head down to the jawbone.

"The Saxon standing in the English line beside the dead man turned and watched his companion fall, startled by his fate. As he watched his comrade die, I lunged forward, low, my shield raised to cover me, and with my sword, Biter, I cut his legs from under him." As Harald described his attack, he crouched and lunged, acting it out for us.

"Roaring now like some great, wild beast, Hrorik charged forward into the hole he and I had cut in the English line. I, and those of our crew standing closest to us, quickly followed him. We broke the English line there like a speeding arrow breaks the iron rings of a mail brynie, our warriors driving forward in a wedge that forced aside the linden-wood walls of the Saxons' shields, while our spears and swords reaped a bloody harvest inside their lines.

"Seeing our attack, all of our ships' companies gave a great cheer and surged forward against the Saxons' shield-wall. Like a great wave, we struck them, and our steel sought their life's blood, hewing and stabbing. English blood stained the white English sand red, and the battle seemed to be ours.

"Then I looked up and saw, not twenty paces away, the Saxon leader Eanwulf. He was standing behind the main battle line of his army, surrounded by heavily armed warriors of his household guard. A rider was beside him, leaning low in the saddle, shouting to be heard. I could not hear the rider's words over the din of battle, but at his message, Eanwulf smiled a grim smile, then nudged one of his companions and pointed beyond the fight raging in front of him, toward the river that lay behind us.

"As he did, I heard cries of alarm from among our own forces. Men were shouting, 'The ships! The ships!' At their cries I turned and looked behind me. From two separate points, in the direction where our ships were moored along the river's banks, columns of dark smoke were rising above the trees.

"Up and down our line, our chieftains tried to regain control of their frenzied men, and pull them back from the fight. 'Fall back!' they cried. 'Reform the shield-wall and fall back! Fall back toward the ships! We are attacked in our rear!'"

Many in the hall of the longhouse gasped at hearing of the assault on the ships, and murmuring spread across the room. All knew the greatest danger that could befall a raiding party was to lose their ships and become stranded in a hostile land. Death or slavery was certain to follow. Harald waited for the talking to subside, then continued his grim tale.

"The English, only moments before on the verge of breaking, now found new courage and rallied, surging forward against us as we fell back. 'Eanwulf! Eanwulf and Osric,' they shouted, and from their new battle cry I realized what had happened. We fought not one English army, but two, and we were caught between them.

"Though in desperate danger, our army fought bravely. The Saxons attacked furiously across the front of our shield-wall, but we held as we fell back toward the ships, step by step in an orderly retreat. Hrorik and the other chieftains shouted their orders and warnings above the din of battle. 'Hold formation! Maintain the shield-wall! Retreat to the ships!' they cried, and though the battle was clearly lost, as men we were not beaten.

"Then behind us, three more plumes of smoke billowed up above the tree line along the river. Three more ships were dying under Saxon torches. It was then that one of the ship's companies betrayed themselves and all of their comrades through their cowardice. Their fear and weakness doomed us all."

Harald paused and spat upon the floor to show his disgust. "Perhaps one of the new columns of smoke rising above the trees was from their ship," he said. "I do not know, nor do I care. We all must die some day. We cannot avoid that fate, but we can meet it with courage and honor. But those men did not. They turned from our shield-wall and fled down the beach, heading for the ships. Their fear spread like a fever through our army. At the sight of them running from the battle, two more crews turned and fled, then three more followed after them.

"The Saxons chased the retreating men like wolves after deer, stabbing and hacking at their unprotected backs. Thus do cowards die. But doom also stalked those of us whose courage held, for now there were large gaps in the line of our shield-wall. English warriors poured through the gaps and circled behind so that in an instant we were under attack from all sides. Our battle line disintegrated, as each ship's crew tried desperately to form into its own defensive circle.

"The warriors from the *Red Eagle* did not shame themselves. Though our further retreat was now blocked by a howling mob of Saxons, our crew fought fiercely. We formed into a tight circle, our shields and spears facing out on all sides, and soon the beach around our position was thick with English bodies. Seeing that we could not be overwhelmed in a quick rush, the Saxon warriors encircling our crew pulled back a brief distance to regroup.

"When they did, Hrorik formed a plan. 'Take some men and cut a path through the Saxons behind us,' he shouted to me. 'Clear a passage, then let half of our crew run for the ship. Tell them to cast off and ready oars, while I and the rest of our warriors try to hold off these dogs. When the ship is ready, those of us still standing will run for it.'"

After he recounted Hrorik's words, Harald looked around the hall at the faces watching him. "Thus does a true leader of men face danger," he said. "Thus did Hrorik, a chieftain of the Danes, boldly choose to risk his own life, that at least some of his followers might survive."

I glanced over to where Hrorik lay on the platform near the fire, covered in furs. His head was resting in Sigrid's lap, and her hand gently stroked his brow, but her eyes were on her brother Harald. Hrorik's eyes were closed. For a moment I thought he might already be dead, but then I saw the slow rise and fall of his chest as he breathed.

"I moved from man to man through the press of our crew," Harald continued. "They stood jammed together, shoulder to shoulder, waiting for the Saxons to resume their attack. All knew that those I picked were most likely to survive that day, yet no man dishonored himself by asking to be chosen. All were willing to stay behind and fight to protect their comrades and the ship. When all was ready I moved with my chosen men to the back of our defensive circle.

"The line of Englishmen blocking our way to the river was only a single rank deep. The main fight, and the thickest press of Saxon warriors, was still on the side where the original battle lines had been. At my signal, the warriors who'd gathered with me in the rear of our circle suddenly surged forward in the direction of the ship. We caught the English by surprise. A few ran and escaped. Those who tried to stand against us were badly outnumbered, and we cut them down quickly. When they died, there was nothing between us and the *Red Eagle* except open beach, and we sprinted for the ship.

"When the mass of English at the front of our circle saw some of our crew running across the beach toward the ship, they must have thought our courage was breaking, for they howled triumphantly and surged forward anew against our line. Though other ships' crews also still stood and fought on the field in their own circles, the battle was fiercest around our men, for where Hrorik stood the pile of Saxon bodies grew deepest, and their bravest warriors pressed forward against him, all wanting the honor of cutting him down. The Saxon leader himself, and the warriors of his household guard, joined in the attack against him.

"When our ship was freed from the shore, its mooring lines pulled aboard and our men ready at the oars, I leapt onto the shore and ran back to where Hrorik and those of our crew who still stood were fighting. The English line was still thinner on the side closest to the river, and all of those Saxons were facing our dwindling circle, looking for openings to strike. They did not see me approach. With three quick blows I felled three of them.

"'Hrorik,' I cried. 'Come now, quickly, before the way is blocked again.' He swung his axe back and forth in two great sweeps, felling one Saxon and driving the rest back beyond its reach. Then he and the men with him turned and we all ran for the ship, the Saxons racing in pursuit.

"Two of our men stood in the prow of the *Red Eagle*, armed with bows to cover our flight. As we neared the ship, they began loosing arrows over our heads at our pursuers. The English behind us were howling in anger and frustration that we might escape. A spear whistled past my head and thudded into the back of the man in front of me, felling him at the water's edge. It was Gunnar the blacksmith. He died only steps away from safety. More spears flew among our men, striking them down. Close behind us, I could hear the Saxons' leader, Eanwulf, urging his men forward with hoarse shouts.

"The Saxons caught up with us as we entered the shallows at the water's edge and were slowed, wading out toward the *Red Eagle*. Hrorik and I turned to hold our pursuers back, while the rest of our men—and only a few had survived the run— clambered over the sides into the ship.

"Eanwulf himself led the assault against us. As the Saxon leader closed in, Hrorik struck at him with his axe, so mighty a blow that it split the Saxon leader's shield, the axe's blade cleaving through the wood and leather down to the iron boss in the shield's center. The force of the blow drove Eanwulf to his knees. But while Hrorik struggled to free his axe blade from the shattered Saxon shield, one of Eanwulf's houseguards, standing at his leader's side, lunged forward with his sword and swung a mighty cut at Hrorik's arm, chopping it through above the elbow.

"Hrorik staggered back, a fountain of blood spouting from the stump that remained. His sev- ered arm, the hand still clutching the shaft of his axe, hung down across the front of Eanwulf's shield.

"I swung Biter, my sword, and cut through the neck of the warrior who'd wounded Hrorik. He dropped, dead, into the shallow water, but I was too late for aught but revenge. Even as I swung my blade and killed the Saxon warrior, Eanwulf stabbed forward with his spear, driving it through Hrorik's mail shirt and into his chest.

"Spears and arrows began to rain down on the Saxons as more of our men rushed to the *Red Eagle*'s prow to cover us. In moments, three more Saxons fell, and the rest, including Eanwulf, staggered back onto the shore.

"Hrorik was bleeding badly, and by now could barely stand. Pulling him with me, I waded to the ship's side, where eager hands reached down and pulled us both aboard.

"Our oarsmen backed us out into the river while I ran to the stern and seized the steering oar. The ship turned and we headed toward the sea and safety. The men who'd been shooting from the ship's bow at the retreating Saxons now took their seats and ran their oars out into the water, and we picked up speed. As we pulled away from the river's mouth into the open waters of the bay, I looked back upriver at the carnage we'd left behind. Of the forty ships in our fleet, only three others besides the *Red Eagle* had left the shore and were underway. One of those had been boarded by

Saxon warriors, and fighting was raging on her deck. I do not know if she managed to escape. Of the other ships still moored along the riverbank, most were aflame or surrounded by English warriors. Back on the beach, four ships' crews still remained, formed into circular shield-forts, selling their lives dearly in a brave but hopeless fight against the ever-increasing numbers of the enemy who swarmed around them."

Harald looked around the hall, silently gazing at the faces staring intently at him. When he spoke again, his voice sounded hoarse with emotion.

"For the English, the battle we fought that day was a great victory. Many of our warriors fed the carrion birds, and their bones now lie bleaching white in the sun on the sands of that distant beach. Many of you here tonight have been robbed of kinsmen, of husbands and fathers, brothers and sons, by the Saxons' victory over us. Yet though your menfolk may have lost their lives, the Saxons did not take all from them. Every man who sailed this voyage on the *Red Eagle* fought bravely in the face of doom. Be assured that the Valkyries have carried the spirits of all of your men who died that day to the feast-hall of the Gods. Be comforted that their courage will live forever, honored in songs sung by the skalds of the gods in the halls of Valhalla."

THE BARGAIN

After Harald ended his tale and sat down, many among the folk in the hall approached him with questions, seeking to learn the details of their own kin's death. Harald could not have witnessed every man's fall, yet he assured all who asked that their loved ones had fought and died heroically.

From the tale he'd just told, I knew that some who'd died had been speared in their backs while they were running for the safety of the ship. To me, nothing seemed heroic about such a death. But men and women tended to believe what Harald said, just because he was Harald. Being able to make folk believe what is obviously untrue is one of those special qualities often possessed by a leader.

It was late by the time the last guest left and we slaves could wearily begin the task of restoring the hall of the longhouse to order. Even before the last guest had gone, Gunhild, ever frugal, began snuffing the oil lamps hanging from the row of great posts—each the trunk of a tree that had been stripped of its bark—that supported the beams and rafters of the longhouse's roof. I thought it churlish to send the last of the guests off in near darkness. As soon as the thought entered my head, I could hear Gunhild's reply in my mind: It was they who were ill-mannered, for staying so late. Gunhild always had a quick reply to any criticism and always managed to find a way to blame someone else for wrongs she did.

Gunhild, of course, would not have considered leaving the lamps lit until we thralls had completed our work. Oil was too expensive to waste on mere slaves. And so we labored in the shadows, the only light coming from the dimly flickering flames of the remains of the fire on the main hearth.

As I worked, my mind was filled with visions of the battle Harald had described. I imagined myself fighting beside Harald, against great odds. That was a life of honor and glory! My mind was so filled with my foolish fantasies that, unseeing, I tripped over one of the hounds and spilled a half-empty cup of ale I was carrying. It splashed across the back of one of the serving girls. She cursed me, and the dog snapped at my leg. I shook my head to clear my thoughts, and looked around me. I was not in England or some other distant land. I was not a warrior. I was just a thrall, working for my masters in the longhouse where I'd grown up. That was my reality. That was my world, a small one, and was the only one I'd ever know. Thralls do not live heroic lives.

While the slaves cleared the hall and the other members of the household stumbled off to their sleeping positions on the platforms along the walls, Gunhild, Harald, and Sigrid stood huddled around Hrorik, where he lay near the main hearth and the warmth its dying fire provided. I was helping my mother take down one of the feast tables when Harald broke away from them and walked over to where we were working.

"Derdriu," he said. "Hrorik would speak with you." He hesitated, looked at me, then added, "Perhaps you should come, too."

As we approached, I saw that Hrorik appeared even weaker than when he'd been carried into the hall that afternoon. When he spoke, his voice was no more than a hoarse whisper.

"Derdriu," he rasped. "Soon now I will leave this world and journey to the land of the Gods and the dead. I do not wish to make that journey alone.

"Gunhild is a noblewoman and wealthy in her own right. Life still holds many prospects for her after I die, and she is not ready to make the journey I must travel.

"You have given me much pleasure in this life, and for that I thank you and would honor you. It would comfort me now, in my passing, to know you will be at my side, to give me the comfort of your companionship and the pleasure of your body in the next life, too. I wish you to travel on the death ship with me."

It was a high honor that Hrorik offered my mother, to accompany a great chieftain on his death voyage. In my thoughts, though, I damned him for it. I damned Gunhild, too. She was his wife. Why couldn't she die, to comfort him in the next life? Of course I knew that women of noble birth did not sacrifice their own lives at their husband's graves. Their lives mattered, so slaves accompanied the rich and powerful on their final voyage. But why should I lose my mother?

Mother paled, and for many moments was silent. Then her back straightened and she raised her head and spoke.

"Since first we met, Hrorik Strong-Axe, you have been as a thief and a robber to me. I was born the daughter of a king in Ireland, but you stole me from my home. I was a princess, and might some-day have been a queen, but you made me a slave. I hoped someday to be wed, but instead you made me your concubine. Now you plan to steal my very life, so that your death can be more comfortable. Why should I care if you are comforted in your death?"

I was astonished by my mother's boldness, but proud of her courage. Sigrid gasped in surprise and raised her hand to cover her mouth. Harald's eye-brows rose and a muscle in his cheek twitched. But only Gunhild spoke.

"She is a slave. You do not need to ask her," Gunhild snapped to Hrorik. "I'll gladly tighten the knotted cord around her neck myself when the time comes."

Ignoring his wife, Hrorik asked my mother, gasping at the effort it took him to speak, "Have you known no happiness in your life with me?"

I could not believe his words—he who had stolen my mother from her home and family, made her a slave, and raped her. Should she be grateful to him for that? Should she be pleased to have had his attentions? Is a dog thankful for the foot that kicks it?

My mother turned away, her head hanging down and her hands covering her face. I thought she, too, must have been astonished by Hrorik's words. She stayed so, silent, for so long I thought she did not intend to answer. What would have been the point anyway? What difference would a slave's words make? When did a master care about a slave's feelings?

Finally, my mother turned back to Hrorik and raised her eyes to meet his. When she spoke, her words surprised me even more than his had. "No, not totally," she told him. "You are right. You know it is so, and my heart will not let me deny the truth about the past, though bitterness may fill it today. We did share some happy times, when first you brought me into your home. When your first wife had not long been dead. When your children, Harald and Sigrid, were young and sad and alone. When I became as a mother for them. When I became as a wife to you. And soon enough my belly filled with a child of my own—our son, Halfdan.

"During that time, those first years, you did treat me with kindness and affection. But those days have long been past. I've often wondered what path our lives might have taken had you not married Gunhild. But now the only attention you pay me is late-night visits to my bed, whether I wish it or not. And Gunhild does her best to fill my days with sorrow, from jealousy over the number of nights her own bed is cold and empty because you are in mine."

At this, Gunhild's face flushed red with anger and her eyes flashed dangerously.

My mother covered her face with her hands again and stood with her head bowed. I could see her lips were moving, as if to speak, but they made no sound. Had her voice failed her in her fear? All eyes were on her, but no one spoke.

"Very well, Hrorik," she finally said, looking up. "I will sail on the death ship with you. But in exchange I will extract a bargain."

At that, Gunhild stepped forward and struck my mother hard across the face—so hard that it turned her head.

"A slave does not bargain with a chieftain," she snarled. "You forget your place."

My mother shook her head to clear it, then looked at Gunhild with a cold gaze.

"I have endured much at your hands, Gunhild," she said. "I, who was once a princess, of greater rank than you will ever achieve. It appears I am soon to die, so now I have little to lose. It would be wise for you to tread carefully around me until I am gone."

Gunhild drew back her hand to strike Mother again, but Harald stepped between them.

"Stay," he said.

My mother turned back to Hrorik.

"I know that I can be forced against my will to accompany you on your death voyage, Hrorik. No doubt any of your men would willingly slay me on your bier. Gunhild herself is eager to speed my passing. But to do so would be unwise. I would die cursing you to my God and his angels of destruction. The afterworld is the realm of all the Gods. On its voyage to the lands of your Gods, your death ship might not escape the wrath of my God and His angels. Their anger would fall upon it like a storm batters a ship trapped on the open sea. And even if you did safely reach the hall of your Gods, you would find little comfort in me there if you force me on this journey against my will. I swear on all that is holy to me I would be a companion who would seek to bring you eternal misery rather than pleasure."

Mother paused, took a deep breath, then continued. "I will go willingly with you, though, if you grant me this request. My son Halfdan is the grandson of a king in Ireland. He is your son, too—the son of a great chieftain of the Danes. He should not be a slave. Free him this night, so that you and I can look on him together and see him as a free man. Then in the afterworld, we can remember him proudly and listen for tales of his exploits. Acknowledge Halfdan now as your son, and have him raised as a chieftain's son should be."

I could not believe my mother's words. My mouth fell open and I gaped like a fool.

Hrorik nodded his head slowly, as though he was thinking on the words my mother had spoken. Then he looked at me and spoke, and in that brief moment my world changed.

"Halfdan, you are this day a free man," he said, "and I acknowledge you as my son. I should have done so long ago."

He turned to Harald and added, "This is your brother. I entrust him to your care. Do for him what I cannot."

4

DERDRIU'S TALE

"Wake up, Halfdan."

The words roused me from a deep and dreamless sleep. Someone was shaking my shoulder. When I opened my eyes, I saw Harald standing above me, looking down at me with a tired smile. Behind him I could see a bright beam of sunlight shining through the smoke hole in the roof, cutting through the dim light of the interior of the longhouse. From its angle, I could tell I had slept long past dawn.

"We have much work to do this day," he said.

I sat up, my mind still confused from sleep. I could not understand why Harald would be waking me. He did not concern himself with the doings of slaves.

"What work?" I asked him.

"We must build the death ship. Our father, Hrorik, is dead."

At those words, the memory of the night before rushed back into my head. I was free.

Long after I'd gone to my bed I'd lain awake, too excited to sleep. My mind had been filled with visions of myself as a warrior, wandering in foreign lands across the seas. All my life I'd expected only to hear tales of such adventures, but now I might actually live them. When I'd finally fallen asleep, it had been from sheer exhaustion, which even my excited imaginings could no longer hold at bay. Looking back, I'm shamed now to remember that during that night I thought only of my own good fortune. Not once did I regret—or even think of—the price my mother would pay to buy it. In the light of morning, though, as the fog of sleep cleared from my thoughts, the fantasies that had filled my wakeful dreams the night before scattered before the realization that my mother was to die.

Harald continued, "I could tell Hrorik had little time left in this world, so I sat up with him after the rest of the household went to their beds. We spoke of many things. Late in the night, he told me he wished his death ship to be built on the hill behind the longhouse, overlooking the sea. He said it was his favorite place on these lands. Then, as dawn approached, he asked me to give him his sword. He grasped it tightly to his chest and tried to sit up, but was too weak. I reached out to raise him, but by the time I did he was already dead."

The news of Hrorik's death elicited no sorrow in my heart. My mind might know he was my father, but in my heart he was still my owner, even though now I was free. His passing did fill me with dread, though, for it meant that soon my mother must pay the price of the bargain she'd made.

Harald had spoken of a death ship. I wasn't certain what he meant. I had seen funerals before, of course. Death, after all, is a part of life, and is ever present. The funerals I'd seen, though, had been simple things. The dead were buried in the earth, sometimes with a few of their favorite possessions to give them comfort in the next life. I had never seen a chieftain's funeral. I did not know what was required.

"What do we do?" I asked. "What must I do?"

"I've already been up on the hill this morning and planned where we'll build the burial ship," Harald said. "I took three thralls and showed them where to dig the earth out. Ubbe has taken a cart and two other thralls to collect stones to build its hull with, and Gudrod is in the forest cutting wood to build the death house. This household has been busy this morning while you've slept. Now you and

I must go supervise the building, to make certain that all is properly done. We are Hrorik's sons. It is our duty to see that he is honored as befitting his rank."

I still did not know what Hrorik's funeral would entail. My ignorance embarrassed me. "I do not know what to do," I told Harald again.

"I will show you, my brother," he replied.

My brother. To Harald and others of his rank, slaves, though essential to the work of the estate, were property. More than beasts perhaps, but less than men. I wondered if Harald even knew the names of the slaves whose tasks he'd ordered this morning. Yesterday I, too, had been just a thrall. Today I was Halfdan, a free man. Today Harald called me brother. How did he feel about my sudden change of status? Did he feel shamed to be brother to a former slave? Did he resent me? Nothing showed on his face except a tired smile, but folk often mask their true feelings with a smile. It is one of the less noble characteristics that distinguish men from beasts.

Angry voices erupted in the longhouse. Harald sighed in exasperation and strode down the hall toward the source of the noise. I quickly pulled on my clothes and ran after him.

My mother and Gunhild were arguing.

"What is the cause of this?" Harald asked them,

46

irritation obvious in the tone of his voice. "Why do you disturb the peace of this household on this day of mourning?"

Gunhild spoke first. "There is much work to do to prepare for the funeral feast. I have ordered this slave to come and help. She will not obey me."

Harald turned to my mother. "Is this true?" he demanded.

Mother nodded her head. "It is." In a bitter voice she continued. "I am to die tomorrow for the honor and pleasure of your father. May I not have this last day of my life to compose my heart and make peace with my God? Gunhild would work me until the very moment I step into the death house."

Harald was quiet for a moment as he pondered my mother's words. Then he turned to Gunhild. "Derdriu is right," he said. "The time that remains to her should be hers alone, so she may embark on the voyage with Hrorik with her heart at peace."

"But I have already given her orders," Gunhild snapped angrily. "I have already decided."

I saw the muscles in Harald's jaw clench at Gunhild's words. "No, Gunhild," he said in a quiet voice. "I have decided. Now I am the master of this household. Do not again forget."

Gunhild recoiled as if she'd been struck. Without another word, she turned and rushed

47

away. Watching her go, I knew her rage would soon be felt by some unsuspecting and undeserving thrall. I was glad it could no longer be me.

"There is one other thing," my mother said as Harald turned to leave. He turned back to her, anger still visible in his eyes.

"Yes?" he asked impatiently.

"This shift is the only garment I have. It is a threadbare rag. If I am to enter the great hall of your Gods at Hrorik's side, should I not be dressed in a manner more befitting the consort of a great chieftain?"

I was amazed at my mother's boldness. It was a side of her I'd never seen. Harald stared at her, also startled, then laughed aloud.

"You are right. A new dress you should have, Derdriu. When Hrorik enters the hall of the Gods, he would want the Gods and heroes there to gaze with respect upon the woman who enters at his side.

"Can you sew a dress in one day?" he asked her.

"I can," Mother answered.

"Then this is what we will do," he said. "When we raided along the coast in England, before we reached the Severn Bay and the doom that awaited us there, among the booty Hrorik took was a bolt of fine red linen he found in the house of a Saxon thegn. It lies in his sea chest still. I will fetch it for you now."

Harald winked at her.

"Hrorik intended the cloth as a gift for Gunhild, but we'll not tell her that." He put his hand on my shoulder. "Come, Halfdan. Let us fetch the linen from Hrorik's sea chest. Your mother has a dress to make."

Harald strode away. I paused, abashed, before my mother. Tomorrow she would die. I knew it would happen. Yet at the same time, it did not seem real to me while she stood and lived in front of me. I felt there was something I should say to her, but no words came.

"Mother . . .?" I whispered.

"Go now," she told me. "Go with Harald. He is your brother, and a fine man. You and he have much work to do this day, and you must begin to learn each other's ways. And I must sew a dress. Tonight we will talk. I have much I wish to say to you."

After I gulped down a bowl of cold porridge, Harald and I climbed the grassy hill behind the longhouse.

Three men, all thralls who worked on the estate, were digging on the hilltop with wooden shovels. Fasti, who usually cared for the cattle and horses, had once been a free man, a Svear who'd been captured years ago by Hrorik in a raid on the Kingdom of the Sveas. Hrut and Ing, thralls by birth, worked the fields. Since I was a toddler, Fasti had been a special friend to me—almost an uncle. When he would milk the cows, he'd often scoop a cup of fresh milk out of the pail for me. As I grew older, it was Fasti who'd taught me to ride, setting me on the back of a horse and walking beside to keep me from falling.

When we drew near, I hailed them, wishing them a good morning. The three men turned their eyes to the ground, and none answered.

"Fasti?" I said. "Fasti, what is wrong?"

He continued looking down and picked at the ground with his wooden spade as he answered. "There's nothing wrong, Master Halfdan."

He turned to move away. I grabbed his sleeve and stopped him. "What is bothering you?" I demanded.

"Nothing," he insisted, his eyes still averted. "It's just that you are changed."

"What do you mean, I'm changed? I'm the same Halfdan I was yesterday. Remember? Just yesterday morning you told me a story you'd heard about a woman in the village. How she sleeps with a piglet in her bed, to keep her warm when her man is away. We laughed together till tears ran down our cheeks. Now you will not even look me in the face. You and I have always been friends, Fasti. Look at me and tell me truly what is wrong."

Fasti looked me in the face then. Perhaps he felt he had to, because I had ordered it. When he raised his gaze, I saw there was sorrow in his eyes.

"Forgive me. I did not mean to give offense. I am happy for your good fortune, Halfdan. But whether you know it yet or not, you are greatly changed. You have crossed over a gulf almost as wide as that between the living and the dead. I know. I crossed that gulf myself, years ago, when I was stolen from my home by Hrorik and made to work his lands as a slave. Yesterday you were my companion, one of us, a thrall. Today you are a master."

"But can't we still be friends?" I cried.

Fasti looked at me sadly. "I will always think with fondness of the boy I helped to raise. You were a good-hearted boy, and I have watched you grow into a fine young man. I am sure you will make a kind master. But the way of things now is that we are no longer equals. When you speak, I must do as you say. You are a master and I am a slave. I am your property, not your friend."

Although Fasti did not mean to cause injury with his words, they cut through me like a sharp knife. The thought of my freedom had initially filled me with excitement and joy. Now I found my new status was also filled with pain. My freedom, my dream, was taking my mother and my friends from me.

Harald, who'd stood quietly behind me watching my exchange with Fasti, stepped forward and put his arm around my shoulders. It felt strange to me that he did, for yesterday I'd been but a thrall to him. He hadn't even considered me a man. Perhaps it felt strange to him, too, for after a moment he removed his arm. When he spoke, though, his voice was gentle, and his words kind. "Come, Halfdan," he said, pulling me away. "Look here. Do you see how they've cut the outline of the ship in the earth?"

The grass on the hilltop was thick, with deep roots. The three workmen—the thralls—had cut the turf in strips and lifted them from the ground. The strips of turf were stacked some distance away in a pile. The area of bared earth they'd exposed on the hilltop was indeed in the shape of a longship, broad across the middle and tapering to a point at either end. Harald walked out into its center, pulling me with him.

"This will be the bow," he said, gesturing toward the end nearest the edge of the hilltop. "See how it looks out from this hill over the sea? We'll stand tall stones at the bow and the stern, to mark the stemposts of the ship. The rest of the stones that Ubbe collects we'll use to outline its sides."

With his foot, Harald scraped a line in the soil, marking off a large square in the center of the outlined ship.

"Come here," he called to Fasti. "We will build the death house here. The earth must be dug out deeper in this square, as deep as my leg, from my foot to my knee. Pile the soil you remove beside the stack of cut turfs. We will need it after the fire."

"I do not understand what we are doing," I confessed to Harald. "I have never seen a chieftain's funeral. What fire? Will we not bury Hrorik in the earth?"

"Our people, Hrorik's line, come from the north, above Jutland, across the water," Harald replied. "It has always been our custom, for as far back as men can remember, to honor the deaths of our chieftains and heroes by burning their bodies in a great fire. We believe the smoke rises to the heavens, and signals the Gods and heroes in Valhalla that a great warrior is on the way to join them. We burn them in a ship, either a real one, or a death ship we build specially for their final voyage. The flames and smoke launch the ship and the dead on their final voyage, and speed their journey to the feast-hall of the Gods."

❖ ❖ ❖

We labored till dusk. Harald was pleased with our progress, and said we should easily finish the following day.

At the evening meal, my mother ate little, then retired to her bed-closet. Few who lived in the longhouse slept in the privacy of an enclosed bed. Most, slave and free both, made their beds at night on the long platforms built against the side walls of the longhouse. Hrorik and Gunhild had a small private chamber walled off in one corner of the longhouse at the end farthest from the animals' byre, and Harald and his sister, Sigrid, had bed-closets—beds with paneled enclosures for privacy. My mother, Derdriu, also had a bed-closet. It had been something of a scandal and had caused a terrible fight between Hrorik and Gunhild, when Hrorik had told Gudrod the Carpenter to build a bed-closet for my mother, a mere slave. But Hrorik came often to her bed, and did not choose to do his rutting in full view of the entire household.

That evening, Mother and I sat together on her bed late into the night, talking, the doors of her bed-closet open for light. It was a familiar place to me, and comforting, for when I was younger I had often slept there, secure inside its walls, snuggled close to my mother for warmth—except when Hrorik would come in the middle of the night and turn me out, claiming for himself my place at my mother's side.

To me, Mother appeared far more at peace that night than I felt, though she left no silence long unfilled.

"I do not want you to die, Mother," I told her. "Let me remain a thrall. It's wrong that you die for Hrorik, after all the harm and pain he's caused you. You owe him nothing. I hate him for what he's done to you."

My mother took my face between her hands and gazed into my eyes. "My dear Halfdan," she said. "I do not die for Hrorik. I die for you. I am grateful I have the chance to give you this gift.

"Sometimes, though rarely," she said, "I am visited by the second sight. My grandmother in Ireland possessed it to a very high degree. When my grandfather was king, he would often consult her before he acted. It passed through her blood to my mother, and through my mother to me, though weakly. Perhaps it has passed to you, too. Time will tell.

"I knew before the *Red Eagle* returned that Hrorik was dying. In the same way, I know that there is greatness inside of you. But that greatness can only be realized if you are a free man. And I know that only I can set you free.

"You must not hate your father. There was

both good and bad in him, as there is in all men. There is much about him, and about what passed between him and me, that you do not know. I must tell you now, while there's still time. The past is like a great stone that lies on the bed of a river, hidden from view but shaping the currents of the water as it flows by. You cannot read the currents in the river of your own life, and navigate them safely, if you do not understand what causes them. You must know your past, for it will shape your future.

"I have never told you the full tale of how I became a slave—the story of my capture and the first years of my life in Hrorik's household. By the time you were old enough to understand, Hrorik had already wed Gunhild and the paths our lives were following seemed a doom that was set and could not be changed. To have told you this tale before now would have only made you bitter. Now . . . you should know."

My mother settled back against the end wall at the head of her bed-closet and began. "The summer when Hrorik stole me from Ireland, my home, I was only fifteen years of age, just barely older than you are now. My father, Caidoc, was a king over lands along the River Bann, under the High King of Ulster. I was his only child.

"My father wished to form an alliance with the ruler of the neighboring kingdom, a king named

56

Frial, so the previous winter he had betrothed me to Kilian, Frial's oldest son. We were to be wed at the end of the summer, at the harvest feast. Kilian was strong and tall, with a gentle manner and pleasing smile. I was considered the greatest beauty in our two kingdoms, and we were both well pleased with the match. Had the marriage occurred, one day I would have been a queen, and the two kingdoms would have eventually been united and ruled by Kilian's and my son, if I'd borne him one.

"Because I was his only child, my father doted on me and gave me more freedom than was enjoyed by most well-born young women my age. One of the ways he indulged me was in my desire for learning. From a young age, I was allowed to study at a nearby monastery whose lands adjoined my father's. I craved the knowledge contained in the books and manuscripts there, many of them hundreds of years old. And the abbot, who was a kindly man, was willing to humor so avid a student, even though I was not a male. To unlock the secrets contained in the monastery's library, I learned to read and speak Latin, the language the ancient books were written in.

"We all were aware, of course, of the pirate raids by the Northmen that had been occurring more and more frequently along the coast.

However, my father believed our lands were safe, being so far inland from the sea. Like many folk in our land, he misjudged the Northmen's greed and daring.

"It happened on a day late in the waning summer. I was reading in the library at the monastery. Suddenly I became aware of cries of alarm coming from out in the courtyard. When I ran to the window and looked out, I saw that Northmen were attacking and had already breached the gate. A few of the monks tried to resist, but they were not warriors. The Northmen cut them down without mercy, and the rest surrendered without a fight.

"I tried to hide. I pulled a chair into a corner of the library, stacked it and the floor around with books and scrolls, then crouched behind, trembling with fear and praying desperately to God to make me invisible to the heathen eyes of the pirates. My efforts were, of course, to no avail. One of the pirates found me. I still remember how he looked, and how he smelled of sweat and blood. He dragged me from my hiding place, threw me on my back on the table in the library, pulled my skirts up over my head and was going to rape me then and there. I was screaming—I did not know so much sound was in me. The pirate's chieftain heard the noise and came to investigate, and stopped the man from raping me.

"The pirate chieftain was Hrorik, your father. He was thinner then through the body, and his beard and hair were still a rich, yellow gold, without a trace of gray. By the other pirate's deference to him, I realized he must be a leader, and by his grand appearance I could see he was a man of substance: a highly polished helm crowned his head, and a fine shirt of mail covered his breast, with a richly woven red cloak pinned at one shoulder and hanging down his back. It is strange how vividly that first image of him still lives in my mind. I remember, too, that he carried a long Danish war-axe in one hand. It was the first time I had seen such a weapon.

"When Hrorik stopped my attacker from raping me, I thought perhaps he had been sent by God to save me, in answer to my prayers. I thought perhaps he was a Christian, and that was why he'd intervened. I soon realized I was wrong. He began touching me, feeling the cloth of my dress, and turning my head from side to side, studying my face. Then he ran a hand through my hair and bent down and smelled it. When he did that I believed he had stopped the other man merely to take his place, and I began screaming again.

"Hrorik looked startled for a moment by the volume of noise I was producing. Then he smiled.

It was not an evil smile. He was genuinely amused, and his humor showed in his eyes. He put one hand across my mouth to muffle me. His other hand he freed by hooking the blade of his axe on the edge of the table, then he raised a finger to his lips and spoke a word that was common to both our languages.

"'Shush!' he said, then 'shush' again. It was the first word your father spoke to me. It is a word I've heard from him many times since."

"Why did he stop the warrior from raping you?" I asked.

"Much later, after I learned the language of the Northmen, I asked Hrorik that. He told me he could tell I was a valuable prize, either the daughter or wife of a noble, and worth much ransom. He said he'd stopped the man only because damaged goods bring a lower price at market. He had not intended to show me kindness, only to protect my value."

If my mother believed her tale would improve my opinion of my father, so far it had not.

"I was taken down to the courtyard of the monastery," she continued, "where the pirates were tying the hands of their captives, and roping us together in pairs. Abbot Aidan was among the prisoners, and I was tied together with him.

"Aidan was a very learned man, with a great

gift for tongues. As a young man, before he dedicated his life to God and the church, he'd left home seeking adventure and had sailed the northern seas for many years on a vessel owned by a Frankish merchant from the trading port of Dorestad. During that time he'd learned the language of the Northmen. His knowledge allowed him, during those early days of our captivity, to converse with our captors and to explain to me their plans for us. He confirmed to Hrorik that I was indeed of noble birth, and in fact was the daughter of King Caidoc who ruled over the surrounding lands. Hrorik was much pleased by the news.

"'The Lord is watching over you, Derdriu my child,' Aidan told me after speaking with Hrorik. 'You will be freed unharmed. It is only a matter of time, for the pirates' chieftain must contact your father and arrange for a ransom to be paid. The pirates intend to ransom me, too. Your father and the abbots of the other monasteries across the land will all contribute to free a churchman of my rank who has been taken captive.'

"Aidan sighed heavily and looked sadly at the monks standing near us. 'My children are not so fortunate. I fear no one can afford to pay for the safe return of all of them. Some at least, perhaps all, are doomed to a life of slavery.' Aidan was a kindly man, and the fate of the monks he'd led worried him. I could feel only relief for my own fate, knowing that soon I would be free."

Mother shook her head sadly. "It was not to be," she said. "The pirates marched us like a herd of stolen cattle across country toward the river where they'd left their ship. My father learned of the raid on the monastery and my capture. He had no way of knowing, of course, that Hrorik was protecting me from harm and intended to exchange me for ransom. Gathering such force as he could assemble on short notice, he set out in pursuit. Because of the necessity for speed, only those warriors wealthy enough to own war-chariots or fine, fast mounts joined father's would-be band of avengers. By chance—unfortunate chance, as it proved—my betrothed, Kilian, and his father, King Frial, were out hunting with a small retinue of their followers, and encountered my father and his men as they were racing after the Danes. They, of course, joined in the pursuit, though they were not equipped for war.

"My father and his men caught up with the pirates before they reached the safety of the river and their ship. As they neared, Father's men signaled their coming with peals of their war-horns, perhaps thinking to give us captives hope and to throw fear into the hearts of the pirates.

"A shallow stream cut through the meadow we were crossing when the horns first warned of the approach of Father and his men. Because of the dryness that summer, the water in the stream came no higher than our ankles, but in wetter seasons the stream ran swiftly. Over many years, its waters had cut the channel of the streambed as deep as the waist of a grown man. At Hrorik's command, the pirates crossed it and began forming for battle on the far bank. Hrorik assembled half of his men in a battle line, standing shoulder to shoulder with the prisoners huddled behind. The other half of his force concealed themselves below the edge of the stream's bank. All of the men who lay hidden were armed with bows or spears.

"Barely had the pirates concealed themselves when Father and his men swept into view. When Hrorik saw them as they rounded the base of a low hill, riding in their chariots, he threw back his head and laughed. His laughter chilled my heart. A cheer burst from the throats of my father's men when they saw us. Because fully half of the Danes were hidden from sight, my father's warriors must have thought their victory was assured.

"What followed was not so much a battle as a slaughter. The chariots could not cross the barrier created by the streambed. As they drew nearer and saw it, their drivers began sawing furiously at their reins, trying to slow their horses' headlong charge. The warriors on horseback galloped on, undeterred. Then the hidden pirates rose from their place of concealment below the edge of the bank and let their missiles fly.

"Almost the entire front rank of horses in the charge went down, felled by the deadly fire. The chariots and horses rushing behind could not stop in time to avoid them. Instantly all was chaos as the second wave of the charge collided with the sudden barrier of dead and dying mounts. Some of the chariots flipped, cart over horse, flinging their drivers like stones shot from a catapult. Others, trying desperately to turn aside, skidded sideways till their wheels caught in the soft turf and their carriages rolled, crushing their human cargo. A few skilled riders on horseback—my betrothed, Kilian, was among them—vaulted over the mass of wreckage and injured, raced past the first group of Danes, and crossed the streambed to the battle line beyond on the far bank. They were too few, though. The pirates' line held firm and cut them down. I saw Kilian fall with a spear through his side.

"Not all of the Irish warriors were killed, of course. Those in the rear of the charge were able to turn aside in time. But when they saw so many of their own men get cut to ribbons, and realized how large was the band of Danes who opposed them, they turned and fled.

"Unfortunately, my father and King Frial, who were both brave men, had been leading the charge. In a few brief and bloody moments, everyone who might have paid ransom to the pirates and won my freedom was killed.

"We prisoners waited beside the streambed all afternoon under guard, while the Danes pillaged the battlefield. They stripped the bodies of their valuables, their weapons, and sometimes even their clothes. We stood and watched, numb and despairing, making no sound except when Abbot Aidan led the monks in prayers for the dead. It was when the pirates were robbing the bodies of the slain that they found two men wearing circlets of gold. Hrorik realized the significance of the find. He brought Abbot Aidan and me to where they lay, and we confirmed that one of the dead men was my father, and the other King Frial. After we did, Hrorik spoke a while, then pointed at me, indicating that Aidan should tell me what he'd said.

"'The chieftain says to tell you that he is sorry, for your sake, for the death of your father, but such is the way of war,' Aidan said. 'He also said it will be awkward if there is no one left to pay your ransom.' Abbot Aidan looked uncomfortable as he spoke these last words. Well he should have, for they filled me with fury.

"I answered Hrorik, while Abbot Aidan translated. 'Awkward? It is far more than awkward,' I told him. 'For both of us your victory will prove costly. On this field of battle not only does my father lie slain, but also my betrothed, and his father, too. My doom is upon me. I who was once a princess shall now become a slave, and no doubt shall die as one. I can only pray that death finds me soon. You have but lost a ransom. I feel as though my heart has been ripped from my breast.'

"That night, the Danes held a great feast on the bank of the river where their ship was moored. They roasted meat from the horses killed in the battle, and drank heavily from casks of ale they'd forced the monks to carry from the monastery.

"We captives were forced to sit huddled in a tight group, off to one side of the bonfire the Danes had built. There were more prisoners than just those of us who'd been taken in the attack on the monastery. The pirates had apparently raided as they'd moved upriver, for more than a score of other prisoners who'd been previously captured, mostly women and a few children, were confined with us.

"As the feast wore on into the night, several times Danes left the circle of their fellows around the fire, staggered over to the prisoners, and, after searching among the frightened faces, led one woman prisoner or another off into the shadows, to the sound of sobbing and occasional screams. After this had happened several times the awkwardness which Hrorik had spoken of manifested itself.

"The pirate who had found me in the monastery, a tall, lanky Dane with long greasy black hair hanging down around his shoulders, dressed in a dirty brown woolen tunic and trousers, stood up and forced his way into the crowd of prisoners. He stopped in front of me and spoke some words. There was no reason he should have expected me to understand, but he was obviously drunk, so perhaps his wits were dimmed by ale.

"'What does he want?' I asked Aidan in a frightened whisper, though in my heart I knew.

"'He is telling you to come with him,' Aidan said. 'He says since no one can ransom you, you are his property now.'

"Hrorik, who was seated on the far side of the fire, stood up and strode over to where my captor was standing. The two of them argued back and forth for a time, their voices growing louder and angrier. Finally the black-haired Dane shook his head, shouted one final word, and grabbed me by my arm, pulling me to my feet. I was sobbing by this time, and pleading with him to leave me alone, though of course the Dane could understand nothing I said.

"Suddenly Hrorik slapped my captor hard across the face with the back of his hand. The man staggered back and shouted furiously at Hrorik. Whatever it was that he said brought a grim smile to Hrorik's face. Then both men turned and walked away.

"'What is happening?' I asked Aidan.

"'The chieftain,' he explained, 'offered to buy you from the other pirate. He kept offering a higher and higher price, but the black-haired Dane refused. Then the chieftain slapped him. Among their people, it is a deadly insult. The other Dane had no choice but to challenge the chieftain to a duel. They have gone to arm themselves.

"The fight was brief. My captor was armed with a spear and shield, plus a long knife stuck in his belt. He had no helm nor armor. I suspect he was too poor to afford them. Perhaps to make the fight appear more fair, Hrorik also wore no armor, and did not even carry a shield. He entered the ring the pirates formed around the fire armed only with his sword, yet the thin Dane clearly was afraid. He kept moving away from Hrorik, backing around the circle while Hrorik followed, stalking him. Suddenly, with a fierce cry, my captor leapt forward, stabbing his spear at Hrorik's chest. Hrorik also lunged forward, slapping the spear aside with the flat of his sword. With his empty hand, he grabbed the rim of the black-haired Dane's shield and, heaving mightily on it, slung him to the ground. As he struggled to regain his feet, Hrorik's sword swung down, and the duel was ended.

"A short time later, Hrorik approached us, pushing his way through the prisoners, who by now were huddled tightly together against the coolness of the night air. I cowered behind Abbot Aidan, fearing Hrorik had come to claim the prize he'd won. When he reached our position and stood over me, though, he did naught but hold out a heavy woolen cloak. After I cautiously took it, he spoke briefly with Aidan, then returned to the celebration at the fire.

"Abbot Aidan and I wrapped the cloak around our shoulders, grateful for its warmth. 'What did he say?' I asked.

"'He said the night would be cold and the cloak would keep you warm.'

"'Is that all he said?' I asked, suspicious.

"'He said you need fear no longer. He said to tell you his name is Hrorik, and now you are under his protection.'

"The next morning, the Danes rowed their ship back downriver to the sea. When they reached the coast, they raised the sail and set a course away from land. The other women prisoners, and even some of the men, began wailing and crying. I was silent, though. I had no strength left in my spirit for such displays. I just watched quietly as the green hills of Ireland slowly receded until finally I could see them no more. In my heart I knew I would never see my home again.

"Abbot Aidan became quite agitated when we sailed away from land. He called frantically to Hrorik, reminding him that the church would pay ransom to win his freedom. Hrorik, who was manning the ship's steering oar and setting our course, ignored him until we had passed beyond sight of land. Then he called another of the crew to take over steering the ship, and came to where Aidan, now dejected and silent, was sitting beside me among the other prisoners.

"Hrorik squatted down beside us and spoke. When he'd finished, Aidan told me what he'd said. 'This black-hearted pirate has told me I am not to be ransomed after all. He says he finds my knowledge of the different tongues of men to be of value, and he's decided to keep me for himself as a slave in his own household. He says he wants me to teach you to speak the tongue of the Northmen, too.'

"Hrorik spoke again briefly to Aidan, then looked expectantly at me.

"'The chieftain asks that you speak your name to him, so that he may learn how to say it,' Aidan told me.

"'Derdriu,' I said. Then, because Hrorik looked puzzled at the sound, I repeated it again, more slowly: 'Derdriu.'

"Hrorik nodded. 'Derdriu,' he repeated softly several times. Then he spoke rapidly for a few moments with Aidan, and rose as if to leave.

"'The chieftain has ordered me to begin your lessons immediately,' Aidan said bitterly. 'He said he hopes to be able to speak directly with you by the time our voyage is ended. To speed our progress, neither of us will have any other duties while we are onboard his ship.'

"I looked at Hrorik with disbelief. 'Am I to understand that conversation is all that will be required of me?' I asked.

"Abbot Aidan said nothing. Hrorik indicated that he should translate my words, and waited impatiently for him to do so. When Aidan had finished, Hrorik answered brusquely.

"'When we reach land, you also are to be a slave in his household,' Aidan translated. 'There, everyone works, including him. You will care for his children. Their mother recently died.' Aidan looked embarrassed and paused for a moment, then continued. 'He said to tell you that he understands what you fear. He said that if he wished to take you by force, he would have done so already. It is not his desire. He says he does not understand his own heart and head in this matter, for you are very beautiful, and he is used to taking what he wants.'"

My mother drank some water from a cup she'd brought to her bed. Her tale left me astonished. I did not recognize the man she'd been describing as the Hrorik I'd known, and I told her so. I, too, thought of Hrorik as a man who had cared little for the wishes of others, and had claimed as his own whatever he wanted.

"That is why I felt the need to tell you this," she replied. "Whatever else Hrorik was, or what he became, he is your father. And I would not have you go through life believing you were a bastard-child who was the result of rape, rather than conceived in love."

"In love!" I exclaimed. This was too much to believe. "How can that be so?" I demanded.

"In those days, Hrorik did not have this large estate, which he acquired with Gunhild's dowry. Then he had only a smaller farm in the north on the Limfjord. Although it was small, there was a homey air of comfort about it that this greater estate lacks.

"By the time we reached Hrorik's lands, I was

already speaking halting phrases in the Northmen's tongue, and such was Hrorik's eagerness to converse with me that my knowledge quickly progressed under the constant practice he gave me. He took great delight in simple things, such as teaching me the names for plants and trees, for different beasts, or foods, or farm implements. So obvious was his pleasure in speaking with me, and so gentle and kind his manner, that I, too, came to enjoy the times we spoke together, though I felt guilt that I could feel anything but hate for the man responsible for the death of my father.

"As my understanding of his tongue grew, Hrorik told me about his own life. He talked with great pride of the accomplishments of his two young children, Harald and Sigrid, and he told me of their mother, Helge. Hrorik and Helge had known each other since childhood, and their families had always expected that they would marry. From what he told me of her, Helge was a merry-spirited woman, whom he had enjoyed and respected greatly. She died of a fever when Harald and Sigrid were five years of age, during the winter before the raid on Ireland when I was captured.

"My duties at Hrorik's farm were light. Primarily, I was to be as a mother to Harald and Sigrid. I found that caring for them was no burden, for they were sweet and affectionate children, and over time I gave my heart to them completely. I could do so without guilt, for unlike their father, their hands were not stained with blood. So I was a mother in Hrorik's family, but no more, for by his manner toward me, Hrorik acted almost as a brother would toward a beloved sister, with great kindness and affection, but nothing more.

"Then came the night that changed everything. We had had a merry dinner, with much laughter and too much drink. When there were no guests, as on that night, Hrorik would insist that I eat at table with him, though I was but a thrall. That night Abbot Aidan had joined us, too. It was his telling of tales, some quite bawdy, from his days as a Frankish merchant-sailor that had caused our merriment.

"I put Harald and Sigrid to bed while the kitchen thralls cleared away the remains of the supper. When I was done, I saw Hrorik still seated at the table, now alone, and I went to him. His expression had turned somber.

"'Where has your recent mirth departed to?' I teased.

"'My thoughts are better left unspoken,' he replied, 'lest they be misunderstood.'

"The jollity of the evening, and perhaps also the amount I had drunk, had left me bold. 'Misunderstood?' I asked. 'Do you still consider me so poor a pupil of your tongue?'

"'It is the language of my heart I would have you understand,' he replied. Hrorik took a deep breath and released it slowly. 'Derdriu,' he asked, 'will you come to my bed this night?'

"I felt startled and frightened by his words. My face must have shown it, for he looked away as though dismayed. When he turned back to me, he kept his eyes downcast. 'I must know,' he said. 'What thoughts filled your mind at my words and made you look so?'

"I searched my thoughts and heart carefully before I answered.

"'The first thought that entered my mind,' I told him truthfully, 'was a recollection of the day I was stolen, and how I feared that day that I would be raped, and hated you and your men for what you had done and what I feared you would do.'

"Hrorik pounded his fist upon the table, and Abbot Aidan, from across the hall, looked over in concern.

"I was silent after that for a time," Mother said, "as I searched further through my thoughts and deeper into my heart. I marveled as I realized that the anger I'd long felt toward Hrorik, because he'd stolen me from my home and caused the death of my father, had faded.

"'The other thought that now enters my

mind,' I told him then, 'is to wonder what has taken so long for you to ask me?'

My mother smiled, and I could tell that for a moment she wandered in her memories.

"That night," she said, "was one of the sweetest of my life. And there were many more nights, and days, too, over the next three years that were as sweet as honey. You were born during that time, less than a year after I first came to Hrorik's bed."

"What happened?" I asked her. "What changed?"

"I thought Hrorik would marry me. I believed he would free me and we would wed, and you would stand next to Harald as his son. But then he led a great raid on Dorestad, the Franks' trading center on the coast of Frisia, using knowledge of its defenses he'd gained from talks with Aidan about his life among the Franks. Dorestad was captured and sacked, and all who went on the raid won much wealth. Men began to flatter Hrorik, telling him that if he continued to grow in wealth and renown as a chieftain, he was surely destined to someday be made a jarl by the king and rule over a district.

"Alas, their words of flattery went to his head. A chieftain named Orm had been killed in the Dorestad raid, leaving a rich widow. Her name was Gunhild, and she was the daughter of Eirik, a wealthy jarl who lived on the island of Fyn. All of Eirik's son's were dead, and it had been widely believed that when Jarl Eirik died, Gunhild's husband, Orm, would be appointed jarl by the king to replace him. Although he loved me, Hrorik paid court to Gunhild and wed her to gain the wealth of her dowry and the hope of her father's title.

"My heart was torn apart the day I saw Hrorik and Gunhild wed. It should have been me, not her, standing by his side. It should have been you, not Toke, her son by her first husband, who was accepted into Hrorik's family as a son. But instead we remained thralls.

"Poor Hrorik. Jarl Eirik still lives, but now Hrorik is dead. He sacrificed our happiness but never gained his prize. Though he treated Gunhild with respect, it did not take her long to realize that his heart belonged to another. She argued often with him that he should sell me, but he would not. After a time, he began visiting my bed again. I think he hoped to recapture the happiness we'd known, but that part of my heart that had once held love for him was now filled with only bitterness."

My mother paused and caressed my cheek softly with her hand.

"And now, my son," she said, "you understand the truth of the lives that your father and I have shared. Because he is your father, much of him is in you, so it is good you know the tale."

She was wrong. I had heard my mother's words, but I still did not understand. As far back as my mind could find memories, I had known love for my mother, and she had always shown her love for me and tenderly cared for me. That kind of love I understood. Even thralls, who possess almost nothing, can feel such love. But I did not understand what could ever cause a woman to feel aught but fear and loathing for a man who'd stolen her from her home, killed her father, and made her a slave. I did not understand how my mother could ever have come to love Hrorik. To me, it seemed obvious he had never truly loved her. If he had, he would not have betrayed her by marrying Gunhild, and dooming Mother and me to lives of slavery. That was no way to show love.

Even though Hrorik had freed me before he'd died, I did not believe I could ever come to think kindly of him. Too many years of slavery had gone before. My mother and I had suffered too much, for too long. My mother might forgive him, but I never would.

5

A FUNERAL PYRE

By noon on the second day of our labors, the death ship and death house were completed. We embedded tall stones, each almost as large as a man, in the ground at either end of the outline of the ship that had been cut into the thick turf on the hilltop. It took six of us—Harald, Ubbe, Fasti, Hrut, Ing, and me—to wrestle them into place. The two tall stones formed the stemposts of the death ship, as the curved wooden timbers rising from the keel formed the stemposts on a real longship. Smaller boulders, knee-high or slightly larger, spaced an arm's length apart, curved in two arcs from the stern to the bow, marking the death ship's sides.

Where Fasti, Hrut, and Ing had dug out the

square hole in the center of the death ship, we'd built a rough shed of logs. It was windowless and had a single low doorway. Inside, against the wall opposite the doorway, we'd built a bier of loosely spaced, stacked layers of small logs and thick branches, with twigs and brush stuffed in the gaps between the larger timbers. The top of the bier, which was waist-high, was a platform of rough planks, draped with cloaks, to lay the bodies on. We leaned stacks of dry, dead wood against the outside walls of the death house, as high as the roof. When lit, it would make a bonfire that could be seen for miles.

I'd worked hard, wresting boulders and chopping and stacking wood. I'd hoped that if I worked hard enough, I wouldn't think about what would follow when we finished our labors. My hopes were in vain. Images of my mother snuck constantly into my mind. I was building her funeral pyre. She still lived, but I was preparing for her funeral. I felt as though I was trapped in an evil dream which I was powerless to wake from.

Such thoughts apparently did not trouble Harald. He stood, hands on his hips, surveying the product of our labors.

"It is good," Harald said. He turned to me. "At Lindholm Hoje, a village in the north near the Limfjord, not far from where Hrorik's people first settled after they came south from the lands of the Norse, there is an entire field of stone death ships, a great fleet of the dead who have sailed from this world into the next. It is a strange sight to behold."

Harald called to Ubbe, who'd helped us complete the death house after we'd finished with the stones for the ship's hull.

"It's done. Send messengers out to the folk of the village. We will have the funeral this afternoon, when the sun begins to fall, and feast afterward."

Then he looked at me. "There is not much more time," he said. "Sigrid and I must prepare Hrorik's body. You should go to your mother."

I found my mother sitting in her bed-closet with Sigrid, Harald's sister—my sister now, too, I realized. Both appeared to have been weeping, but they rubbed their cheeks when they saw me approaching, and spoke in cheerful voices.

My mother had on the new red dress she'd made. She lifted the hem to show me the shift underneath.

"Look, Halfdan. Sigrid has given me this fine white linen shift to wear under my dress." She raised her hand to her throat. "And look. This amber necklace. She gave me this, too."

"They are nothing," Sigrid said. "The love

you gave to Harald and me when we were young, when two children who'd but recently lost their mother were lonely and afraid, is the treasure beyond price."

My mother's eyes filled with tears. Sigrid put her arms around her and held her.

"On this day," Sigrid said, "in this world and the next, you will take your rightful place at my father's side. This day, may I call you Mother?"

My mother opened her mouth, but no words came. She nodded her head, her eyes glistening with tears. Then both women began weeping. I stood beside them, silent and embarrassed, not knowing what to do. Finally Sigrid kissed Mother on both of her cheeks, then backed away. She turned to me, smiling through her tears.

"Derdriu and I have something for you, also."

A stack of folded garments lay at the foot of my mother's bed. One by one, Mother handed them to me. There was a white linen tunic with embroidery around the neck opening and the ends of the sleeves, a pair of dark green woolen trousers, a leather belt with a silver buckle and tip, and a short cloak of gray wool with a large circular silver brooch, cast in the shape of a fanciful serpent, to pin it.

"We had no time to make new clothes," Mother said. "These were Harald's, that he gave us for you. They are in fine condition, not worn out at all. Sigrid has helped me remake them to fit you."

"We did not want you to attend the feast looking like a thrall," Sigrid added.

"I . . . I thank you," I stammered. I'd given no thought to my own appearance, until Sigrid mentioned it. I would have shamed myself at the funeral and feast, had I worn my tattered and filthy tunic—the only clothing I possessed. No doubt I would have shamed Harald and Sigrid, too. A small, graceless voice in the back of my mind wondered if that was the real reason for my new clothes. I might be free, but in my heart still lived the suspicious, petty spirit of a slave.

Sigrid embraced me. "I am happy to have you as my brother," she whispered. When she released me, she turned to my mother.

"You will want to spend the time remaining with Halfdan," she said, and hurried away.

Mother took a deep breath, and let it out slowly.

"So. It is time?" she asked. I looked down, embarrassed.

"Soon. The work is completed. Messengers have been sent to summon the villagers."

What do you say to your mother when she is about to die so that you can better your own life?

83

I felt struck dumb and said nothing.

Mother took off her linen cap, unpinned her hair, and let it fall down her back. Although it infuriated Gunhild, Hrorik had let her keep her hair long, unlike the rest of the thralls, who wore their hair cropped short. Mother did keep it pinned up and concealed under her cap, though. Gunhild was not a woman to anger heedlessly.

"Will you comb my hair for me, Halfdan?" she asked. "I shall wear it down today, as a princess of Ireland would on a feast day. Hrorik used to love to run his hands through my hair. Years ago, when we lived in the north, sometimes he would sit behind me and comb it for me. I would feel a man's hands in my hair once more in this lifetime."

At first we sat in silence as I ran the comb through her long hair. It was as black and shiny as the feathers of a raven, without a trace of gray. After a time, she spoke to me over her shoulder, as I stroked the comb through her tresses.

"I have little to leave you. This bed-closet shall of course be yours. You must move it up to the other end of the hall, away from the animals' byre, as befitting your new status. Poor Gunhild. How it infuriated her that I, a mere thrall, should have a bed-closet, when none of the carls who live in the longhouse had one. When Hrorik had Gudrod build it for me, I think he intended equally to spare

Gunhild embarrassment when he came to my bed as he did to benefit himself and me. All Gunhild could see, though, was this bed standing in her house every day as a monument to his affection for another woman.

"My comb was also a gift from Hrorik. It is well made. The teeth are fine and close together, and catch even the smallest lice. It will serve you well. And these two other things I want you to have most of all. They're all I have left of Ireland."

Lifting her hair up from the back of her neck, Mother exposed the leather thong around it from which hung a small silver cross she wore, under her shift.

"Untie the knot," she said.

It seemed wrong. I'd never seen my mother remove the cross from around her neck. But wordlessly I obeyed.

When I'd untied the knot for her, she said, "Turn around." Then she took the cord from my hands, raised it over my head, and tied the thong in a knot behind my neck.

"This is the sign of the Lord Jesus Christ, the one true God," she told me. "Wear it always, and perhaps He will watch over you and protect you, even in this heathen land. And this," she said, as she placed a small sealskin pouch in my hands, "contains the words our Lord spoke during His lifetime."

I recognized the pouch. I'd learned to hate seeing Mother bring it out over the years. It contained a small parchment scroll, relating the life of the man-god the Christians worshiped. Hrorik had taken it as plunder in a raid many years ago, and had given it as a gift to my mother. She'd spent many hours using the scroll to teach me about the White Christ, and also teaching me to read, write, and speak in Latin, the language of the Christian church. I'd hated those lessons. I'd hated wasting the little free time a slave is given to learn Latin. Why should a thrall learn to speak and read the language of a foreign people, or study the life of a weak God, who held no power in our lands? If the White Christ was as great a God as Mother claimed, why had he not protected her? Still, I knew Mother valued the little scroll highly, and to her the gift meant much. I stroked the worn leather of the little pouch gently, swallowing hard.

"It is *I* who should be giving gifts to you," I told her, looking down. I felt embarrassed that I had nothing to give her.

She smiled and reached out and placed her hand over mine, on the pouch.

"Every moment of your life has been a gift to me," she answered. "And it is a great gift now to know that you will make your way in the world as a free man. You are growing into a fine man,

Halfdan, and I know you will live your life well. No mother could ask for more than that."

A horn sounded from the hilltop. A shadow of fear briefly crossed her face. Then she forced a smile to her face and spoke, though her eyes betrayed the falseness of her cheery expression and voice.

"Quickly now," Mother said. "That is the first call for the ceremony. Run to the washhouse and clean off the sweat and dirt from your labors. You must present a fine appearance, for all will be watching. We have little time to prepare you."

By the time the horn sounded its second mournful peal, I was clean, or at least relatively so—thralls were not encouraged to bathe or allowed to use the bathhouse, so washing was a new skill I had yet to fully master.

Back at Mother's bed-closet, I quickly dressed in my new finery. She combed my hair for me and pinned the cloak together at my left shoulder with the silver brooch.

"I should have thought to tend to your hair before now," she said, trying to arrange it round my face with her hands. "This short, ragged cut is that of a thrall, not a chieftain's son. But we have no time. As it grows out, ask Sigrid to trim it for you. It would be a sisterly thing for her to do for you."

I could not imagine asking Sigrid to cut my hair. I feared she might recoil at the suggestion. But I said nothing to my mother.

We embraced, and I could feel her trembling. I wondered if she could feel that I was trembling, too.

As we stepped out of the door of the longhouse, Mother put her hand in mine and gripped it tightly. She held her chin high and looked straight ahead as we walked. As we took that final walk together, I glanced frequently at her, at the ground, at the people who were gathering on the hill above—anywhere except at the death ship that awaited us.

The sun still shone brightly outside, though the shadows were beginning to deepen and lengthen as the sun dropped toward the horizon and the afternoon waned. A light breeze rustled the grass as Mother and I climbed to the top of the hill. In the sky above, two gulls circled, calling to each other in their harsh voices, their curiosity no doubt aroused by the gathering on the hill.

Most of the folk of the village were already up on the hilltop, standing together on the landward side of the stone ship, looking across it out toward the sea. As my mother and I made our way with slow, deliberate steps up the hillside, a few stragglers from the village hurried past us, on their way to join the gathering. They stared at us, but did not speak. At the summit their paths parted from ours. The latecomers moved to join the crowd of villagers and folk from the estate.

Mother and I walked toward the entrance of the death house. My legs felt disconnected from the rest of my body, and my steps slow and awkward, like movement in a dream. I wished it was but a dream, a bad dream, and that I could awake from it.

Harald and Sigrid awaited us at the entrance. With them was Ase, Ubbe's wife. She was a shaman, and the local priestess of the goddesses Freyja and Frigg. In one hand she held a staff carved with magic runes and symbols, and something was wrapped around her other hand. I realized it was a knotted cord. I glanced at my mother, and saw that she, too, was staring at the cord.

"Ase must go," she said. "I will not die strangled like some sacrifice to your pagan Gods."

Ase looked at Harald questioningly. He nodded, and she left, joining the crowd standing around the stern of the stone ship. "Safe journey, Derdriu," she said, softly, as she passed us. "Fair winds."

My mother took a deep breath and spoke. "Men say, Harald, that there is no one in the district, and perhaps in all of Denmark, who is as swift and sure with a blade as you are. As a parting gift, to one who loved you as a mother, will you help me on my way?"

"I am honored by your request," Harald replied, smiling gently at her. I did not understand how he could smile. I knew his heart must hold some kind feelings for my mother because she had raised him when he and Sigrid were young. Sigrid had told Mother she loved her. Yet now Harald must kill her. His face showed nothing, though. Harald was a true warrior, who feared nothing. I could never be such.

My mother turned to me and we embraced for the last time.

"Mother . . ." I whispered.

She put her hand over my lips to silence me, then said simply, "I love you, Halfdan."

I wanted to tell her not to go, but it was too late.

Mother turned and with her back straight and head held high, she walked to Harald and Sigrid. Each embraced her in turn.

"It is a fine day," Harald said. "A good day for sailing."

They turned together and began walking toward the doorway of the death house, Sigrid on my mother's right side, her arm about her waist, Harald on her left and slightly behind. As they walked, I saw Harald slip his knife from its sheath with his right hand and hold it down close beside his leg, out of sight.

"Do you remember the day, Derdriu," he asked, "when we still lived up north, on the Limfjord, and you took Sigrid and me down to the big rocks along the shore, and she and I went fishing for the first time in our lives? You were still carrying Halfdan in your belly. Sigrid hooked a fish and you helped her pull it in. Do you remember? It was a beautiful day, sunny with a light breeze, much like today. It is a joyful memory that I carry to this day. Do you recall it?"

They stepped down into the doorway of the death house and passed out of sight. I thought I heard a gasp, and Harald stopped talking. I ran to the doorway and looked inside. Harald was holding my mother in his arms, lifting her onto the platform of the bier. Hrorik's body had already been placed there, his shield at his head and his helm at his feet. When Harald slid his arm out from under Mother's back, after he'd laid her body beside Hrorik's, I saw a smear of blood on his sleeve. Sigrid glanced back and saw me watching from the doorway. She stepped in front of something lying on the floor, and Harald bent over and picked it up.

When Harald turned to face me his knife was

back in its scabbard. Sigrid smoothed my mother's hair around her face.

"She sleeps now for a while," Harald said. "She and Hrorik are resting in preparation for their voyage."

Harald was wearing a horn slung on a leather strap over his shoulder. It was this horn that had summoned us to the hilltop. Now, as he exited the death house, he lifted the horn to his lips and blew two long, slow notes.

At Harald's cue, a procession began to move toward us from among the crowd gathered on the top of the hill. Most were folk of the household who lived in the longhouse, but many also were from the village over which Hrorik had presided as chieftain. All who approached were bearing gifts, save a few who led or carried beasts.

Harald indicated that I should stand with Sigrid and him at the doorway of the death house, to greet the procession of gift bearers.

"It is our duty to receive the gifts and give thanks for the honor they convey," he explained. "We are Hrorik's children."

First in the line was Gunhild. She was bearing, folded in her arms to form a square cushion, Hrorik's heaviest winter cloak. It was a magnificent garment, thick wool dyed a deep green, with a red silk border sewed around the edge. She also bore, lying across the top of the cloak, Hrorik's sword in its scabbard, plus other of his personal items, including a silver comb with ivory teeth, a fine silver goblet, and a small leather pouch of the type men use to carry flint and steel for fire-starting.

She stopped in front of the three of us, but looked only at Harald as she proclaimed her speech.

"I am Gunhild, wife of Hrorik Strong-Axe. I bring my husband his sword, that he may wear it proudly in the halls of Valhalla. And I bring other gifts, for his comfort on his sojourn there."

I watched through the doorway after Gunhild entered the tomb. She laid the sword along the top of Hrorik's body. His one remaining hand she raised and rested on the hilt, clasping it to his chest. The folded cloak she used to pillow his head, then she placed the other items she'd brought on the platform between his body and that of my mother. Even in death, it seemed, she sought to separate them.

"Good-bye, Hrorik," she said, in a low voice. "You were not the best husband a woman might wish for, but you never raised a hand against me and, thanks to you, our life has always been well comforted. Safe journey, and may the mead be sweet and strong in Valhalla."

After she exited the death house, Gunhild

walked to Harald's side, and stood with him to help greet the rest of the procession. Sigrid took my hand and stepped down through the door and into the death house, then indicated I should stand in the doorway. As the other gift-bearers came forward one by one, Harald received their offerings and handed them to me, and I passed the gifts to Sigrid, who arranged them around the bier.

There were many gifts. Astrid, Sigrid's maidservant, who also worked in the kitchen, carried as gifts from Sigrid and herself two wooden platters, piled with two pottery cups, a small knife, a large wooden spoon, and a small iron cooking pot. She sighed and shook her arms wearily after Harald took the gifts from her.

Several of the villagers bore chickens and ducks—and one a goose—all presented with their necks already wrung. Others brought cheeses or slabs of butter wrapped in cloth, or pitchers of fresh milk. Gunulf, a carl who owned a large farm in the village and was locally renowned for his brewing skills, brought a small cask of ale. Hrorik had loved his ale. I thought he would appreciate Gunulf's gift far more than milk.

Ingrid, a kitchen thrall in our longhouse who'd been one of my mother's best friends, brought the only gift for Mother—a small sewing kit, wrapped in a scrap of cloth, consisting of two bone needles and a few lengths of yarn and thread. For a thrall who owned next to nothing, it was a fine and generous gift. Although it earned me a disapproving glare from Gunhild, I let Ingrid enter the tomb herself and place her gift in Mother's hand. She bent and kissed Mother good-bye on her cheek. I saw that her eyes were brimming with tears when she turned to leave.

Each gift-bearer, as they presented their offering to Harald, pronounced, "Good winds and safe voyage, Hrorik Strong-Axe."

Always Harald replied, "I thank you. Your gifts and wishes will speed his journey."

The beasts were brought last, in a short procession led by Ubbe the foreman. Ubbe had a knife—a seax with a long, thin blade—in a scabbard hanging from his belt. At his approach, Sigrid exited the death house and stood watching from just outside the ring of stones, off to the side of the doorway. I joined her.

First came the thrall Hrut, leading a sheep by a short length of rope. He half led, half dragged the poor creature bleating in fearful protest, down into the death house. Ubbe followed closely behind. After a moment the sheep fell silent. A moment later Hrut hurried out.

Ubbe limped into view in the doorway, holding the long knife, its blade now dripping blood.

He motioned to Ing, who was cradling a squirming and squealing piglet in his arms. Ing stopped at the threshold of the doorway, fear visible on his face, and would go no farther. The young pig was wriggling furiously in his arms, and nuzzling at his beard. Impatiently, Ubbe took the pig, holding it under one arm, and turned back into the tomb. I heard a single, brief squeal from inside.

Kark, a house-thrall and Hrorik's servant, led one of Hrorik's hounds by a short length of rope. I saw that it was Clapa, a clumsy, good-natured clown of a dog that was Hrorik's favorite. Kark knelt beside him and scratched the fur behind his ears. I reached over and patted Clapa on the head, and he panted happily. Ubbe reappeared in the doorway of the death house and whistled. Kark released the rope and Clapa bounded to Ubbe, following him into the tomb as Ubbe backed inside. There was a brief yelp, then silence.

The last beast to be brought forward was Hrorik's favorite horse. He was led by Fasti, he who had been my childhood friend, the thrall from Svealand. Fasti tended the horses and loved them, each and every one, as though they were his family. He'd raised horses, he'd told me, on his farm in Svealand before he'd been captured and enslaved. Misery was visible on his face as he brought the horse forward.

Ubbe hobbled up out of the death house. His arms and the front of his shirt were splattered with blood. I knew from experience that there was no way to escape the spurting blood when beasts' throats are cut in a slaughterhouse.

"This one will be difficult," Ubbe said, studying the horse.

As if on cue, the horse, a shaggy brown animal with wild eyes, caught the scent of the freshly spilled blood, and began neighing nervously and jerking its head back and forth against the rope. Harald and Ubbe ran forward and pulled down on the halter. Ubbe snapped at Fasti, "Quick, fool, cover its eyes."

Fasti pulled a length of cloth from his belt and tied it around the horse's head, covering its eyes so it could not see. Then he stroked its neck and whispered in its ear until it quieted.

Ubbe led the horse, which was still trembling but now under control, through the stones of the death ship's side and over to the death house, in front of the doorway. "Boy," he said to me, "come here. We need your help."

We arrayed ourselves along the horse's side: Fasti at its flank, I in the middle, and Harald at the front shoulder. Ubbe, at the horse's head, was holding the halter.

"All together," Ubbe said. "When Harald

strikes, we push, so it topples against the doorway. Watch for the hooves." I put my hands against the horse's side. Its skin trembled under my touch.

Harald eased his long sword out of its scabbard. I'd wondered what Ubbe had intended. A horse is not an easy animal to kill quickly. Its neck is too thick to cut cleanly with a knife.

Harald drew back his arm. The sword's polished blade caught the sun and flashed like fire in his hand. In one swift movement he lunged forward, thrusting with his whole shoulder and body, and plunged the sword's blade deep into the horse's side, piercing its heart. The beast screamed in pain and terror, and I could feel its muscles clench under my hands.

"Now," Ubbe shouted, and jerked down on the halter, throwing his shoulder against the beast's head and twisting it down to the ground. Fasti and I leaned forward and pushed against the doomed creature. It staggered one step sideways and tried to brace its legs against us. Then, suddenly, they buckled, and it toppled sideways against the wall and doorway of the death house. Harald stood as still as a statue, his arm extended, and as the horse fell, his sword slid free from its body and blood gushed from the gaping wound.

The four of us stood for a moment, breathing hard, staring at the fallen creature. Its chest heaved as it gasped a few final breaths, and its eyes began to cloud as its spirit left its body. It occurred to me that when Hrorik had died, he'd spawned an ongoing chain of death. Beasts had died—and even my mother—to honor his passing.

It was the way of things, I knew, for even in the afterworld chieftains must have beasts and followers and possessions to ensure their comfort, and the passing of great men always changes the lives of those left behind. Still, I hoped that the path that led from Hrorik's deathbed would not be stained with any more blood. I hoped that now the deaths were ended.

"Fasti . . ." Ubbe was panting. "You and the other thralls—take the extra wood and lay it over the horse and in the doorway behind. The flames must eat its body, too."

I edged to the doorway and gazed beyond the horse's carcass one last time upon my mother. She looked at peace. I hoped she was.

Fasti stepped past me and threw an armload of brush and cut branches into the doorway, blocking my view, and she was gone.

Harald reached down and pulled free from around the horse's head the strip of cloth that had been used to blind its eyes. He used it to wipe the blood from his sword's blade before he sheathed it, then tossed the now bloody rag onto the stacked brush and wood.

"We must move to the other side now," he said, and set off around the stone ship. Gunhild, Sigrid, and Ubbe followed him. I followed, too, though I did not know what we were doing. As we walked, the free men of the household and village moved forward from the crowd and formed a circle around the stone death ship. They left a gap in the circle directly behind the stern. We took our places there, completing the circle, and stood looking out across the ship toward the sea, sparkling and glinting in the distance below us as its choppy surface caught the waning rays of sun.

All who formed the circle were men. Gunhild and Sigrid stood nearby. At their feet were several large pottery pitchers, and the silverbound drinking horn that Hrorik had used at feasts.

On the ground beside the tall stone sternpost lay two torches, each made of a long branch, with twigs and moss, soaked with seal oil, tied in a bundle at one end. Harald knelt beside the torches and, taking flint and steel from a pouch on his belt, struck sparks onto one until the oily moss ignited. From its flame he lit the second torch, and handed it to me.

"We are the sons of Hrorik," he said. "It is for us to launch his voyage."

Harald and I circled the death house in opposite directions, periodically thrusting our torches into the cut wood and brush stacked against its walls. There was much small, dry kindling stuffed among the larger pieces of wood, and it caught the flames eagerly. By the time we met on the far side, flames were beginning to lick as high as the roof, and the fire was beginning to speak in a low roar.

When Harald and I reclaimed our places in the circle, Sigrid lifted one of the pottery pitchers, and Gunhild held the drinking horn while Sigrid filled it. She passed the filled horn to Harald.

Harald held the horn in both hands and raised it above his head. In a loud voice that all could hear, he called out to the sky, "This is mead, the drink of the Gods, and one of their many gifts to men. We offer it back to you now, that you may join us in toasting Hrorik Strong-Axe and Derdriu, and grant them safe journey. Welcome this warrior, All-Father Odin, into your feast-hall."

Harald poured some of the mead onto the ground, then raised the horn again. "I drink to Hrorik Strong-Axe, a chieftain of the Danes, a fierce warrior and a cunning leader. In battle, his axe smote his foes like Thor's thunderbolts thrown from the sky. His wise counsel led many successful raids, and won us all much plunder. To Hrorik first fell Dorestad, trading center of the Franks, a great victory and a rich prize. I drink this cup in honor of Hrorik, my father, and to Derdriu, his consort, a princess of Ireland, a woman of great beauty and a beloved foster mother."

Harald put the horn to his lips, and as he drained it, the men in the circle shouted, "To Hrorik and Derdriu."

Harald passed the horn back to Gunhild, and Sigrid refilled it. This time Gunhild herself held the horn aloft and said, "I pray, you Gods, grant fair winds and safe voyage to this ship." Then as Harald had done, she poured some of the mead onto the ground.

"To Hrorik," she said as she raised the horn again. "Wise chieftain and fierce fighter who feared no man; successful in battle and generous afterward dividing the spoils. Long will it be before the Danes again see such a man."

When Gunhild offered her toast, I thought the words she failed to speak revealed the shape of the bitterness that lingered still in her heart. She described Hrorik as a great leader, a fierce warrior, and a bold and cunning raider. From her words, one might have thought she was one of his warriors, rather than his wife. She spoke nothing of love, nor wifely affection, nor did she praise him as a father, though for a time he had sheltered and raised her own son by her first marriage. And of my mother, who'd died so Hrorik, Gunhild's husband, would not be alone at the Gods' hall in the after-world, she spoke no words at all. A more gracious woman would have expressed gratitude for Mother's gift to Hrorik, but Gunhild did not.

Sigrid filled the horn a third time, and Gunhild placed it in my hands. I raised it high. All eyes were on me. I hoped my voice would not quaver or squeak from the fear I felt at speaking in front of so many people.

"To all the Gods," I said, "To Odin, the God of my father, and to the White Christ, the God of my mother, grant this ship a safe voyage."

I poured some of the mead onto the ground. Thankfully the horn was no longer full after my offering to the Gods, for my hands were shaking from my nervousness as I raised it again.

"To Derdriu," I said, "daughter of Caidoc, a king of Ireland. She was my mother, and a more loving mother there has never been. In this land, she was but a thrall. She will never be sung of round the fires at evening time when tales of courage are told. Yet she was as brave as any warrior who has carried shield and swung sword. She offered her own life so that I could be free and be acknowledged by my father as his son. And when the time came for her to meet her death, she embraced it willingly, with head held high. To Derdriu, to her courage and her love!"

The men in the circle echoed their approval, shouting, "To Derdriu!" as I drank. I drained the horn and offered it back to Gunhild.

I realized that the warriors in the circle were still staring expectantly at me. Harald leaned over and whispered, "Your toast brought much honor to your mother. It was a fine thing you did. But you must also offer a toast to Hrorik. He was your father and our chieftain. If you fail to do so, you will dishonor him and yourself."

Sigrid poured more mead into the horn. I took it from Gunhild and again I held it aloft. I searched my mind for words to say, for my heart held no kind feelings for my father.

"To Hrorik. I cannot praise him as a warrior or a leader, for I did not know him as such. I knew him only as a slave knows his master, until the last hours before his death. Then only did I know him for but a moment as a father. Yet I know this of Hrorik: Toward my mother, there was in him kindness and affection, and perhaps even love, so to this I raise the cup and toast him. To Hrorik!"

"To Hrorik!" the circle echoed, though with muted enthusiasm. I supposed my toast did not sit well with all—certainly not with Gunhild, for anger was evident on her face. I did not care. I refused to lie at my mother's funeral, to honor the man who'd asked for her death.

By now the death house was engulfed in flames. A dark column of smoke rose above it, carrying the spirits of my mother and Hrorik up into the sky. High above the hilltop, the wind caught the smoke and blew it out over the sea in an ever lengthening plume.

Round and round the circle, the toasting horn passed. Long before the death house at last collapsed in upon itself in a shower of sparks, my head was spinning from the strong mead. By then the farthest reaches of the trail of smoke, and the spirit ship that sailed upon it carrying my mother and father, were far out over the ocean, lost in the deepening dusk. As I watched my mother's spirit sail away from our shores, I did not feel as though I'd gained what I'd dreamed of all my life. I felt as though I'd lost everything.

6

LESSONS

I can remember few details of the feast following the funeral, even though it was the first feast I attended as a free man, and as such should have been a new and exciting experience for me. Harald insisted I sit by his side, and made certain my cup stayed filled. I think he believed it better that I had a spinning head than a grieving heart. His strategy worked well that evening, but the morning after was a different matter.

I awoke fully dressed, sprawled across the bed in my mother's bed-closet, with no recollection of how I came to be there. There was a pain in my head, the likes of which I'd never known, and the first thought that came to me was to seek out my mother for a remedy. At that, memories of the day before rushed in. I would never see my mother again. She was dead. Even her body was gone, consumed by the flames. The reality of it settled on me like the weight of a great stone pressing into my chest. Though I'd learned at a young age not to shed tears—it is a mistake for a thrall to be weak, but even more of one to let weakness show—that morning I wept, for her and for myself.

I was still dressed in my new feast clothes. Today they seemed hateful to me, a symbol of the bargain my mother had made. I removed them and dressed in the stained, rough tunic that had clothed me as a thrall. I felt it was all I deserved.

Though it was long past dawn, most of the household still slept, recovering from the feast. A few thralls moved quietly about the longhouse, cleaning up the wreckage and leavings from the previous night's celebration. I stopped at the hearth and helped myself to half a loaf of bread, a pot of soft cheese, and a large wooden tankard, which I filled with cool water from a waterskin hanging from one of the roof-posts. Then I staggered out into the bright sunlight and made my way up onto the hilltop.

Inside the stone boundary of the death ship, all that remained of the death house was a large pile of ashes, speckled with scraps of dark charcoal and the charred stumps that marked where the corner-posts had stood. Somewhere among the ashes were the charred bones of my mother and Hrorik and the beasts who'd been sacrificed at their bier.

Fasti, Hrut, and Ing were already at work, covering the ash heap with the loose earth they'd excavated two days ago. Though the thralls had shared in the feast honoring Hrorik and Mother, and each had even been given a single tankard of ale, that was yesterday. Today they were back at their toils again, for work is the only life a thrall knows. I gave them a wide berth, for I felt no desire for human contact that morning.

I walked back to where the grassy hilltop met the edge of the forest, and sat in the edge of the tree line. The food and water had soothed my stomach and dulled the pain in my head a little, but my heart felt like it would break. My mind tormented me with visions of my mother. Too late, my thoughts were filled with things I wished to tell her—with all I should have thanked her for.

Shortly before midday, Fasti and the others completed their work. They laid the strips of cut turf over the earth-covered ash heap, forming a low grassy mound in the center of the deathship. Not long after the thralls left the hilltop, Harald climbed into view and walked over to where I sat.

"I have been looking for you," he said. "Fasti

told me I could find you here."

"She's gone," I told him, "and her death was because of me."

Harald sat on the ground beside me, looking toward the death ship, and the sea beyond it.

"You do Derdriu honor by grieving her loss," he said. "But you take honor from her by blaming yourself. The decision she made was hers alone. It was her wish that you come into your birthright and become the son of a chieftain. It was her choice to give her own life to achieve that wish. Her death will be meaningless if you do not seize what she has given you."

I pondered Harald's words and saw there was truth in them. Though I now regretted Mother's choice, it would be wrong to rob it of meaning. I'd been wishing I could say more to her—could tell her how much I loved her—now that it was too late. My actions would have to speak for me now. I could only work to make myself what she'd wanted me to be: the son of a chieftain and, perhaps, some day a man of note in my own right. I hoped that somehow, in the afterworld, she would know.

"What must I do?" I asked Harald. "How do I seize my mother's gift?"

"In truth," he answered, "we have a difficult task ahead of us. All your life you've been a thrall. Now you must become a warrior—and quickly.

You are far behind. By your age, most young men have been practicing the skills of war for many years. It is fortunate you have me to teach you, or you might never catch up."

I looked at Harald. He was everything I'd ever secretly dreamed of being. He was tall and handsome, possessed of a cheerful disposition, and was a great and fearless warrior. Almost everyone, men and women, loved Harald, and he in turn was friends with all, except those few who were foolish enough to insult his honor. Those men, of course, he killed.

Strangely, I felt no anger or resentment toward Harald for killing my mother. I understood that he'd done it out of kindness. Her doom was set when she'd made her bargain with Hrorik. Harald had only eased her passage, by giving her as swift and painless a death as possible. How could I resent it? I believed it was an act of love.

"Do you resent me?" I asked him suddenly. He looked puzzled by my question.

"Why should I?" he asked.

"You've been forced, by Hrorik's charge to you, to accept a thrall as your brother."

Harald pondered my words for a time before he answered. "In truth," he said, "I had not thought of it that way. My father, on his deathbed, told me he wished for you to be raised up, and for me to care for you and train you. I would be dishonored if I did not obey my father's dying wish."

I was not satisfied with his answer. "But what do you feel in your heart?" I asked. "For though your honor ensures you will act toward me as a brother, your heart might still resent having to treat a former slave as your equal. All my life you have known me as a thrall. Will you not always, in the back of your mind, think of me that way?"

"Ubbe and Gunhild manage this estate," Harald said. "I've always left the management of our thralls to them. If you had been a bad thrall, lazy or insolent, I might have noticed you more. Perhaps then, as you say, in my heart I would not welcome you. But as far as I can recall, you've always been industrious and well-mannered.

"It was the Norns who spun your fate and made you born into slavery, and now they've changed the weave of your life and you have become a free man. No man chooses his own fate. We do not have that power. We can only react to what our fates lay before us. Why should I think less of you for a fate you could not control?

"And there is another thing. My mother died when I was very young. I have few memories of her. Your mother, Derdriu, raised Sigrid and me, and she was as loving to us as though we were her own children. I loved her. You are her son and

Hrorik's. I am glad you are my brother."

Harald was a good man. My heart was not as open and generous as his. I was glad he'd never concerned himself with the management of the estate and its thralls. I was glad he'd never beaten me as a thrall, for had he, I did not think I could forget it. I knew I would never forgive Gunhild for all her acts of cruelty toward me and my mother. Though I was now her equal and we must, by necessity, act with politeness toward each other, anger still burned secretly in my heart over the thrashings I'd received at her hand or direction.

"Do you think I can do it?" I asked Harald.

Harald looked puzzled again. "Do what?" he replied.

"Be the son of a chieftain. Become a warrior. I am just a thrall."

"It is the fate the Norns have now given you," Harald replied. "The fates that the Three Sisters weave for us are sometimes strange and twisted. Derdriu was born the daughter of a king, yet she lived much of her life as a thrall, and died as one. You were born a thrall, yet now you've been raised up and acknowledged as the son of a chieftain. Noble blood fills your veins. Your mother's father was a king of the Irish, and she was a princess. Your father was a great chieftain among the Danes. That for a time you were a thrall was just a quirk of fate woven by the Norns. You have more right to call yourself of noble blood than most who were born free."

Harald stood and stretched, then extended his hand to me. I took it, and he pulled me up. As I stood I swayed a little and winced at the throbbing that surged anew in my head. I grimaced and squinted my eyes at the pain.

"Mead is sweet in the cup at the feast table, but can be bitter in the morning," Harald said, noticing my expression. "We will start your lessons as a warrior tomorrow. This afternoon we'll take one of the small-boats out on the fjord. I, too, need the wind and salty air to clear my head after last night's feast. And while we sail, I'll tell you the memories I have of Derdriu from when you were but a babe and she was mother to Sigrid and me."

Harald did not boast when he'd said I was fortunate he was to be my teacher. Most Danish free men—even chieftains like Hrorik—were farmers, and generally they farmed more of the year than they raided. Though no man was a more avid warrior when battle called than Hrorik had been, he'd also enjoyed the physical labor of wresting the fruits of a harvest from the land and, when at home, could often be found working in the fields alongside the thralls.

Harald, by contrast, did not enjoy the labors of a farmer. Though he would join in the work at times, such as harvest when all were needed, his true loves were weaponcraft and war, and he practiced their arts constantly. Although he was but twenty years of age, he was unquestionably the finest swordsman in the district, and some opined he was one of the finest in all of Denmark. He'd already fought and won five duels—more than most men fight in a lifetime. In three of them he'd killed his opponents, two of whom had been berserks—dangerous killers of men.

My first lesson, Harald informed me, would be to learn the correct way to cut with a sword. Inwardly I groaned, though I didn't show my frustration on my face. If I was to make up for years of missed training, surely I needed to begin somewhere further along in the process. I was certain I knew full well how to cut, for I was already skilled with an axe—I could chop through a seasoned oak log faster than many grown men. Surely, I thought, oak wood was far harder to cut than flesh. I expected my first lesson to be brief.

We started early in the morning, tramping across the fields until we reached an area at the edge of the woodlands where many small saplings grew, as the forest tried to reclaim the cleared land. The mature trees had seeded heavily here. Their numerous offspring ranged in diameter from a single finger to as large as a man's wrist.

Harald was carrying a battered-looking sword in a rough scabbard.

"I took this from the body of a dead Frank in Frisia," he explained. "The hilt and the scabbard are finished roughly, but there's good steel in the blade. It takes and holds a sharp edge. I use it for practice. Never," he continued, his voice and expression serious, "cut wood, even saplings, with a fine sword. Swords are not made for such work, and over time the shock will shake the handle loose, and may damage the blade."

Unsheathing the sword, Harald used its edge to scrape a small patch of bark off of a sapling at a height slightly above my shoulders. Then he handed the sword to me.

"This tree is an enemy facing you," he said. "That mark is his unprotected neck. With one blow, strike off his head."

I'd never held a sword before. I shifted the handle until it felt comfortable in my hand. Eyeing the mark, I drew the sword back at shoulder height, much as I would have drawn back an axe, and gave it a full, hard swing with all the strength of my arm and shoulder. The blade hit just above the mark Harald had made and stuck, embedded halfway through the sapling's trunk. The force of the blow left the blade vibrating and jarred my arm.

If it had been an axe, I told myself, the weight of the blade would have cut the sapling through. I began to suspect that the sword was an overrated weapon.

"The sword," Harald said, "is a weapon of skill and precision. Its blade is thin and sharp. It will give poor service if used with naught but brute force, like a woodcutter's axe. Did you feel the shock in the blade?"

I nodded.

"A proper cut will not shock your arm or the sword. You swung the sword with all your strength, did you not?"

Again I nodded.

"Had you missed, the force of your blow would have carried your arm far out of position, and your foe could have killed you before you recovered. A properly struck blow will do more damage, with less force, than one such as you struck. Your blows must be powerful enough to kill if they land, but light and quick enough so you can recover and defend yourself, or strike again quickly, if you miss."

Harald reached up and grasped the sword's grip. He worked its blade free from the trunk of the sapling.

"Another thing," he added. "If you aim your cuts into your target at an angle, rather than swinging straight on as you did, and if you pull the sword ever so slightly back toward yourself as it strikes, its blade will be far more likely to slice through your target rather than merely chop at it."

As he spoke these last words, Harald positioned himself in front of the sapling, his left foot forward, his body slightly turned, and his right foot back. His left arm was in front of his body, as if it supported an invisible shield. He held the sword loosely in his right hand, its blade pointed upright, the hilt held close to his body and slightly above his waist.

Suddenly, as if it moved of its own accord, the sword's blade leapt up and swept down diagonally across the sapling, shearing at an angle through the trunk exactly where the bark had been scraped away. Scarcely had the blade cleared the wood than Harald whipped the blade in a loop, bringing it back overhead then down again, striking the sapling from the opposite side, again slicing cleanly through the trunk at an angle, a hand's length below the first cut. The top of the sapling had just begun to topple sideways toward the ground as, halting the downward swing of his blade, Harald whipped his wrist and the blade backward and up in a rising backhand cut. He slashed through the sapling's trunk a third and final time at thigh height.

I stared awestruck as the sections of the sapling dropped around its stump on the ground.

"Do you see now the importance of learning the proper way to cut?" Harald asked.

I nodded silently. Harald grinned.

"There is another thing you must understand about the sword—and cutting with it: A sword's edge must be thin and sharp to cut through clothing, flesh, and bone. A sharp edge can cut very well, but it is not intended for anything else.

"Never, if you can avoid it, use your sword to parry another blade. That is what your shield is for. Sometimes, of course, you will have no choice. A blow may come at you from an unexpected direction and catch your shield out of position, or sometimes you may have to defend yourself when you are not carrying a shield. If you must block another sword's cut with your own sword, be sure you catch the attacking blade with the flat of your blade, not its edge. The flat is slick and hard, and a striking edge will slide off of it, not bite into it. If two swords strike hard against each other edge to edge, the best that can happen is both edges will be badly chipped. At worst, such a blow can break a blade, even a fine one."

For three solid days, I practiced cutting until I'd sliced to pieces every young tree growing in the vicinity of the estate. After the first day, I bore a large, circular shield while I practiced. Harald showed me how to hold it by its grip in the center behind the iron boss, and how to adjust the shield's long strap over my neck and shoulder so I could let it hang, my shoulders supporting some of the weight, whenever I was not actually maneuvering it in combat.

"For now," Harald explained, "I want you to practice holding your shield as if you were in single combat. Hold it tilted, like this, with the bottom edge angled forward and the top slanted back toward your head. Crouch behind it. This extends the shield's protection farther out from your body than if you hold it straight up and down. It will also help you deflect your opponent's strikes off as glancing blows, rather than receiving them as solid hits that might damage your shield, or even cut through it. When fighting in a shield-wall, of course, it is often necessary to hold the shield straight up and down, for in the shield-wall there is little room to maneuver, and each man must help guard his fellows who fight beside him. But we will practice that later. Battle is different than single combat in many ways. You must learn the skills necessary for both."

Though I was large for my age and my muscles were used to hard labor, by the end of each day of Harald's training, my arms and shoulders felt exhausted, and I welcomed the failing light of evening. Yet even at night, lessons of other kinds continued. Sigrid and Harald taught me to eat with the manners of a noble, rather than the manners—or lack of manners—of a thrall. And at every evening meal we drank ale.

"You are a warrior now, and highborn," Harald explained. "When you dine with others, they will serve you ale or mead, or perhaps even wine. It is important to develop a tolerance for strong drink, so you do not become a witless fool when it's served to you."

Each night, after we ate and the table had been cleared, Harald and the other housecarls who lived and supped with us in the great longhouse would tell me of battles they'd fought in or had heard tales of. Hrorik's warriors, who were Harald's men now, would line up nuts across the tabletop to show the positions of the armies, and how they'd maneuvered, and would explain to me the tactics that the commanders had employed to achieve victory, or the errors they'd made that had brought them defeat.

❖   ❖   ❖

On the morning of the fifth day after the funeral Harald announced that we would begin sparring practice. This day our "swords" were long, thin oaken slats, padded with wool, then wrapped with leather. Two old and battered helms and two shields completed our gear.

All morning we practiced cuts and parries at slow speed. "Strike at my head," Harald would say, or "Make a low cut at my legs." I would swing my weapon as he directed, but slowly, and he would demonstrate how to parry the cut with his shield, and how to follow with a counterattack. Then Harald would make the same cut at me and I would practice the parry and counterstrike.

We rested briefly at midday and fortified ourselves with slabs of buttered bread and long draughts of cold water. When we'd finished, Harald grinned.

"Now, little brother," he said, "your real training begins."

After we'd rearmed ourselves, Harald faced me and said, "Halfdan, defend yourself."

He moved toward me, his weapon at ready. The words he'd taught me sprang into my head: "Distance is the key to both defense and attack. You cannot hit what you cannot reach." I retreated as he advanced, keeping my eyes focused on his sword.

Suddenly he lunged forward and cut at my head. Swinging my shield up and over, I knocked his blade aside and cut low at his extended leg. Harald pushed his own shield downward, blocking my blow, then we both leapt back out of range.

Harald laughed. "Excellent, Halfdan. Excellent!" he exclaimed.

This time he began circling me, periodically feinting with his shoulders as if he was preparing to strike, watching my reactions to his movements. As before, I watched his sword hand, which I knew must move to initiate any real attack.

Or so I thought. His sword hand never moved, but suddenly Harald charged at me. Too late, I back-stepped furiously, still watching for the attack to come. When it did, it was not with the sword. Harald crashed against me, shield against shield, and knocked me sprawling to the ground. As I struggled to get up, his sword arm finally swung. Desperately I tried to block the blade with my own, but Harald changed his aim in mid-stroke and his oaken slat smacked across my forearm. Though the wooden blade was padded, the pain made me gasp and my weapon sailed from my grip. A split second later, another blow descended on me, clanging against the side of my helm and knocking me flat to the ground, my head spinning.

Harald laughed again, though it sounded as

though it was coming from a distance.

"Do not feel discouraged, little brother. It takes many bruises to learn the skills of a warrior. This was an important lesson. Anything—a shield, butting with your helm, kicking, even throwing a rock or handful of dirt—can be used to attack with. If you become too focused on only the obvious weapons, such as your opponent's sword, you may leave yourself open to some other assault. Had this been real combat, and my sword steel rather than practice, my first blow would have severed your arm, and with my second cut I'd have struck through your neck, not against your helm."

Over the days that followed, I took many more hard blows than in all the beatings I'd ever received as a thrall. Yet all were accompanied by Harald's good-natured laughter and an explanation or a lesson. I did not regard my pummelings as beatings. Those times were, in fact, some of the happiest days I'd lived, for as we worked together Harald and I grew ever closer as brothers and comrades. Harald laughed often and complimented me, and seemed to genuinely enjoy my company. Secretly, he had always been my hero. Now he was my brother, too, and—best of all—he seemed glad that I was his.

✦ ✦ ✦

I was a quick learner. Within a fortnight I had developed sufficient skill to defend successfully against all but the most persistent and skilled of Harald's attacks. A week later, I won my first victory.

I made my plan while we sat drinking water and catching our breath. We'd just completed an unusually long exchange, where we'd traded blows fast and furiously, none striking home, until finally Harald's wooden sword had thumped across my ribs. While my fingers tenderly probed my newest wound, Harald tilted his head back and gulped down a long swallow of water. Then he looked over at me and chuckled.

"You seem very serious. What grave matter do you contemplate?"

"The imbalance," I replied. "I have many bruises and you have none."

As was his wont, Harald laughed. "View them as love taps, little brother. Why, my affection for you has grown so great that your body is virtually covered with signs of my love."

I strapped on my helm and stood. "It's a method of showing love I would share with you," I said.

We squared off again. I launched an attack by lunging forward and swinging a low cut at Harald's legs. He reached down with his shield to block it, while swinging his sword in a high cut that arced downward toward my head.

My attack had been a feint, though, with little force behind it. When Harald lowered his shield to parry, I stepped in close and hooked my sword arm over it, pinning his shield to my chest and immobilizing it. As I did so, instead of parrying his sword cut by sweeping it aside with my own shield, I raised my shield over my head like a roof, and let Harald's hand and blade thump down flat across it. It must have seemed a clumsy, hasty block, borne of desperation. I hoped it did. Ever quick to react, Harald began to whip his blade around the edge of my shield to strike, for my entire side was now left open and unprotected by my unconventional maneuver.

For once I was quicker. Still holding my shield level, I punched it straight forward. Its rim struck the front of Harald's helm, ringing it like a bell. His eyes crossed and he staggered back, both arms dropping limply by his sides. I lunged forward and rammed the tip of my padded sword into Harald's stomach, driving his breath out with a *whoosh*, then completed my victory with a solid thump across his back when he doubled over.

When he regained his breath and wits, Harald was—if possible—even more excited by my victory than I was.

❖ ❖ ❖

That evening in the longhouse, he told the story over and over, to Sigrid, to Ubbe, and the other housecarls—to anyone who would listen.

"Halfdan was truly born to be a warrior," he would say in each retelling. "These were not moves I taught him."

Harald and I sat at table, a pitcher of fine Frankish pottery filled with ale between us, long after the dishes and remnants of food had been cleared away, and most of the rest of the household had retired to their beds. We had refilled the pitcher several times, for Harald was in an especially jolly and talkative mood that night.

"I must show you my sword," Harald suddenly said. "It is a very fine one, and very special."

Harald staggered off to his bed-closet and returned with a long, narrow bundle wrapped in sealskin. He unwrapped it and revealed a long sword in its scabbard. I'd seen it hanging at his waist many times before, but had never paid particular attention to it. The scabbard was wood, covered in deerskin tanned to a buttery soft finish and dyed a dark brown. The chape that covered and protected the toe of the scabbard, and the scabbard's throat where the blade entered, were of silver, cast in a complex design of intertwined serpents. Three evenly spaced, wide bands of thick

126

cowhide, dyed a dark green, decorated the scabbard's body. On the band immediately below the silver throat of the scabbard, two straps were attached as hangers.

The sword's handle was simpler than I would have expected on a fine weapon. I'd seen swords worn by Hrorik and others with hilts that were intricately carved and decorated with silver or copper or gold. On Harald's sword, the hilt and pommel were of simple iron, though I could see that the workmanship on them was very good. No hammer-marks or pitting had been left by the smith who'd forged them, and the finish of the metal was smooth and highly polished. The hilt was a simple straight bar, as long as my longest finger, tapered to a point at either end. The grip was wood, wrapped with leather, and the pommel was made of two large, heavy pieces of iron. The piece closest to the grip was a bar, similar in design to the hilt, but only half as long. Attached to it by two heavy rivets was a large, heavy oval of iron, divided into three lobes in the fashionable style. The surface of the iron on the hilt and pommel was simply decorated with a pattern made of small holes drilled into the metal and blackened with carbon from the forging process.

"This is Biter," Harald said, and slid the blade from its scabbard. When he did, I saw that he was right. It was a very fine sword indeed. The blade was pattern-welded. It had been forged by hammering together bars of steel and iron, beating them at high heat into a single piece of metal, then folding that bar back upon itself and repeating the process hundreds of times until the blade was composed of a single piece of metal made of thousands of thin layers of steel and iron. Such blades were supposed to be almost unbreakable, and could take and hold the sharpest of edges.

Since I was ten, I'd served as a helper for Gunnar, the blacksmith on Hrorik's estate, whenever he'd needed to fire up his forge. It was one of the benefits my clever hands and quick mind had won me. Gunnar had told me about pattern-welding and of the legendary swords made with the technique. Gunnar, of course, did not possess such skills—he said only a few specialized blademakers, most of them located deep in the eastern Frankish kingdom, did. Gunnar, though, was skilled at working metal, and could readily forge farm tools or simple weapons or hardware needed for harnesses or ships and the like. Over time he'd taught me all he knew.

"Hrorik captured this blade when he led the first great raid on the Frankish trading center at Dorestad," Harald explained to me. "When the city was sacked, Hrorik came upon a swordmaker's shop and took its contents as plunder. It contained mostly completed swords of good quality, but nothing extraordinary. He found, however, five pattern-welded blades such as this—blades only, not finished swords. Any man wealthy enough to afford such a blade would wish to choose the design and decoration of the hilt himself. The Frank who owned the shop willingly surrendered the swords and blades in exchange for his life, and he told Hrorik the five blades had been made by a famous smith who lived on the Rhine River, deep in the Frankish heartland.

"Two of the blades Hrorik kept for himself. A third he presented later that year to the King of the Danes, and the remaining two he gave as gifts to two of the chieftains who'd accompanied him on the Dorestad raid. By such generous gifts, alliances are often forged.

"One of the blades Hrorik kept was made into a sword for himself. That was the sword that accompanied him on his voyage to Valhalla, on the death ship. The funeral fire consumed it, and it will serve no other man. This blade Hrorik gave to me as a gift, at the Jul feast in the year I turned eighteen. I spent much thought on the design of the handle. Though I considered a rich hilt and pommel decorated with silver like Hrorik's, in the end I decided on simple iron, finely executed, to reflect the purity of purpose of so fine a weapon."

Harald passed the grip of the weapon across the table to me. "Hold it," he said.

I knew by its size that this sword must be at least as heavy as the practice sword I'd used to slay so many saplings with, yet it felt half the weight.

Harald smiled broadly at my surprised expression. "The magic is in the balance," he told me. "The swordsmith at Hedeby who hilted the blade for me made two other lobes for the pommel, each of which I rejected, before he made this one. This pommel has just the right weight to counter that of the blade, balancing it perfectly in the hand. Perfect balance creates a sword that feels lighter than its actual weight—and is quick to strike or recover."

Harald was in an expansive mood that night. He drank much ale, and because he was pouring and his high spirits were so contagious, I did, too. I sensed some subtle change in his attitude toward me, but not until late into the evening did my mind realize the sign my ears had earlier registered. That evening, and thereafter, Harald addressed me as "Halfdan" or "my brother." Never again did I hear the words "little brother" pass his lips.

7

THE BOW

In the days that followed, we continued to work with the padded practice swords and shields, and I continued to improve. As weeks passed, more swiftly than any I'd ever known, the land was transforming around us. Though by count of days from the Jul feast it should have still been winter, everywhere signs of spring began appearing. Branches of the trees tipped themselves with buds, waiting to open into tiny new leaves. Above us in the sky, flights of birds passed daily, returning to the north after their winter sojourns in southern lands. The first shoots of the earliest plantings sprouted into bright-green rows in the fields, to be carefully tended by the thralls under Ubbe's watchful supervision. All around us, the folk of the estate welcomed the reawakening of life, while Harald taught me my lessons of killing and war.

Harald began to vary my studies now. I learned to fight with a spear, using a long, wooden shaft with a padded leather sack tied over its end. I learned that with its quick jabs, a spear could often strike more swiftly than the slash of a sword, and its reach was far greater. I quickly discovered, though, that maintaining distance when fighting with a spear was even more critical than when using a sword. If a swordsman was ever able to press forward inside the reach of the spear's point, an opponent armed with a spear might as well be unarmed.

Other days, Harald enlisted the help of Ubbe, the foreman, and others of the estate's housecarls. We formed two short shield-walls of four men each, and fought mock battles all day with padded weapons, so I could learn the skill of fighting while holding a position in line with warriors to either side of me.

One afternoon, a stranger rode onto the estate and sat for a time watching us spar from his horse's back. He wore a mail brynie, and carried a helm tied to his saddle and a shield slung across his back. Harald halted our practice, and we walked over to where the stranger waited. Harald and I were both dressed in simple woolen tunics, and were using our battered practice helms, shields, and padded wooden swords. Though clearly we were warriors, we no doubt looked to be no more than simple housecarls.

"Greetings," the stranger called out as we neared him. "My name is Arnulf. I bear a message for your chieftain, Hrorik, from his kinsman, Horik, King of the Danes." I noticed that the stranger held a single arrow, painted red, in his hand.

I saw that Harald was eyeing the arrow, too. He unstrapped his helm and removed it, then wiped the sweat from his brow with the back of his arm.

"You have a long ride still to travel, to deliver your message to Hrorik," he replied. "He lives now with the Gods in Valhalla."

Harald's answer clearly surprised the stranger, but did not appear to dismay him. Perhaps his duties led him to call on many chieftains. Among the warlike Danes, no doubt some were always dying.

"How and when did he die?" Arnulf asked. "The king will want to know. He knew nothing of this when he dispatched me, but I've been traveling for many days now and have covered much ground."

"In England," Harald answered. "We raided

early, because of the mildness of the winter. Our fleet numbered forty ships. It surprises me the king does not know of the outcome, for one of the chieftains with us was Haakon, one of the king's sons. Few on that ill-fated voyage survived. Did Haakon escape?"

The rider shook his head. Now his face did show distress.

"I cannot say. We knew, of course, of the raid Haakon had sailed on. One of my comrades departed with him on his ship. They have not been gone so long, though, that we looked for Haakon's return. What you have told me is grave news, indeed. You must tell me more so I can carry this tale to the king. If Haakon and the warriors who journeyed with him may be lost, the king will want to know."

"If you have been traveling for so long you must be weary," Harald said. "I am Harald, eldest son of Hrorik, and this is my brother, Halfdan. These are my lands now. You are welcome to break your journey and rest here, and I will tell you all I know of the raid on England, though I cannot say with certainty whether Haakon was one of the many who found their doom there."

That evening after we'd dined, we sat around the main hearth drinking, while Harald recounted his tale of the ill-fated voyage to England.

"You carry the red arrow that summons chieftains to serve the king in war," Harald said, when he'd finished his telling. It was a statement, but a question, too.

"Aye," Arnulf answered, nodding his head. "The king is calling a war council. All of his jarls and many great chieftains are being summoned. Hrorik was one of the chieftains whose counsel he sought. The king wishes to carry war to the Franks. Travelers from the Frankish lands have told him that the Frankish kings fight among themselves and weaken their own defenses."

I was surprised to hear Arnulf speak of Frankish kings. I knew little of the Franks—slaves have no need to learn of foreign kings and lands, and Harald's lessons so far had not included any such instruction. Though I had, in years past, heard tales told in the evenings about the Franks. They were the most powerful of the enemies of the Danes. As all Danes did, I knew our lands had been invaded many years ago by their King Charles, he whose vanity led him to call himself the Great. And the land of the Danes had been attacked again by the son who had succeeded him. I'd always thought, from the tales I'd heard, that the Franks had only one king, and I said as much to Harald.

"For many years that was true," he said, "but no more. The old King Charles ruled all of the Franks' lands. He was a fierce warlord who slew many of the Saxon tribes who once lived to the south of our kingdom and took their lands for his own people. His son was a doughty warrior, too, and also ruled the Frankish kingdom alone. But the old king's grandsons could not agree among themselves who should rule when their father died. They carved the Frankish lands into three kingdoms, each claiming one."

Arnulf nodded his head. "But they are greedy men, and all three still dream of being the one king of the Franks, so they fight each other constantly. It is a good thing when your enemy sheds his own blood and weakens himself before you even attack."

"Perhaps we should go to this council, my brother, and hear of King Horik's plans for war," Harald said to me, nudging me in the ribs with his elbow and grinning. "Perhaps we can show the Franks how well you've learned your lessons."

"That will not be possible," Arnulf said.

Harald looked at him coldly. It was a strange thing about Harald. His countenance usually displayed his mood for all to see, when he was in good spirits. But if he felt someone had insulted his honor—something few who knew him dared to do—all signs of emotion vanished from his face and bearing. I personally had seen it happen only once before, when Toke, Gunhild's son by her first marriage, still lived on our estate. There was no brotherly affection between Harald and Toke. But then, Toke had seemed to feel no affection for anyone, or anything. He was a berserk.

"I am chieftain here, now that Hrorik is dead," Harald said in a quiet voice. "Why should I not attend the king's council in his stead?"

"It is but a small council the king has sent me and others to summon," Arnulf replied. "Only his jarls and a few chieftains whose counsel he has found to be wise in the past. Your name is not on the list. I am sorry, and mean you no offense. It is not my decision, though. I have no power to invite you in the stead of Hrorik, your father. But I am certain that if the council does vote for war, your sword, and those of the men you command, will be welcome."

"No doubt," Harald said. He said no more that evening. A short time later he excused himself and retired to his bed.

Arnulf left early the next morning. All that day and the next, Harald seemed in an ill humor. It was a side of him I had not seen before. He did not laugh or even smile during our practice bouts, as was normally his wont, but slashed and hacked at me with grim intensity.

All in the household could sense Harald's simmering anger, and felt uneasy because of it.

The second night, as we sat at dinner, Sigrid took it upon herself to try and lift his spirits.

"I have a taste for venison," she said and sighed. "I tire of salted pork and smoked fish. I feel as though we have been eating them all winter."

Gunhild, who was standing by the hearth, chimed in. "I, too, would love fresh game. It has been long since we've had some. Perhaps, Harald, you and Halfdan could do something useful for a change and go hunting."

Leave it to Gunhild. Sigrid had hoped to distract Harald from his anger at the slight he felt Arnulf had given his honor and status, but Gunhild, in trying to assist, managed to insult him.

Harald, who'd been drinking heavily that night, drained the last of the ale in his cup and set it down with a loud thump on the table. He belched loudly in Gunhild's direction. She frowned in response and turned away, which seemed to please him. Sigrid smiled sweetly at him, though I thought her eyes betrayed a nervousness behind the smile.

"Well then, Halfdan," Harald said to me.

"Since my sister has a taste for venison, I suppose that tomorrow I must begin teaching you to shoot a bow. It will be difficult. A bow is not an easy weapon to learn. We can only make a beginning. But after I show you the rudiments of shooting a bow, we will take a rest from your lessons and hunt. Hopefully we'll find a deer, and I can show you how it is done."

Both Sigrid and Gunhild hid smiles behind their hands, but the ale in his belly and head kept Harald from noticing.

"Let me show you my bow," Harald added and left the table. A few moments later, he returned bearing the bow, and handed it to me. "Is it not a fine one?"

I looked at it briefly, then laid it on the table and resumed eating. It was a well-made bow that stood as tall as Harald's shoulder, with broad flat-tened limbs that tapered to a rounded grip in the center. I would not call it a fine bow, though.

"It's a good bow. It should be," I said, between mouthfuls. "I made it."

Harald sat back and frowned. "How can this be? For years, Gudrod the Carpenter has made all of the bows and arrows for our household. He made this bow. He made Hrorik's bow. He makes the bows for all the carls who live here."

I shook my head. "When I was just a young

boy," I told Harald, "Gudrod showed me how to cut a stave from a tree, and shape the stave into a bow. He showed me how to split out shafts and turn them into arrows. He showed me because my hands have a cleverness in them, and he wished to train a helper to aid him with the carpentry work on this farm. It was not long after Gudrod taught me, that he told me I could find the bow hidden in the wood better than he. For more than three years now, it has been I who has made every bow in this household."

Harald shook his head in amazement. It did not surprise me that he had not known. The doings of thralls had never interested him. I'd been virtually invisible to Harald until I became his brother.

"Well, for tomorrow's lessons, and afterward for our hunt, you can use Hrorik's bow. I suppose you made it, too?" he asked. I nodded. He shook his head. "A thrall that makes bows," he said. "I have never heard of such a thing. I suppose we're lucky you did not make one for yourself."

I grinned. "Let me show you my bow," I told him. I left the longhouse and walked to the carpentry shed where Gudrod had stored the bow he'd allowed me to make for myself. I had not thought to bring it into the longhouse since I'd been freed.

It had been a little over a year since Gudrod had told me I could make a bow for myself. I'd chosen to make a longbow. Gudrod had one, and had showed me how. It was more difficult, he'd explained, to shape such a bow's limbs, for they were rounded rather than flat, and had to be carefully tapered from grip to tip to bend in an even arc when the bow was drawn. With such a shape, the limbs needed extra length to achieve a smooth and even draw, and powerful cast. Most men, Gudrod had explained, found the length of such bows unwieldy, and chose to shoot a flatbow instead, despite the fact that a well-crafted longbow was capable of greater power and range.

I'd lavished care in my bow's crafting, for as a thrall, it was the only thing of any value I'd possessed. It was made of yew, as all our bows were, and stretched, tip to tip, almost two hands taller than I stood. I'd wrapped its center, where I gripped it with my hand, with leather. The end of each limb I'd capped with a tip of horn, which I'd notched to hold the ends of bowstring. I'd sharpened the horn tips to fine points on their ends, and had decorated the socket of each where they joined to the end of the wood limb with a narrow ring I'd hammered from scraps of bronze Gunnar the Blacksmith had given me. Gudrod had smiled at that touch. "You are making a bow fit for a jarl," he'd said. "Be careful. If you draw attention to this bow you are likely to lose it."

I knew Gudrod risked Hrorik's displeasure had it become known that he'd allowed a thrall to own a weapon. All owners fear their slaves rising up against them. I think Gudrod did so because he and I shared a love of shaping wood, of finding the object that lay hidden within. Gudrod had no sons to share his passion for the wood with. He warned me that if ever the bow was discovered, we would have to claim it was his, and he'd say he'd just allowed me to use it.

My bow had remained a closely guarded secret, which at first only Gudrod and I were privy to. Whenever time permitted, he would take me out into the forest, beyond the reach of spying eyes, and teach me to shoot it. Under Gudrod's tutelage I learned quickly, and we discovered I had a natural eye for aiming, and an affinity for the bow that allowed me before long to become a better shot than my teacher.

I quickly progressed to shooting at small game—fowl, squirrels, rabbits, and the like—and practicing on such small and often moving targets sped my progress with the bow even more. Before long, it was a rare occasion when our trips into the forest did not produce some amount of meat, which Gudrod contributed to the estate's larder. Sharp-eyed Ubbe was the first to discover our secret. Gudrod, it seemed, had never been that eager or successful a hunter before. Ubbe was troubled at first when he learned it was actually I who was shooting Gudrod's fine new bow. He allowed us to continue, though, and eventually began allowing me to go into the forest alone and hunt.

Oddly enough, I had Gunhild to thank for that. She enjoyed varying her diet with fresh game, and as Hrorik mostly chose to ignore her nagging, she'd turned her tongue on Ubbe, Hrorik's foreman, and burdened him with her complaints about the lack of industry and hunting prowess of the men on the estate. When Ubbe realized that I always returned from the forest with some game in hand, he decided the simplest way to silence Gunhild was to relieve me from my other chores and dispatch me into the woods whenever she sought him out.

I, of course, loved it. Being alone in the forest was the only freedom I knew. Eventually Sigrid, her maid, Astrid, and even Gunhild—the three women in charge of preparing the meals for Hrorik's table—learned the true source of the game procured for the table, but their desire to keep the influx of fresh and varied meat in their diets had enrolled them in the conspiracy of silence.

When I returned to the hall of the longhouse, I handed my bow proudly to Harald for his inspection.

Its pull was stronger than most men's bows, but I could draw it easily, for I practiced at every chance. The only thing I'd loved more than my bow was my mother. Even on days when Ubbe did not send me into the forest to hunt, I would sneak off to the carpentry shed in the evening, after my chores were done, take my bow from its hiding place, string it, and practice my draw, standing inside the darkened shed and aiming imaginary arrows at targets that crossed my view through the open door.

I waited excitedly while Harald studied the bow, running his hands along the limbs and feeling their smoothness and strength, touching the horn tips to feel their sharpness, and rubbing his thumb across the hammered-bronze bands that decorated them. I was proud of my bow, and expected Harald to be pleased with it, and proud of me for making it. But when he looked up across the table at me his expression was strange.

"This is a very, very fine bow, Halfdan," he said. "Very fine indeed. There is an important lesson for you to learn from this bow. Someday you will own lands and own the thralls that work them. If you do not watch them constantly, they will steal from you every chance they can."

I felt the blood drain from my face and my stomach turned as though I had been struck. From the first day he'd become my brother, I'd felt gratitude toward Harald for his willingness to undertake the task of training me. Gradually I also came to feel trust, then friendship, and finally love. But now a cold anger swept over me and as it did, it was as though Harald changed before my eyes. No longer did I see my best friend and loving brother sitting across from me. I saw him again as through the eyes of a thrall viewing a master. He was one of them; different from me, and he always would be.

"No, Harald," I said in a quiet voice. "That is not the lesson here. The lesson is that if you see your thralls as little more than cattle, and treat them as such, that is the only value you will ever get from them. But thralls are men, not beasts. Each is different. Like any other men, some have special talents and gifts. You and others like you who own other men can only know your thralls' full worth if you possess the wisdom and kindness to treat them like men, and encourage them to find and use their talents. All your life you've been too blind to see this. You live your life of ease only because it has been built upon the thankless toil of thralls, but you do not even have the grace to think of them as men.

"I did not steal from this household when I made this bow. Before I put my hands to it, this was only a worthless piece of wood. You certainly do not possess the skill to have brought a bow to life from it. In your hands, it would have had no more value than a piece of firewood. What did I steal from you, Harald? A scrap of firewood? And tell me, when you dined on wild goose or duck or hare, where did you think they came from? I hunted them with this piece of firewood, often in the early, cold hours before dawn, while you were still warm in your bed, sleeping off the night's drinking, or satisfying your lust with a kitchen thrall."

I had no more appetite for food. I stood up and carried my bowl to where one of the hounds lay, and let him eat the remains of my dinner.

The room was silent. No one else moved. No one spoke to Harald that way. No one. He was a jolly and good-humored man, except when he felt his honor had been impugned. Then, though, his anger was a thing to be feared, for it could be deadly. The kitchen thralls stared at me in shock, and Sigrid sat still as a stone, her eyes wide with alarm.

Finally Harald spoke. "Halfdan," he called in a stern voice. "Come here."

His face was twisted in a deep scowl. I began to regret my words. I hoped my angry outburst had not cost me the love of my brother. Even more, I hoped they would not cost me my home—or even my life. I walked slowly over and stood before him, where he sat at table.

His face was beginning to turn red. I feared it was a very bad sign. Then his shoulders began shaking—and a moment later he burst into laughter. Tears ran from his eyes down his cheeks.

"I could hold it no longer," he gasped. I realized then his anger had been feigned. He had been trying to frighten me, as a jest. He had succeeded.

When Harald was finally able to cease laughing and compose himself, he continued, "You are right. My words were unjust. I am greatly sorry. Today you are the teacher, not I." He began laughing again. "But the look on your face, after you spoke, and realized what you had done . . ."

This time, all of us, Sigrid, I, the kitchen thralls, and even Gunhild, joined in his laughter. And afterward, even the lingering traces of the anger Harald had been carrying since Arnulf's visit were gone.

Harald picked up my bow and looked at it again. "I suppose," he said, "that this also means I do not need to teach you to shoot a bow before we can go hunting. Good. Tomorrow we shall try to find a deer for Sigrid."

I woke Harald long before dawn the following morning.

"Surely," he said as I shook him awake, "the deer are all still asleep at this hour. We should follow their good example."

Harald had never been a serious hunter. On the occasions when he did hunt, he favored using hounds or thralls to drive the deer, wild pigs, or other game to him. Today I did indeed intend to be the teacher, though, and show him the skills of a true woodsman. When I'd been sent into the forest to gather food for the table as a thrall, I'd had no hounds to sniff out the quarry, nor thralls to beat the underbrush and drive it to me. I'd had to rely on my eyes, and ears, and wits. I'd learned to use them well.

I collected bread and cheese and a small skin of water, and was waiting outside the longhouse with my bow and quiver when Harald finally emerged.

"Where are the others? Where are the dogs?" he asked.

"There are no others," I told him. "Only you and I are hunting."

"But how will we find the deer?"

"I will find one for us," I said and set off. Harald ate the food I'd brought as we walked.

"If it was later in the year, closer to summer, we could hunt where the forest runs down to the edges of the fields," I explained. "At dawn, the deer like to sneak out from the forest to feed upon the crops. But the earliest spring plantings have barely begun sprouting in the fields, so there is little there now to draw the deer from the protection of the trees. We will have to hunt deep in the forest.

"In late winter and early spring, forage is scarce. The deer will scrape the forest floor under oaks, looking for the last of the acorn drop, hidden by fallen leaves, or feed on the tender tips of green branches where they are just beginning to sprout, or on new rushes and grass along the edges of streams. This morning, we will follow the stream that empties into the fjord near the base of the death-ship hill. Back in the forest along its banks, there are large stands of oak trees. I think it will be a good place to look."

"How did you learn the ways of the forest creatures, Halfdan?" Harald asked.

"Gunhild and Sigrid enjoy variety in their meats at table. On rare occasions, you and Hrorik and the housecarls might schedule a hunt, and if you were lucky you would bring in venison or wild pig. But none of you like to hunt hares, or wild fowl, or other small game. You never considered that to be noble sport. Gunhild and Sigrid enjoy such fare, though, and so, for that matter, do you.

"When I was still a young boy, Ubbe would sometimes send me into the forest to set snares for rabbits. That way, he would not lose a day's work from a grown thrall. It was then I first began to learn the ways of the forest and the creatures that live there. Later, after Gudrod taught me how to make and shoot bows, I began harvesting the creatures of the forest with arrows. By then I'd learned to move through the forest as silently as the beasts themselves.

"Did Ubbe know of your bow?" Harald asked.

"Eventually," I answered. "But he was glad to have a source of game for the larder, and no one else had the skill or interest to supply the farm with wild meat. Whenever my services as a hunter were requested, I lingered in the forest as long as possible. It was the only place I felt free."

"Was it hard being a thrall?" Harald asked. "It is difficult for me to imagine."

"If every day you could only do those things that Gunhild or Ubbe ordered you to do, but all around you others could do whatever they wished, would you find it hard?" I replied.

Harald was silent for a long time. Finally he answered. "I do not think I could stand it. I think I would kill someone." He grinned. "Probably Gunhild," he said. "At least to start with. Then perhaps others. I would not like always being told what I must do.

"How many deer have you taken, in your hunts

in the forest?" he asked, changing the subject.

"None," I answered. "You and Hrorik and the housecarls ate duck or hare or goose without wondering where it came from, but the sudden appearance of venison on the table, when none of you had been out hunting, would raise too many questions that Ubbe might find difficult to answer. I have followed many deer, though, for hours, just for the pleasure of watching them. I have come to know their ways."

"So," Harald said, looking pleased for the first time since I'd roused him out of bed that morning. "As to deer, at least, I am the more experienced hunter between the two of us. I have killed many."

I smiled but said nothing.

We walked for a time in silence, then Harald spoke. "It must have been difficult," he said. "All these years that you hunted meat for the table, yet as a thrall were allowed to eat none of it."

My face reddened. "Well," I said, "You know you must watch thralls constantly, or they'll steal from you every chance they can. If Ubbe told me Gunhild needed four hares, I would take five, and cook one in the forest. I'd eat my fill of meat in the forest as if I was a free man, and smuggle the remainder in to my mother. Gunhild was never the wiser, and if Ubbe suspected, he did not care."

We'd reached the point where the stream

flowed out from the border of the forest, so we ceased our chattering and began moving quietly, as though we belonged in the forest with the other creatures. A gentle breeze was blowing downstream into our faces as we advanced, carrying our scent away from the area we hunted.

Inside the forest, the limbs of the trees were still mostly gray and naked from winter, though numerous unsprouted buds on the tips of their branches gave promise of the foliage soon to show itself. Wisps of mist hovered over the stream. Dawn was rapidly approaching and as the sky lightened, we could see farther and farther upstream.

Just ahead, the stony shoulder of a low hill blocked the stream's course, forcing it to curve in a wide bend around the rocky obstruction. When we rounded the foot of the hill I saw—far ahead in the distance on the opposite bank—a stag pawing the earth beneath a stand of oaks.

I touched Harald's sleeve, held a finger to my lips, and pointed to the distant deer. Slowly and silently we backed out of sight behind the shoulder of the hill. Harald crept on his hands and knees to where he could raise his head and peer at the deer over the top of the rise. He whispered over his shoulder to me.

"Gods, but it's a fine deer, Halfdan. Sigrid will think us heroes if we can bring this one home, for she loves her venison. I wish we had beaters to drive it to us. I think we'll have to stay behind this ridge and try to stalk close enough for a shot. It will be difficult, though."

While he talked, I slipped an arrow from my quiver and nocked it on my bowstring. I took a deep breath and blew it out, then stood slowly and, pushing my bow forward with my left arm and pulling back on its string with my right, brought my bow to full draw.

Harald caught a glimmer of my movement and turned as I came to full draw. His eyes widened, as if he was seeing a disaster play out before his eyes. He whispered, "No, Halfdan, no! It is too far!"

In truth, it was a long shot, a very long shot. I would not have attempted it had I not desired so much to impress my brother. I stared at the deer, then at its front shoulder, then at a tiny tuft of fur just behind the bend of its front leg. When I could focus my sight no tighter, I released.

The arrow arced through the air, seeming to take forever to cover the distance. When the twang of my bowstring reached the stag, it raised its head and looked downstream toward us, searching for the source of the sound. I felt as though it was looking straight into my eyes, and I whispered, "Godspeed to your spirit."

The arrow struck. The great stag turned as if to

flee, staggered a few steps, and collapsed.

Harald was silent as we walked to where the deer lay. The arrow had passed completely through it and was embedded in the ground several paces away. Harald stood over the carcass and looked back downstream to the shoulder of the hill from whence I'd made the shot.

"Halfdan, my brother," he finally said. "I have never seen such a shot, nor even heard of its equal in song or tale. I have known no man who could accomplish this. I know not what your destiny will be. No one can know what fate the Norns are weaving. But I believe you have been touched by the Gods and given a great gift. Truly, I mean this."

8

TOKE

When Harald and I appeared from the forest, carrying the deer slung between us on a sapling we'd cut, we were greeted with as much excitement as though we were heroes returning from a quest. Astrid, who was at the stream filling waterskins when we first appeared, ran to the longhouse, calling for Sigrid and Gunhild.

They clapped their hands excitedly when they saw us as they emerged from its doorway, and Sigrid, who especially disliked dried fish and salted pork—meat that had been the basis for most of our meals, since Harald had begun my training—ran to us and danced round the deer as we carried it to the meat shed to be skinned and butchered, planning what she would cook.

"It's so big!" she said. "I'll take the long strap muscles that run along the spine and wrap them in a pastry dough, and bake them with a sprinkling of ale and herbs. From this great stag, there will be enough meat from the straps alone to feed us all."

By now, Ubbe and others had gathered round. Harald was excitedly telling the story of my shot that had felled the deer, with some exaggeration—though in truth, little was needed. I drew my knife and squatted by the deer's body, starting a cut near the breastbone. Ubbe put his hand on my arm and stopped me. He bent close and spoke softly in my ear.

"Let Fasti do this. It is a thrall's work."

Ubbe beckoned to Fasti, who came over, took Ubbe's long knife from his hand, and knelt beside the carcass. With a quick slash of the blade, he opened up the deer's belly and began pulling out its entrails. He kept his eyes averted from mine as I wiped my knife clean and sheathed it. I, too, made a point of avoiding his gaze. It felt strange—and somehow wrong—to watch my old friend doing what should have been my work.

I stood up, glancing around as I did. No one but Ubbe seemed to have noticed my mistake. For that was what it was. I was a free man, but had unthinkingly acted like a slave.

Harald was laughing and talking to Sigrid. Astrid emerged from the longhouse carrying two tankards of ale.

"Refreshment for the returning hunters!" she announced with a bright smile. Her hand lingered a moment when it brushed Harald's as she passed one of the cups to him.

Gunhild may have noticed it, too, for she wrapped the deer's liver in a cloth and handed it to Astrid.

"Here. Take this and go inside," she told her. "Cut it into chunks, skewer them on sharpened branches, and throw more wood on the cook fire. We shall have roasted deer liver now, as a special treat, to celebrate the successful hunt. Go on. Get to work."

Harald tipped his head back and drained his tankard in one long, continuous gulp. It was a skill he possessed that all the men of the estate admired. When he was finished, he belched, slapped me on the back, laughed, and said, "Life is good, is it not, my brother? It is still early morning, but you have wakened me early and worked me hard. Today we shall rest for the remainder of the day from your lessons. It is right, since this day you have been the teacher to me. Besides, I would have a soak in the bathhouse to drive the chill of the forest from my bones, and perhaps even a nap afterward. I have worked hard these recent weeks, trying to teach you all I know about being a warrior. It is a lot to teach."

The bathhouse was attached to the longhouse, running off from it in a separate wing. While the wooden soaking tub was being filled with heated water, Harald and I disrobed and rinsed ourselves, shivering, with washing cloths and a basin of fresh, cold water. When we'd scrubbed ourselves clean, we gratefully lowered ourselves up to our necks in the tub of steaming water.

Sigrid entered, carrying a heavily laden wooden platter.

"Today," she said, "I intend to treat the two of you like kings. You have saved me. If I'd had to eat one more mouthful of dried fish, I should surely have choked on it!"

She handed each of us a large silver goblet. Mine was warm to the touch.

"I've mulled Frankish wine with spices and honey," she explained, then handed Harald and me each a wooden skewer on which chunks of deer liver, roasted over the open fire, had been speared. The hot juices ran down my chin as I hungrily tore bites of the fresh liver from the skewer.

When he'd finished his meat and wine, Harald stepped from the water and wrapped himself in his cloak. The rest of his clothes he left lying on the bench of the bathhouse. His long blond hair hung wet and dripping down his back, and his legs and feet showed bare below the hem of the cloak. But he pushed his chest out, and with a grave dignity that belied the informality of his appearance, he turned to Sigrid, and said, "Thank you, my sister, for the royal repast you provided." He turned to me and added, "Teacher, with your permission, I will go now and seek the sleep you robbed me of this morning."

I felt no inclination to leave. The mulled wine and hot water were leeching the pain and stiffness from weeks of battering and bruises from my body.

A low fire was burning on the hearth in the bathhouse, under an iron kettle suspended from a tripod. Sigrid lifted the kettle from the fire and added more hot water to the tub.

"Give me your cup," she said. "I'll refill it."

When she returned, she bore in one arm a stack of clothing.

"I have been sewing again," she said as she handed me my wine. "You must have more than just the feast clothes I made before, and your old tunic."

She held up the first garment, a long cloak of thick gray wool.

"I've made this of our thickest weave, to protect

you in harsh weather. The wool's natural oils will make it shed water in all but the hardest of rains. And this silver ring brooch, to clasp it, was Father's. It is from Ireland, in the style that Derdriu's people wear. I'm sure Father would have wanted you to have it. And here, this tunic I've made for you is also wool, though of a lighter weave. I did not dye it, but left it gray, like the cloak, for I know you love the forest, and I thought the natural color of the wool would better blend there. These trousers, though, I dyed brown—we cannot have you dressed all in gray. And last, I asked Ubbe to make you these new shoes."

I reached out and felt the shoes. Their tops were of deerskin, very soft, and the soles were from the thickest cut on the back of a bull's hide. Ubbe was the most skilled on the estate at working leather. I'd never had shoes such as these, for he did not make shoes for thralls.

My mother had loved me all her life, and had protected me as best she could from the hurts life inevitably brings. No one, though, had ever showered me with gifts the way that Sigrid did.

"Sigrid," I told her, "I do not know what words to say to thank you. I am more than just at a loss for words. I do not even know what to think. I am not used to such kindness."

"Think that you have a family," she said.

"Think that I am your sister, and that these are but expressions of a sister's love."

Sigrid sat smiling quietly at me after she spoke those words. A family. It was a strange thought. I'd never had a real family. I liked it.

Before, as a thrall, the only sense of belonging I'd ever felt was the knowledge that I belonged to Hrorik, that I was his property. But now I belonged to a family. I had a brother and a sister. It was a totally different kind of belonging. We were bound to each other by bonds of love, not ownership.

I studied my sister as she sat there smiling at me. In appearance, Sigrid was completely unlike my mother—the only other person who'd ever loved me. Mother had been of but average height, with raven-black hair and gray eyes. Sigrid was tall and willowy like Harald, who was her twin. Her hair was golden, the gold of morning sunlight rather than the metal, paler even than Harald's, and her eyes were a deep blue.

"Sister, may I ask you a question of a personal nature?" I said.

"Of course. There should be openness between brother and sister," she replied.

"You possess such great beauty, both of appearance and spirit, and as the daughter of a famous chieftain, you are of the highest social standing.

How is it you are not wed?"

Sigrid laughed merrily. "Perhaps because I have rarely been the recipient of such pretty words, and certainly never from young men seated only an arm's length away, wearing no clothes."

I blushed at her answer, and sank lower in the water.

"The true reason is this," she continued, smiling at my sudden discomfort. "I have almost no memory of my true mother, who died when I was very young. Your mother, Derdriu, was the only mother I knew. Later, when Father wed Gunhild, and I grew older, Derdriu remained very dear to me. She was a thrall, and I a master, and we both knew it. There was no escaping such difference in status, particularly with Gunhild as the mistress of the household. Though there was much we could not share, within our hearts we continued to feel friendship and love.

"Many times Derdriu told me the story of how love grew in her heart for Father, and how the relationship between them blossomed and grew like a flower in the spring—until Gunhild came. I saw with my own eyes the happiness love can bring to a man and woman. And I have also witnessed, with Father and Gunhild, the unhappiness of an arranged marriage where there is no love. I resolved that when I wed, it would be to a man I loved."

I marveled that Sigrid had known so much more about my mother—about her feelings, dreams, and disappointments—than I had. Had I been a bad son, so concerned with my own wants and needs that I never stopped to wonder about Mother's? Mother had given me everything, even her life, and I had given her so little in return.

Sigrid continued. "I remember clearly the evening that I announced my intention to Father. He'd been talking at dinner of a chieftain who lived on the island of Fyn, and how he was looking for a wife. I expected Father to react with rage, for he was prone to great fits of anger whenever someone disobeyed his will, and I knew that arranging my marriage to form an alliance was a thing he could use to great advantage. That night was not the first time Father had speculated aloud on who might prove an advantageous match for me. Instead of anger, though, a sad expression crossed his face. Then he clasped my hands between his, kissed my forehead, and gave me his blessing. 'On this matter,' he told me, 'you should indeed follow your heart.' I think he spoke so because he regretted that he had not followed his. Thus far, my heart has not spoken, so I am not wed."

Hrorik had always seemed to me to have the disposition of a bear awakened from his hibernation slumber. The pictures of him painted by my mother and Sigrid did not fit at all. In what other ways, I wondered, had I failed to understand the truth that lay behind what I believed I was seeing?

"And Harald?" I asked. "Why has he not wed?"

Sigrid laughed again. "I suspect it will be some years before Harald is ready to assume the responsibilities of wedded life. I believe he views the female sex as a platter of delicacies to sample, and he does not lack for willing partners to indulge him. His current affection is for Astrid. Indeed, if you had not been keeping Harald so busy these past weeks, I do not know how I would have kept her out of his bed long enough to do her chores."

What Sigrid told me was no surprise, of course. It is difficult to keep secrets living in a longhouse.

Sigrid stood and straightened her apron.

"I must go prepare my roast. When you finish your bath, it would give me pleasure if you would wear your new clothes, so I may see how they fit you."

My bath—and the mulled wine—left me feeling relaxed and lazy. After I dressed, I was lounging on the bench along the longhouse wall, contentedly watching Sigrid and Gunhild at the main hearth preparing the venison, when Ing flung the door open. He paused a moment while he panted for breath, and gasped out, "Ubbe sent me. He sent Hrut to warn the village. A ship has entered the fjord under full sail. Where is Harald?"

The doors of Harald's bed-closet swung slightly open, and Harald's head emerged, peering out between them.

"What kind of ship?" he asked.

"I could not see it clearly enough to tell," Ing replied. That was no surprise. Ing's vision was notoriously bad. If a hawk was hovering in the sky overhead, he rarely could see it, even after you pointed to it. "But Ubbe said it was moving too swiftly across the water to be a trading vessel," he added. "He said it must be a longship."

Harald pulled his head back in. A moment later he climbed out, clad only in his trousers. Standing beside his bed, he pulled his tunic over his head, sat on the bed's edge, slipped his shoes on his feet, and laced them to his ankles. As he did so, three of the carls who lived on the estate rushed in, ran to where their shields and weapons were hanging on the wall, and took down their swords. One also retrieved Ubbe's sword from where it was hanging. Harald stood up and buckled on his own belt and sword.

"Halfdan," he called to me. "Get your bow and quiver and follow me to the shore."

Harald was already running out of the doorway.

As I passed the open doors of Harald's bed-closet on the way to retrieve my bow, I saw Astrid inside, arranging her clothes.

Harald and the three carls had slowed to a fast walk. I caught up with them before they reached the shore.

"Do you think it's raiders?" I asked. "Shouldn't you have your armor and shield?"

Harald shook his head. "It is unlikely to be raiders. They'd be foolish to approach like this in broad daylight, in this area where there are other villages and estates not a great distance away. It may be an acquaintance of Hrorik, or a ship that has gone i-viking and now has goods to sell or trade."

"Then why did you and the others get your swords?" I asked.

"A wise man keeps his weapons with him, and is careful when entering any door if he knows not what lies beyond. We do not know who comes on this ship. If we greeted it unarmed, with no sign that we are cautious and watchful men, our laxity might tempt the crew to take advantage."

Ubbe was standing on the small rise beside the boathouses, his hand shading his eyes.

"I believe I recognize the sail," he said. "It looks to be the *Sea Steed*." There was disgust in the tone of his voice.

Harald squinted for a time at the ship, then responded. "Ubbe, you've always had eyes like a falcon. Now that you've told me, I can just make out the sail's pattern." He sighed. "Brother Toke has returned."

Harald turned and saw that Sigrid and Gunhild were standing at a distance, back near the longhouse.

"Gunhild!" he cried. "Your son has returned."

It had been almost two years since Toke had left. I remembered it clearly. It had been a harsh winter with many deep snows, and we'd often been confined to the longhouse by the weather. It was difficult for everyone, but especially for Toke. He was a berserk, and the darkness lay on him heavily that winter.

Some believe berserks are not really men at all, that they're shape-changers who sometimes walk among folk in the form of men, but in the dark of night can turn into beasts. It is the beast's nature, they say, that makes berserks so difficult of disposition and savage in combat. Personally, I do not believe it, but it is certain that berserks are not like other men. Many men, in the heat of battle, have at one time or another lost themselves in a fury of blood and killing. But with berserks, it's as though that fury is always there, lurking just below the surface, like a great pike lurks beneath the surface of the water, waiting to strike at a moment's notice.

That winter, most of the thralls, and even one or two of the carls, had felt the weight of Toke's fists during his moods of black anger. Toke and Harald had bristled at each other often, but had never come to blows.

Seeing Toke's ship racing toward us, I remembered the trouble that had occurred between Toke and Hrorik that had led to Toke leaving. It had started late one night, when during one of his frequent drunken binges, Toke had caught Astrid alone and unawares. Clapping a hand over her mouth to keep her from calling out, he'd dragged her out into the animal byre and there had taken her against her will, and roughly. Afterward, the girl had fled crying and screaming to Sigrid, who, blazing with anger, had awakened Hrorik.

When Hrorik confronted him, Toke—who by then was already a huge, hulking brute of a man, though he was only a year older than Harald—laughed in his face and dared Hrorik to do anything about the rape. I think it was that night when Hrorik realized for the first time that in a fight without weapons, Toke might win. I can think of no other reason why he would not have attacked Toke after his insolent challenge. At any rate, Hrorik did nothing but shout and threaten, to which Toke responded in kind.

The air in the household stayed poisonous after that, but violence did not erupt again for several weeks. Then one afternoon, when my mother went to the byre to check the chickens' nests for eggs, she encountered Toke lurking there, drunk again. He doubtless did not expect so much resistance from so small a woman. When he grabbed her from behind, ripping her shift open and clutching at her with his rough hands, Mother clawed at his face, drawing blood in long stripes across his cheeks and temporarily blinding his eyes. She broke free from his grasp, but Toke roared in anger and lumbered after her like an enraged bear.

Mother grabbed a pitchfork from a stack of hay, turned, and stabbed it into his thigh, just as Toke swung and caught her a glancing blow on the side of her face with the back of his hand. She was knocked almost senseless, and stumbled backward, falling onto the loose hay on the floor of the byre in front of the hayrick. She would have been defenseless had Toke continued his assault, but his wound distracted him from the chase.

I was in the main hall of the longhouse when Mother staggered, weeping and clutching at her torn dress, from the byre. Her face was already red and swelling from the force of Toke's blow. Hrorik and Harald were seated at the large table near the fire, playing hnefatafl, while Sigrid, Gunhild, and

Astrid were preparing the evening meal at the hearth. I sat nearby, plucking the feathers from a duck.

All eyes turned toward the door of the byre at the sound of Mother's weeping. Sigrid dropped the pot she was holding and ran to her. Hrorik sat motionless and silent, but I watched his face growing a darker and darker red. When Sigrid brought Mother near, he uttered in a strangled whisper a single word: "Who?"

"Toke," Mother gasped. As she spoke his name, Toke emerged, swearing, from the entrance to the byre, holding his leg to stanch the blood, and limped across the hall to his bed-closet. Seeing that he was wounded, Gunhild uttered a cry of distress and ran to him.

Hrorik stood up from the table and stalked down the hall to his sleeping chamber. When he reemerged, he was carrying his war-axe. The handle was as long as a man's leg, and the blade, though thin and light, had a broad, curved edge as long as the span of a man's hand.

Toke was sprawled crosswise on his bed, cursing angrily, his legs stretched out from the closet onto the floor. His trousers were pulled down, and Gunhild was kneeling in front of him, binding his wound with a strip of cloth she'd torn from the hem of her dress. She looked up and saw Hrorik approaching, axe in hand.

"No, Hrorik! Do not!" she screamed and ran to intercept him. Hrorik swept her aside with one arm, so forcefully that she fell to the floor. All in the longhouse—carls seated idling along the side benches, and the thralls at their work—stared, motionless, as though frozen in their places. I was certain—and hopeful—that I was about to see Toke chopped into bits. I could not look away.

As he reached the bed-closet, Hrorik swung the axe sideways in a great sweeping blow that smashed through the side planks of the closet wall on one end, slightly below the top, showering Toke with shards of splintered wood. Toke tried to stand up before Hrorik could swing the axe again, but Hrorik kicked him in the face, knocking him back into the bed. Hrorik swung the axe again, once, twice, three times, chopping at the sides and back while Toke cowered inside, till the boards of the closet's sides were all chopped through and those of the top collapsed upon Toke.

Hrorik raised one foot high and smashed his heel down on the boards lying across Toke's chest. I thought I heard a muffled gasp from beneath the shattered lumber.

"Hear me," Hrorik shouted, leaning forward so his face was close to Toke's. "Since I married your mother, I have raised you as if you were my own son, and I have tried to show you every kindness. But you are as a wild animal in my household. You respect nothing and no one. I will tolerate it no more. I give you my smaller ship, the *Sea Steed*. It is a parting gift far more generous than you deserve. Take her and be gone tomorrow. After this, you have no claim upon me. If you do not go, if you choose to remain and there are any more incidents, I will not restrain myself as I did today. Blood will be spilled."

It was a tense night. My mother did not sleep at all. She stayed by the main hearth and kept the fire blazing. I stayed at her side, helping her feed the fire. I sat close to her and told her not to fear, that I would let nothing happen to her. It was an empty promise. But I, too, was filled with fear. I hoped that Toke would leave us alone, because I knew I would be powerless against his great strength. Most grown men would be, and I was but a child. Toke had beaten me too many times before, just for the pleasure of causing someone pain, for me to have any illusions that I could resist his force and will.

Toke had sailed away the next day with a skeleton crew of only ten. None of the carls from Hrorik's household who'd lived in close vicinity to Toke would accompany him. All of his meager crew were from the village, disaffected sons at odds with their parents or younger brothers with little hope of fortune at home.

Neither Hrorik nor Harald nor Sigrid came to see Toke off that dreary, late winter day that he departed. Only Gunhild came down to the water's edge to witness his leave-taking. Only Gunhild and I, for my curiosity led me to sneak down to the waterfront and watch from behind a corner of the boathouse.

"Where will you go?" I heard Gunhild wail. "How will you survive with so small a crew?"

"We will survive," he snapped. "We'll sail for Dublintown in Ireland. I've heard that there they do not lack for men with stomach for a fight. I'll fill my crew in Dublin."

At Toke's command, his men had used their oars to push the ship away from the wharf. A stiff wind was blowing off of the land. They'd raised the yard, letting the sail billow and fill, and pulled in on the sheets to trim the sail to the wind. The ship had moved away, gathering speed, Toke standing in the stern at the steering oar. For as long as I could make him out, he stood unmoving at the helm and never looked back. I'd hoped to never see him again.

He had not returned during the two years since. I wondered what brought him back now.

When the ship neared, I could make out the

detail on the gilded, wooden horse's head, mounted on the stempost at the bow, from which the *Sea Steed* drew her name. It had been carved by Gudrod, the Carpenter, with great care and skill, so that it was at once both recognizable as a horse, a familiar beast, yet at the same time appeared some strange and fanciful creature, wild and dangerous.

A beast of a different nature, and far more frightening and dangerous than a carved statue, was in the stern of the ship. There Toke stood, arms folded across his chest, beside the steersman.

Where Harald was slender and supple, with the dangerous grace of a cat, Toke possessed the build, disposition, and power of a bear. His shoulders were so broad, and his chest so thick, that his head, perched above them, looked to me too small for his body. Perhaps Toke thought so, too, for he'd let his black beard and hair grow long, and they blew unbound and wild around his head like a mane.

As the ship continued its approach to the shore, I could see that judging from the treasure he was displaying on his person, the two years since he'd left had been profitable for Toke. Silver rings hung from each ear, and multiple silver bracelets graced each thick wrist. Around each of his upper arms, he wore a torque of thick, twisted silver wire. If he'd had a neck, doubtless he would have decorated it, too, with a silver neck ring. All in all, Toke was wearing a chieftain's ransom in precious metal. In addition to the jewelry, he was dressed in a sleeveless tunic made of the coarse, brown fur of a bear, belted over a woolen shirt and trousers, both dyed a deep red, and high, black leather boots.

Toke headed his ship straight for the wharf. The *Red Eagle*, Hrorik's ship—now Harald's—had long since been pulled ashore and stored under cover of the boathouse. Toke's crew looked rough, but they handled his ship skillfully, and brought it smoothly and gently in against the wharf. Ubbe directed two of our men to help them secure it.

Toke disembarked alone and swaggered down the plank walkway of the narrow wharf. We greeted him where it met the shore. Harald nodded his head coolly.

"Toke," he said. "I had expected we might meet again in England, but the fates chose otherwise."

"Son," Gunhild added, "your father is dead."

Toke stared coldly at Gunhild, the mother he had not seen in two years, and responded, "My father died years ago, in the first great raid on Dorestad. I heard, though, that the man you married is dead, or close to it, and that is why the *Red Eagle* fled from the battle with the English and abandoned the others who fought there."

Clearly, time had not mellowed Toke. I hated him. Hated and feared him.

Sigrid was standing close behind me. I could feel her body jerk and hear her quiet gasp when Toke said that the *Red Eagle* had fled the battle. Harald had killed men over lesser insults.

We all stood silently, waiting for what would happen next. Even Gunhild looked appalled. Toke stood smirking, his hands on his hips, watching Harald for a reaction. Harald stood motionless, no expression on his face, staring at Toke as if deciding where best to cut.

Suddenly Harald smiled and spoke. He acted as if he had heard no insult.

"How heard you news of the battle? I've often wondered since that day how many other ships escaped the trap."

I heard Sigrid let her breath out in a long sigh of relief. Toke looked confused, as if unsure how to judge Harald's response, for he showed neither anger at the insult nor fear at the implicit challenge by Toke.

"Two other ships escaped the English that day," Toke finally responded. "Some of the crew on one of them saw Hrorik being hoisted aboard the *Red Eagle*, spouting blood. From what they saw, I reckoned he was dead, or close to it."

"Hrorik died the night after we reached this

shore," Harald said quietly. "Why have you come? Do you wish now to offer him the honor and respect, at his tomb, that you never gave him in life?"

Toke hawked and spat upon the ground. "Two days after the battle, our ships from Dublin found the two ships remaining of the Danish fleet that had fought the English, and we joined forces. The English army had already withdrawn, but we harried the English countryside hard. Whatever respects I had to pay to Hrorik, I did so by spilling English blood upon the ground."

"So then," Harald asked, with a humorless smile on his lips, "If your respects to the dead have already been paid, why are you here? Surely you did not expect, even with Hrorik gone, to be welcomed?"

The bluntness of the question plainly caught Toke by surprise.

"Do you deny that this was for many years my home, too?" he blustered.

"I deny nothing. It was you who chose, by your actions, to make this place no longer your home."

"I came," Toke said, "to see if there was an inheritance."

Harald shook his head, smiling disdainfully. "So you've come to seek an inheritance from a man you say was not your father, but merely the man your mother married? A man whom you insulted and showed no respect or honor to—though he raised you as a son and treated you fairly? From a man who finally banished you from these lands, and told you never to return—you expect an inheritance? It is a strange view of the world you carry, Toke. Your journey was in vain. The only inheritance Hrorik left you is what bore you here. The *Sea Steed* was your inheritance. And in giving you that much, Hrorik was truly a better man and more of a foster father than you deserved."

Harald and Toke stood glowering at each other. Each hated the other, and had for years. When both were young boys, Toke—a bully even then—had relentlessly picked on Harald, who was slighter of build and not nearly as strong. The beatings had stopped the year Harald had turned nine. That was the year when Harald gave up trying to match strength with Toke.

One afternoon, when Toke bloodied Harald's nose and knocked him sprawling one too many times, Harald got up from the ground holding a stone in his hand, as big as a grown man's fist, and hurled it into Toke's face. Toke dropped on his back, knocked senseless. Harald leapt upon his chest, picked up the stone, and commenced pounding Toke's face and head to a bloody pulp.

Only the thickness of Toke's skull, and the fact that Hrorik had quickly arrived and pulled Harald off, had saved Toke's life. He'd been unconscious for an entire day, and his face still bore scars from the beating.

Their fight was a memory I'd cherished in the years that followed when Toke turned his bullying on me. He picked on everyone smaller than him—on everyone who feared him—but he seemed to hold a special hatred for me. Perhaps it was because I'd witnessed his defeat and humiliation at Harald's hands. That fight was the first time I'd realized that Toke was not invincible, that he could be defeated. It was also the first time I'd realized that lurking within Harald's gentle manner was a willingness to kill if sufficiently provoked.

Gunhild stepped forward. "You do not intend to turn Toke away without offering him the hospitality of our home this night?" she asked Harald. "You would do as much for a total stranger who had traveled so far. Toke is my son. I have not seen him for two years. Do not turn him away. Let him and his men stay and rest, just this one night. To do otherwise will reflect badly on you."

Harald sighed. There was a code of hospitality that was expected. Personally, I thought he should ignore it. Harald was a more well-mannered man than I would have been. Braver, too.

"You and your men may rest here this night," he told Toke. "You may dine with us in the longhouse tonight. But you'll sleep on your ship and leave at morning light."

Harald turned to me and said, "Come, Halfdan. Let us return to the longhouse. We need to talk."

For the first time since coming ashore, Toke looked at me. "Things have changed greatly since I left," he said, surprised. "Now thralls wear fine clothes and carry weapons. I always felt Hrorik ran a slack household, but this surprises even me."

Sigrid put her arm around my shoulder and spoke up.

"Halfdan is a free man, and our brother. Hrorik acknowledged him before he died."

"The old fool," Toke said, shaking his head disgustedly. "The more piglets there are to suckle at the teat, the less milk there is for all. And the boy's mother?"

"She accompanied Hrorik on his last voyage, on the death ship," Sigrid replied.

"That," Toke said, "is a pity and a waste. I'd been greatly looking forward to getting to know Derdriu better on this visit, now that the old man is gone."

I could feel the blood rushing to my face. Toke threw back his head and roared with laughter at my reaction to his remark. At that moment, if I'd possessed Harald's skill and bravery, I would have challenged Toke and killed him then and there on the beach. I did not have Harald's skill, however, nor his courage. All I had was anger—my hands were shaking from it. But even stronger than my anger was my fear. Toke still frightened me. I knew I was powerless against his insults, just as in years past I'd been powerless against his beatings. If I challenged Toke to a duel, I knew I would die.

Toke turned and called to his helmsman. "Snorre! You and the men stay with the ship for now. I am going up to the longhouse to visit with my mother."

For the first time, I noticed the ship's cargo. Almost twenty women and female children, and perhaps half as many men, were huddled together in the center of the ship, secured with chains. Toke saw me staring at them.

"They're slaves, boy," he said. "Like you were. Like you should be still. We took them in England. We're bound for the slave market at Birka to sell them. Fair-haired females bring the best price there from buyers for the Araby kingdoms."

"The males look like warriors," Ubbe remarked. "Such men make poor slaves."

"The Sveas will buy them," Toke replied. "They like strong-backed slaves to dig the iron ore."

I looked at the prisoners in Toke's ship. All were dirty, with tangled and matted hair, and many of the men bore fresh cuts and bruises, as if they'd recently been beaten. Toke, I knew from experience, was quick to take his fists or a whip to a slave. The captives stared back at me with pitiful looks of despair and terror in their eyes. I turned away. There was nothing I or anyone else could do for them. They belonged to Toke now. The fates the Norns had woven for them had sealed their doom.

After we returned to the longhouse, Toke retired with Gunhild into the chamber where she slept. Harald had not asked her to move out after Hrorik's death, though as master of the estate he had a right to take the private chamber as his own. He was content, for now at least, with his bed-closet.

Harald sat down at the main table near the hearth. "Sigrid, Halfdan, join me," he said. "There is a family matter we must discuss."

I sat across the table from Harald. Sigrid brought cups and a pitcher of ale. When she'd filled and distributed the cups, she sat down at Harald's side.

"This is the way of it," Harald said to me. "Sigrid already knows this, but it is time you were told. I'd hoped to pick a time of my own choosing, but Toke's coming has taken matters out of my hands. No doubt Gunhild is even now telling Toke what I am about to tell you.

"As you know, Hrorik died just before dawn on the day after we returned from England. Late the night before, he gave these instructions for the division of his property: To Gunhild, he gave the right to live on this estate for as long as she desires, until her death or she remarries. Also, Gunhild possesses a small wooden casket, decorated with plates of ivory and silver, that Hrorik took in his raid on Dorestad and gave her as a gift when they wed. Before he died, Hrorik gave Gunhild the right to fill that casket with whatever jewelry, silver coins, or other valuables she desires from among his treasure. Gunhild's right to choose from among Hrorik's treasure was to be the first, before anyone else took their share."

Sigrid nodded. "And Gunhild has done so. She has chosen what she wished and filled the chest."

"To Sigrid, Hrorik left the two small matching chests of carved wood that he took once in Ireland. She was to fill both of them with whatever jewelry and silver coins she desired, after Gunhild had chosen. Those chests of treasure are to be her dowry.

"The estate itself," Harald continued, "and the *Red Eagle*, Hrorik gave to me, plus any treasure that remains after his other gifts have been distributed."

"It is all as Harald says," Sigrid added, nodding

her head. "And I, too, have already chosen my share."

I did not understand why Harald was telling me this. It seemed none of my affair. His next words solved the riddle.

"Hrorik left an inheritance to you, too, Halfdan. He still owns a small estate in the north of Jutland, on the Limfjord, though in recent years he has rarely gone there. Hrorik left his small estate to you."

I stared at Harald, my mind suddenly blank from my astonishment. I had not expected Hrorik to give me anything besides my freedom. I could not get my mind around the thought of it. I, a former thrall, now owned lands? And not just lands, but an estate?

Suddenly the sound of Toke's angry voice erupted from within Gunhild's sleeping chamber. "Why am I angry?" Toke shouted. "Why do you not understand, Mother? Your husband left me nothing! Nothing! But he gave lands to a slave!"

Gunhild answered him in a voice loud enough so that we could now hear her, too. "He gave you a ship, Toke. And you are the sole heir of my father, Jarl Eirik, who has vast holdings on the island of Fyn. When my father dies, the king may give all to you."

"Bah!" Toke shouted. "That old man seems

determined to live forever. Besides, you, dear Mother, no doubt will marry again, and might bear your new husband brats who would split my inheritance. And the man you marry could catch the king's eye and be deemed more suitable a jarl than me. I do not possess the patience to fit in at a king's court."

Nor the manners, I thought. Within a week at the court of a king, Toke's rude ways would no doubt cause his head to be displayed upon a pike at the execution ground.

"Toke seems very unhappy about the division of Father's property," Sigrid commented. Harald shrugged his shoulders.

"Toke is a berserk," he replied. "Since he was a young child, that darkness has laid upon him. He is usually an unhappy man, angry about everything . . . or nothing at all."

For a time, Toke and Gunhild's conversation was whispered and could not be understood from where we sat. Then Toke's voice, raised in anger again, roared above the sounds of the longhouse.

"You burned Hrorik's sword? Thought you not of me? This household is rife with fools!"

When she responded, Gunhild's voice was sharp and loud with anger, too. "Yes, Hrorik bore his sword on his final voyage. I myself laid it on his body. He was a great chieftain and warrior. It is his

185

due to bear weapons befitting his rank in Valhalla."

It was perhaps the only time I ever heard Gunhild defend Hrorik. Toke possessed a special talent. He could offend anyone, even his own mother. The evening promised to be a grim one.

I cannot describe the meal we ate that night as a feast, though normally we would have called it such, when the hospitality of the estate was offered to visitors. The air was too filled with tension from the very beginning. Gunhild tried hard to make the best of it. She had a fat sheep killed, and made a rich stew with barley and the mutton, and also served meat from the deer's haunches. The special venison roast that Sigrid had been so excited about cooking was served to the head table, which tonight seated Harald, Sigrid, Gunhild, Ubbe, Ase, and me, plus Toke and his helmsman, Snorre.

Things went badly from the very beginning. Toke's crew arrived at the door of the longhouse bearing their weapons. Harald stood in the doorway and would not let them enter.

"It is not the custom in this house that we dine as though expecting imminent attack," he told Toke. "Your men must leave their weapons out here before they enter."

"That is not our practice in Dublin," Toke

protested. "We are warriors and expect to be treated as such."

"You are not in Dublin," Harald replied. "You are under my roof and under the rules of my household. If they are not to your liking, do not enter. As chieftain, you may bear your sword, but your men must leave their weapons here or this roof holds no welcome for them."

The two stood glaring at each other for several moments. Then Toke gave a signal and his men laid their weapons in a pile at the doorway and filed inside. The feast tables had been set up all along the length of the hall, and at each table, our housecarls sat on one side and Toke's crewmen on the other. Before he took his place at the head table, Harald walked to his bed-closet, retrieved his own sword from where it hung inside, and fastened it on his belt.

Harald made no attempt at conversation during dinner. His patience with Toke's ill-mannered behavior seemed to have worn through, and his mood seemed dangerous, like a pot of water simmering just below a boil. Snorre tried to engage Sigrid in conversation, but his attempts consisted mostly of leering at her and making suggestive remarks. After a short time, Sigrid excused herself from the table to help Astrid at the hearth.

I was sitting between Harald and Ubbe. Ubbe was normally a taciturn man, but he surprised me by keeping Toke occupied with questions about Ireland and details of raids he'd made there. Toke seemed flattered by the attention, and eager to describe his own exploits. He even disclosed that in Dublin he was developing a reputation as somewhat of a skald, and he stood and recited a brief verse:

> Irish wolves
> In packs fast-traveling
> Their teeth sharpened steel
> Hunt the seafarers
> Raiding Northmen
> Catching them
> Away from ocean's steed.
> Too late the wolves discover
> They have cornered a bear
> Who turns upon the pack
> And paints the grassy hills
> With wolves' blood.

The poem brought polite applause from our men, and cheers and toasts from Toke's crew. Even Harald seemed grudgingly impressed. I began to hope that the rest of the evening would pass without incident.

It was not to be. Angry voices erupted at a table down the hall. One of Toke's crewmen, a red-haired Norseman from Dublin, slung the ale from his cup into the face of one of our carls seated across the table from him, apparently angered by some remark he'd made. Our man—Ulf was his name—responded by reaching across the table, grabbing the man's hair with both hands, and slamming his face down into his platter of food.

The Norseman leapt to his feet, cursing. He drew a long knife from his belt and climbed onto the table.

"Sheath that weapon!" Harald roared, leaping to his feet.

The man looked back at Harald, hesitated, then turned to Toke.

Harald drew his sword halfway from its scabbard.

"Sheath it now, or die now," he ordered.

The crewman, his face red with anger, put away his blade and stepped down from the table. When he did, Toke stood up from his chair and pounded his fist on the tabletop.

"No man gives orders to my crew, save me!" he roared.

Some of our carls began backing away from the tables, edging toward the walls where their weapons were hung. Several of Toke's crew, those seated closest to the doorway, began eyeing the pile of their weapons.

"I am the master of this household, Toke," Harald warned, shouting back. "I order whom I please under this roof. Take care, and do not misjudge my patience."

Toke put his sword-hand on the hilt of his weapon but stood, wavering, and did not draw. He looked around the hall as if gauging the relative strengths of his crew against our men. Toke had more men, but by this time many of our carls had reached their weapons and armed themselves.

I left the table and slipped along the wall to my bed-closet. My stomach was twisted with fear, and my hands were trembling. As quickly as I could, I slung the strap of my quiver over my shoulder, strung my bow, and nocked an arrow on the string. I'd known, ever since Harald began my lessons, that someday I would have to fight for real—to kill instead of practice. I'd never expected that it would happen inside our own longhouse.

Staying in the shadows, I moved until I had a clear shot across the hall at the doorway where Toke's crew's weapons lay. If a fight started, I was certain Harald would go for Toke. The danger I feared was Toke's crew reaching their weapons before our outnumbered men had a chance to cut them down.

I saw that Ubbe had already taken a position beside the pile of weapons, a spear balanced in his hand. Between the two of us, no crewman of Toke's could reach the weapons alive . . . unless they all rushed at once.

Long did Toke stand undecided, glaring at Harald and looking around the hall, as if still weighing the strength of his men against ours. His eyes met mine and paused, while he tried to stare me down, but I would not look away.

Suddenly he barked to his men, "To the ship. The air in this dung-hole is foul to breathe."

The first of Toke's men to reach the doorway bent down to pick up his sword. Ubbe pressed the point of his spear to the man's throat and said in a quiet voice, "Get you along now. We'll bring your weapons to the water's edge, after you're back onboard your ship."

By now our men had formed an armed corridor leading from the center of the hall to the doorway. One by one, Toke's crew passed between them and out into the darkness. Toke himself was last to leave. As he reached the door, Harald called to him. "There is no welcome here for you, Toke. Be gone at first light, and do not pass this way again."

Toke glared back at him, but said nothing as he stalked out into the night. After he left, the only sound in the hall was Gunhild, quietly weeping.

That night, we built a bonfire on the small rise overlooking the wharf and kept watch all night long in case of treachery. Toke perhaps feared the same, for we could see sentries moving on his ship, their arms glinting in the light from our fire.

When the black of night first faded to gray, and while the air was calm and the morning mist still lay upon the water, the *Sea Steed* cast off from the wharf. Her oars beat the water's surface in steady strokes, and she slipped through the mist down the fjord and out of sight. I breathed a sigh of relief when she could no longer be seen.

9

HARALD'S DANCE

The confrontation with Toke caused the carls of our household and the men of the nearby village to give thought to the condition of their weapons. As a result of the battle in England, where Hrorik and so many others had found their doom, many had helms that were cut or dented, and shields in need of new planks, or with damaged rims or bosses that required repair or replacement. Many had lost spears and arrows in the battle. In addition, there were farm tools and household implements in need of making or repair. All had gone undone, for Gunnar, the estate's blacksmith and one of Hrorik's housecarls, had perished in the recent battle.

Since the age of ten, most of my work on the estate had been divided between helping Gudrod the Carpenter and Gunnar. Gudrod had been first to use me. I'd been watching him at the tedious chore of splitting out and shaping arrow shafts. He'd let me try my hand at it. We both were surprised to learn how quickly my hands took to the task, and soon Gudrod was using me to help with more and more of his duties. Gunnar saw me working with Gudrod on a day when the thrall who had been helping him clumsily broke the handle of a hammer. He'd borrowed me for that day, but was so taken by my eagerness to learn, and how quickly my hands took to shaping the heated metal, that he went to Ubbe and asked if I could work as his assistant as well as Gudrod's.

The two men shared me. Over time, both taught me all they knew about their crafts. No one else in the village besides Gunnar, and now me, possessed the knowledge of working heated metal. So now, at least until Harald could find a new smith to join his household, this responsibility fell on my shoulders.

Ubbe persuaded Harald that we must call a brief halt to my training, as my skills as a blacksmith were urgently needed. Ubbe urged me to select a helper from among our household to speed my labors, and hopefully begin to learn the smith's craft. My apprentice would need to be someone who would be willing to take orders from me. In my mind, that ruled out our housecarls. I was still too newly a free man, and they, too recently my superiors for me to feel comfortable commanding any of them. My helper would also need to possess sufficient intelligence to be able to learn the complex knowledge and mysteries of forging iron. That eliminated most of our thralls, for a lifetime of doing only what you are told tends to dull men's minds.

I chose Fasti, he who'd shown me kindness as a child. He'd once been a free man who'd managed his own lands, so I knew he could think for himself. Fasti was grateful and eager to learn, for he knew that by mastering a valued craft his chances of someday winning his freedom would be greatly improved.

For six days, we worked as hard as the dwarves that live in the hearts of the mountains—Fasti at the bellows keeping the fire glowing hot, I with hammer and tongs at the anvil. Always I taught him as I worked, showing him how iron, when brought to a bright orange-red, becomes as pliable as a green twig, and how two pieces of iron, when heated sufficiently, could be hammered together into one. I showed him how to quench the heated iron to bring hardness to it, or heat it, then cool it slowly, to draw the hardness back out.

We repaired knives, scythes, axe blades, an iron cooking pot, helms, and pieces of metal hardware for shields. We also made many new spears and arrowheads. It was from that work that Fasti learned most, for I showed him how to use the magic in the heat and coals of the fire to turn a pig of rough, crude iron into steel, and use different blows of the hammer to shape it till a weapon grew from it like a tree sprouts from the earth.

Men had always paid Gunnar for the work he'd performed for them, sometimes with bits of silver, but more often through trade. I knew nothing of what to charge for my services, for as a thrall I'd never bought or sold anything. I left to Ubbe the task of bartering with the folk of the village for the work they needed done.

Harald called a halt after the sixth day. "I've suffered your absence long enough," he said. "I have plans that will wait no longer. I wish to travel to the Limfjord to see the northern estate. It is yours now. I'd originally hoped to make the trip to inspect the lands and surprise you with the knowledge that they are yours after you first saw them. The farm lies in a location that is very pleasant and fair to the senses. When Toke visited, though, demanding an inheritance, I felt you should learn from me, rather than his angry shouts, that Hrorik left lands to you. Still, though I can no longer surprise you with Hrorik's gift, we should go now and inspect your property. All lands are fairest in the spring."

I was excited at the prospect of the trip. I myself had been property, owned by another, until recently. It still did not seem real to me that now I, Halfdan the former thrall, owned an estate.

Harald wished to travel by water. "We can continue your lessons on the journey," he said. "I can begin to teach you how to read the sea and the winds, and how to sail. Among our people, there are few free men of your age, and probably none of your rank, who have never taken a sea voyage."

It seemed there was no end to the things I did not know as a free man, but should.

We were to travel on the *Red Eagle*'s smallboat. Because there was no profit to be made from the voyage, Harald did not wish to take enough men away from the household and the village to man the *Red Eagle* herself, for she required a sizable crew.

Four carls from our household would travel with us. Ulf, he who had forcefully fed dinner to one of Toke's men and almost precipitated a battle, would come, plus Odd, Rolf, and Lodver. Each of them brought their full war gear—shield, helm, and weapons—and stowed them in the boat. Rolf also brought a heavy leather jerkin with small metal plates riveted to it, and Ulf a mail brynie. Harald, too, brought his brynie, carefully wrapped in oiled wool and stored in a sealskin bag, plus his helm and shield, his sword Biter, and a spear. He handed me a shield and the helm I'd worn in our practice combats and a sword in a scabbard.

"This sword is almost a hand's-span shorter than most swords," he said, "and it does not have a fine pattern-welded blade, like Biter. It is well-made, though, with good steel that's flexible enough not to break, yet hard enough to take a sharp edge, and it has a good balance. It will serve until we can get you something better. You should bring your bow, also."

I drew the sword from its scabbard. The blade was wide—wider even than Biter, as wide as three fingers side by side. Unlike Biter, and most longer swords whose blades tapered in width from the hilt to the point, the edges of the sword Harald had given me ran straight until the very tip where they curved in sharply to form a broad point. A wide fuller ran up the entire center of the blade to lighten it. The hilt was a simple straight bar of bronze. The grip was wood wrapped with leather, and the pommel a single, pointed bronze lobe, heavy enough to balance the blade. I tested the edge. It was very sharp.

"I'm surprised it balances so well, because the blade has no taper," Harald said. "It must be due to the shortness of the blade, combined with so large and heavy a pommel. The good balance will give it a quickness that somewhat makes up for its shortness. In my opinion, it's the best spare sword we have. I'm sure it will not be your last, though." He grinned. "I predict that one day you'll win a fine and famous sword, for some heroic deed."

It was my first sword, and I loved it.

"Why are we traveling so heavily armed?" I asked.

"We are but six men in a small-boat, and traveling a far distance. There are men on land and sea who would kill us just to take our weapons, or even the clothes we wear on our backs. And there is another reason. The first man I ever killed in a duel, four years ago now, was the son of a chieftain named Ragnvald, who lives on the Limfjord. It was a fair fight—with witnesses—over insults he'd given, but his family was bitter about his death. They presented a case against me at the Limfjord Thing that year. They asked the assembly to have me declared outlaw, or at least to force Hrorik to pay wergild, but their case had no merit and they lost. Whenever I'm on the Limfjord, though, I take extra care lest Ragnvald and his men come upon me seeking vengeance."

I wondered if I would ever be a warrior like Harald. He seemed fearless and totally sure of himself and of all that he did. What would I do, I wondered, when someday I was insulted by another man? Would I swallow my pride and the insult—as I'd done with Toke—or would I fight to protect my honor? If I fought, would I win?

I had little to pack. I took the arrows from Hrorik's quiver and used them to fill my own, for I had only a few. I left my feast clothes and my rough, thrall's tunic in my bed-closet, and wore the new clothing Sigrid had made for me. At my belt, in a leather pouch I'd made, I carried flint and steel, an extra bowstring, and wrapped in a scrap of woolen cloth, the comb my mother had given me. I carried it as much to remember her by as to keep my hair untangled, for it was still much shorter than most free men wore theirs.

We set sail early the next morning. Hrorik's—now Harald's—estate lay slightly more than a third of the way down from the northern tip of Jutland, the Danish mainland. A large point of land extends out into the sea on Jutland's eastern coast there, above the islands of Samso, Fyn, and Sjaelland. On the sheltered southern side of this point lie numerous fjords, the site of many chieftains' estates and small villages. It was here the estate that was our home was located, and it was from one of those fjords that we sailed. As we headed out toward the mouth of the fjord, the brisk breeze carried a chill across the water, and I was thankful for the thick woolen cloak Sigrid had made for me.

Our fjord, and the forest that surrounded it, marked the boundaries of the only world I'd ever known. Once we passed beyond the fjord's mouth and reached the open sea, I felt as though I'd crossed a threshold that led to the entire world beyond—a world that as a thrall I'd never thought I'd see. The wind became stiffer, and our little boat bucked and surged across the broad swells like a horse fresh out of the byre, impatiently pulling against the reins. The sun was shining brightly and the air smelled fresh and clean with a salty tang. Rolf trailed a line as we sailed, and over the course of the day caught three good-sized fish. I learned, on that voyage, that fishing was Rolf's passion. We stayed always within sight of land, and for most of the day our course headed us into the wind, so our progress was fairly slow, but the adverse wind gave Harald opportunity to teach me how to tack and sail close to the wind.

Late in the afternoon, we passed the last fjord and rounded the promontory that marks the end of the protected southern side of the great point of land. As we turned north, the shoreline now was smooth and unbroken. We had traveled only a short distance when we came upon a deserted stretch of beach, where Harald turned in toward the shore for the night. We beached our boat, turning it up on its side, and built our fire behind it, sheltered from both the wind off the sea and the prying eyes of passing ships. With the sail, mast, and oars we formed a rough shelter facing the fire.

For dinner, we roasted the fish that Rolf had caught on spits over the fire and shared a skin filled with Frankish wine. The wind had blown the clouds away, and the sky above us was filled with stars sparkling like jewels. Their light shone so brightly that even though the moon was but a thin, pale sliver hanging in the sky, I could see easily in the darkness whenever I wandered away from the circle of firelight to relieve myself.

"Tell me your thoughts," Harald asked after we had eaten. I was lying back on the sand, my head in my arms, staring up at the sky.

"I was thinking that the sky above us is the same as it always has been," I said, "yet for me, at least, the world has greatly changed. How can such change occur and the sky take no notice?"

Ulf laughed. "The doings of men have no more import to the heavens than the actions of ants have to us."

As he spoke, a star fell out of the sky in a streak of fire.

"Yet some think the heavens contain signs and portents of things that have yet to occur here on earth," Harald said. "Ubbe's wife, Ase, who serves us as our priestess of Freyja and of Odin's wife, Frigg, often reads signs from the stars. She would say, for instance, that the fall of yonder star foretells the death of some great man."

Ulf shook his head. "Believe in such things if you wish. For me, I say that somewhere there is always a great man dying, whether a star falls or no. If I concern myself with what happens in the heavens, which I cannot affect, I may not see a sign here on earth that gives me warning I can heed."

"The Gods do not ignore men, Ulf," Harald said. "If we do not honor them with sacrifices they become angry. And sometimes, for reasons we may not understand, they show special favor on one man or another."

"It is good you believe that, Harald," Ulf replied. "Now that Hrorik is dead, you are the chief priest for the estate and village. I'm happy that you will deal with the Gods for all of us. Me, I will limit my dealings to men, and the affairs of men. And for now, I will limit my dealings to sleep. It has been a long day."

The next morning, we broke the night's fast with bread and cheese, and Rolf roasted some hazelnuts in the coals of the fire. Before I could partake, Harald put his hand on my arm and pulled it back.

"It would be best if you do not eat this morning," he said. "The sea off this coast is never smooth, and with the wind blowing as it is today, it will be very rough indeed. You've never sailed on such waters before. You should wait and see how it affects you." Though my stomach growled with hunger, I did as he advised.

We sailed due north the entire day. As Harald had predicted, the sea was rough. Our little boat reared and thumped across the choppy waves.

By mid-morning, I understood Harald's warning. My stomach tossed like the sea, and I felt deathly ill. Rolf, Ulf, and the others made jokes about whether the color of my complexion matched the green of the sea. At noon, the fish I'd eaten for dinner the night before returned to the sea. Afterward, I wrapped myself in my cloak, pulled its edge over my head like a hood, and lay in misery in the bottom of the boat, oblivious to all that occurred around me.

As the sky began to dim toward evening, I realized I was feeling marginally better. I sat up, looked around, and croaked, "Have I missed anything?"

Harald smiled. "Just the vast, empty sky, the water changing colors as the sun passed in and out of clouds, and the drifting flight of many seabirds. You have missed the peacefulness of being out upon the sea."

I did not think such seemed worth the ills brought on by sea travel, and said so, leaning against the side of the boat and groaning. "I don't think I am cut out to be a sailor," I added.

Ulf laughed. "We all experienced the sickness from the sea on our first voyages. For most, it happens once and never returns. It is almost behind you now."

It seemed Ulf was right. By the time we made shore and prepared a spare meal of a simple salted pork and barley stew, cooked in an iron pot suspended over the fire, my appetite had returned.

We camped on a barren, windswept strand, where the northbound coast began curving west.

"We have rounded a great point that juts out into the sea from this side of the mainland," Harald said. "In the *Red Eagle*, we could have come this far in one day's sail. Even so, now it will be only two days at most, maybe less, until we reach the mouth of the Limfjord."

We reached the opening of the eastern end of the Limfjord in the early afternoon of the second day. By then, we'd all grown weary of the forced inactivity and cramped confines of the small-boat.

"The Limfjord is a wondrous place," Harald told me as we entered its mouth. "At this end, it opens into the sea through a channel no wider than a river, but it cuts clear across Jutland. And there are areas inland where the water is so broad that a man cannot see across to the other side. It stretches so long that we will not reach the estate until tomorrow, and even then we'll have traveled less than half the Limfjord's total length. Ase has told me she believes that Freyr and Freyja placed first man and first woman of the Jutes—the ancestors of the Danes—into the world at the Limfjord, and that we Danes have spread, over time beyond remembering, down Jutland and onto the islands from here."

My heart sank at the news that we would not reach our destination that day. I was weary of sea travel.

"Look," Rolf said suddenly, pointing to a clump of trees ahead of us on the southern shore of the channel. "Deer—coming to the shore to drink."

I did not think the deer Rolf saw were coming to drink sea water, but I did not tell him so. After four days at sea in a small-boat, I didn't care why they were there. Perhaps they came for the view.

"Harald," I whispered. "Pull in to shore quickly, and wait here. If you do, I will get us fresh meat.

Don't any of you move about or make noise. When you see me come out on the shore upstream, sail down to where I am."

The men looked at Harald, questioning that it was I who was giving commands. But Harald nodded to me and then to them.

"Go," he said. "We will wait here for your signal."

When the keel grated on the bottom, I eased myself overboard carrying my bow and quiver. Once in the woods, I paused to string my bow, then moved in a wide arc back from the shore, circling gradually toward the direction where we'd seen the deer. The smells and sounds of the forest and the feel of solid ground beneath my feet were more welcome to me than ale to a weary traveler.

I was well back from the shoreline when I crossed a small stream flowing toward the fjord. I saw a narrow trail where the earth was worn bare of fallen leaves and bracken along its far bank. I knew the trail had been formed by the regular passage of forest creatures. Fresh deer-tracks were visible in its soft soil on the way to the fjord. I crumbled some dry leaves in my hand and let them fall. The air was almost still, but what breeze there was would carry my scent downstream. I would not be able to hunt down the path, for my scent would travel ahead of me.

I moved farther into the woods, as far back from the stream and path as I could go and still be positioned to make a shot from the side when the deer returned from the water's edge to the safety of the deep forest. And return they would, along this path, I was certain of it. Their sanctuary would be in the depth of the forest, and this trail had been created by their regular passage to and from it. Harald could read the sky and the sea, but I could read the forest and the ways of its creatures. I laid an arrow across my bow and nocked it on the string, then crouched beside a tree, waiting. I was as still as a stone, and with my gray cloak pulled around me, from a distance I must have looked like one.

It was late afternoon before I stepped out of the woods onto the shore, and signaled to Harald and the others where they waited beside the boat. As soon as Harald beached the boat where I stood waiting, he said to Odd and Lodver, "Follow Halfdan and help him bring out the deer he has taken."

"He has not spoken yet," Lodver protested. "How can you know he was successful in his hunt?"

"If Halfdan goes into the forest to hunt, there will be meat," Harald said. "It is as certain as the sunrise in the morning."

Harald's praise and faith in my skills filled me

with pride, but I was careful not to show it. I was a free man now, and a warrior in the company of men. Harald had taught me that a warrior accepts praise from his chieftain with dignity.

My taking of the deer left Harald in high spirits. He propped it up in the bow of the boat, its head resting on the stem-post as if it was the dragonhead on a ship. He and Ulf traded jests as to what we should now name our little craft. Based on the time it had taken us to make our journey, Ulf insisted that only the *Slow Stag* would fit. I couldn't help but laugh at their humor, but I also felt a slight feeling of unease. I knew that the forest was a living thing, full of wildness that men could not see or understand. Some God or spirit had graciously given us one of its creatures to feed our hunger. It was ill-mannered behavior to now make the unfortunate beast the butt of our jests. I wanted to say something, but these were seasoned warriors, and I felt I did not have the right to correct them.

That night, we roasted the deer's liver and choicest cuts of meat over the fire, and drank our fill from the last of the wineskins Harald had brought for the trip.

Early the next morning, soon after we set off, the sun broke through the clouds and warmed us. Ulf grinned and nudged Harald with his foot. "Signs and portents from the heavens, Harald," he said. "The sun shines on Halfdan's first visit to his new lands."

As we sailed up the fjord, Harald named the headmen and chieftains whose villages and estates we passed. Most were on the southern shore, which was more heavily forested than the shoreline on the northern side of the broad channel.

When we approached the lands of one estate, Harald steered the boat across the channel so that when we passed it we were hugging the opposite shore.

"That is the estate of Ragnvald, the chieftain I told you of earlier," he said. "From this side of the fjord, they will not be able to see who is in our boat."

I wished that Harald would sit lower in the boat. I did not want him to be seen. I did not suggest it, though. He, of course, would never consider such a thing. It would show fear, and if Harald ever felt fear, he didn't show it. I was afraid, though. I was afraid for Harald, because he had a powerful enemy who wished to kill him. I'd never thought, until that moment, of the possibility that Harald might someday die. I wanted him to live forever. He was my brother, and too fine a friend to lose, now that we had found each other.

Occasionally we passed other craft. Most were small-boats like ours, and the folk on many of them seemed to be fishing. One full-sized ship, loaded with cargo of some sort in barrels and bales, sailed past us, its large sail carrying it at far greater speed than we could manage.

Rolf had kept a line in the water every day of our journey since we'd left the estate. This morning he'd set his hook in a strange-looking bait he'd concocted from the tail of the deer I'd slain. Now he sat, half dozing in the warm sun, with his line trailed out behind our boat. Suddenly the stick Rolf's line was wrapped around jerked from his grasp. It bounced and spun wildly in the bottom of the boat. Ulf grabbed for it.

"Careful!" Rolf warned. "Don't break the line!"

Ulf handed him the stick.

"You take it," Ulf said. "I don't know what you have hooked, but it is very strong."

Rolf let the stick turn slowly in his hands, his thumbs pressing against it to control the rate at which the line paid out, in order to tire the creature pulling against it.

"Thor's hammer!" he said. "It is that bait I made. I thought it might attract a big fish, but it feels as though I've hooked a sea monster."

"Or a great log," Ulf suggested.

It proved, after a lengthy struggle, to be neither a log nor a sea monster, but a salmon—a very, very large salmon, almost as long as a man's arm.

"The old man will love this," Rolf said. "We are bringing him fresh salmon and venison."

"Aye," Ulf said. "Aidan loves his food, for certain."

I looked at Harald in surprise. Aidan was an Irish name, and I'd only ever heard of one man called by that name. "Aidan?" I asked. "My mother told me of a man with such a name."

Harald sighed. "By the time we reach our destination, I will have no surprises left. It is the same Aidan your mother spoke of. He is a very old man now, but still hale. Aidan is the foreman of this estate, as Ubbe is foreman of mine."

"But how?" I asked. "He's a thrall. Mother said he was captured in Ireland in the same raid when she was taken."

"When he was a young man," Harald explained, "Aidan lived for many years among the Franks in the trading town of Dorestad, which lies near the coast in the lands south of Frisia. When Hrorik learned of this, he questioned Aidan often about how the town was situated upon the river, and what defenses the Franks had built to protect it. Aidan thought Hrorik was only curious, and did not foresee the use Hrorik would make of his

212

knowledge. Perhaps he thought Dorestad was too strong to be taken. Hrorik used the knowledge he'd gained to persuade other chieftains to join him in a raid and to plan the attack. The raid was a great success, for it was the first time that Dorestad fell—and the town was filled with rich plunder. The raid brought Hrorik much fame and wealth."

Ulf nodded in agreement. "Every member of every ship's crew gained much plunder. It was a great raid—one that will long be remembered."

"To reward Aidan for his help—though Aidan had not meant to help him—Hrorik freed him. Later, when Hrorik acquired the larger estate in the south, he made Aidan foreman over this estate, which is not large nor difficult to manage."

Clearly, I thought, my father had valued wealth and prestige far above love. Aidan was rewarded with his freedom for unwittingly aiding Hrorik's successful raid, but my mother—who had only her love to offer—had remained a slave and had died as one. Like coals that have been banked for the night, but burst again into flame when pulled clear of the ashes, my bitterness about my mother's death flared anew. Thus I was in an angry mood when we finally reached the estate shortly after noon. Harald sensed that something was wrong, and made several attempts to draw me into conversation, but I sullenly refused to cooperate.

I was prepared to dislike Aidan, out of loyalty to my mother's suffering, but found it difficult to do so. He was a short, jolly man with a round belly and twinkling eyes. His head was bald on top, but a wild, wind-blown fringe of white hair circled his head. He talked incessantly, pausing only to punctuate his words with laughter or to catch his breath.

"Harald!" he exclaimed as we beached our boat on the shore below the longhouse and climbed out of it, stiff from the journey. "Had I known you were coming, I would have prepared a feast. I would have ordered up your favorite delicacy—all the young ladies of the district." At this, he tipped back his head and laughed. His eyes next fell upon Rolf's salmon. "By all the saints in Ireland! You have captured Jonah's whale!"

Rolf looked confused. "It is a salmon, Aidan. A big one, to be sure, but not a whale."

Aidan laughed again. "It was a tale, not a fish's tail, but a fine story I was referring to—about a great fish that swallowed a man whole. I'll tell you the story this evening, while we take revenge for Jonah on this great sea beast you've brought."

"We've venison, too," Harald said. "This is our hunter who brings it to you."

Aidan looked at me for the first time. His jaw dropped, and for a few moments he was speechless.

"Look at that face," he said softly. "You can be no other than Derdriu's lad. And look at your clothes. They are fine. Clearly you're a thrall no more."

Without warning, he threw his arms around me and embraced me. His aged appearance belied surprising strength, for he lifted me off my feet and whirled me around in a circle, to the great merriment of Harald, Ulf, and the others, then set me down and backed away.

"Ah, Halfdan, Halfdan! Let me feast my eyes upon you." He turned to Harald. "So it finally happened? Gunhild's pride would no longer let her share Hrorik—and she divorced him? Hrorik and Derdriu are finally wed? I've always thought it a strange custom you Northmen have that allows a woman to end a marriage, but in this instance I can say with all my heart that I'm glad you have it."

Harald's expression turned grave. "That is not how it happened, Aidan. Hrorik is dead. And Derdriu also. She sailed on the death ship with him."

Aidan's face turned ashen. "Oh, dear God," he whispered. "Oh, dear God. I loved her like a daughter." He dropped to his knees, clasped his hands together in front of his face, and raised his gaze to the sky. "Oh, most holy heavenly Father. Bless the immortal soul of Derdriu, who was baptized and raised in the love of your son, Jesus Christ. Her life was filled with hardship, and she died far from her home in a foreign land. Keep her safe now in heaven with you."

I wondered whether my mother would rather be in the heaven of the White Christ or in the mead halls of Valhalla at the side of Hrorik. If Valhalla, I hoped that Aidan's prayer had not just snatched her away. I did not know the power of Christians' prayers—whether they could touch someone already in the afterworld. Certainly during this life, in the land of the Danes and their Gods, my mother's prayers to the White Christ had had little effect.

My mother had taught me about the White Christ and had tried to persuade me to worship him. I did not think he sounded like a strong God, though. He was not at all like the Gods who were worshiped in our village. He was not a God of storms, like Thor, or of war and death and wisdom, like Odin, or even of marriage and healing, like Frigg. The White Christ seemed to have no special powers. Though my mother said he was a God of love, even there he was not a God of the love between man and woman, like the goddess Freyja. It sounded to me as if he was a God only of liking rather than loving, and of being kind and forgiving. Certainly those could be good things, but they were not all that powerful.

We sat in the sun on a bench in front of the longhouse, drinking ale from wooden tankards that a serving girl brought out at Aidan's command. Harald recounted for Aidan the tale of the battle in England, the voyage home with Hrorik hovering near death, the bargain my mother had struck with him, and the funeral. Aidan sat silent through it all, but when Harald had finished he let out a loud groan.

"This is terrible, terrible. It is what I have feared would happen all these many years. The time has come that I must face retribution for my many sins. I never dreamed that my dear, sweet Derdriu would be part of the price."

I had no idea what the old man was talking about. He seemed to be quick to reach conclusions, with little to base them on.

Harald was puzzled by Aidan's words, too. "What foolishness are you speaking?" he asked, frowning. "What has Derdriu's death to do with you?"

"My God works in mysterious ways," Aidan answered.

"Which apparently include addling old men's minds," Ulf suggested.

"What sins do you speak of?" I asked.

"I helped these heathens take the Christian

town of Dorestad. I, who pledged my life to serve my God and to be a shepherd to his people, helped the wolves break into the fold and get at the sheep. It has tormented me ever since, and I have been waiting for God's vengeance to find me."

It amazed me that Aidan thought Mother's bargain with Hrorik, and her brave death to raise me out of slavery, had anything to do with him. I thought he gave himself far too important a place in the world.

"Then you must continue waiting," I told him. "My mother chose her fate freely, because she wished to see me a free man and acknowledged as Hrorik's son. I suspect she also chose to die because by taking the death-ship voyage, she could finally take her rightful place at Hrorik's side, something that was denied to her in this world. Do not detract from the courage and generosity of her acts by claiming they had anything to do with you."

"Heaven's mercy," Aidan said. "Then it is worse even than I thought. I had assumed she'd died a holy martyr, that she had no choice in the matter. Do you not see, lad? There is no Valhalla. There is only heaven and hell, and I fear that if Derdriu willingly sacrificed her own life in a heathen ceremony, then her soul is doomed forever to hell."

Aidan's last foolish pronouncement pushed me over the brink from irritation to anger. But before I could think of a retort, Harald leapt to his feet and roared, "Silence! You blaspheme!"

In a quieter, but still angry voice, he continued, "Hrorik and I, for all of the years since you left Ireland, have tolerated the practice of your religion. We have allowed you your strange beliefs about the White Christ. We have never insulted your God, though in truth he seems weak and unmanly, for he was never a warrior and he allowed himself to be taken and killed without a fight. But you go too far now to say Valhalla does not exist. Such talk I will not allow. How can you know? You've not seen the afterworld, though if the priests of our Gods hear of the rubbish you speak, you will risk it. I am now the chief priest for our village, since Hrorik has died. It is my responsibility to see that the Gods are given their due and shown proper respect. Such foolishness as you have just uttered will surely anger the Gods. I will not allow it. Henceforth, I do not wish to hear of your religion again. If you must practice it at all, do so in your bed, alone, at night."

I thought our visit did not seem to be getting off to a very good start.

Harald took a deep breath and shook his head. He filled his cup with ale and drank most of it in one long gulp, then he belched and sighed.

"Ale cools the fires of anger," he pronounced. Actually, I'd also seen drink ignite men's passions, but it did not seem a good time to contradict Harald. He turned back to Aidan, who was watching him nervously.

"Come," he said, his voice calm again. "We must not quarrel. I wish this to be a happy occasion. Hrorik left this estate to Halfdan, as a gift from father to son. That is why we have come—so Halfdan can inspect his new lands."

Harald was like Thor, the thunder God, whose rage could fill the sky with darkness and violence, yet a short time later the sun would shine brightly again. As we began to tour the estate, Harald acted as if his anger had never occurred. After a time, Aidan got over his fright at Harald's outburst and acted that way, too.

The estate was situated on a small cove off of the Limfjord. It had been cleared from the forest many years ago, and the woods now encircled the cleared lands like protective arms. A narrow stream flowed through the center of it, running between the fields and into the cove. Along one side of the cove near its mouth, a great slab of stone reared up out of the water and leaned against the shoreline.

"There," Harald said, pointing at the giant boulder. "Sigrid and I used to sit on that great stone as children. We would fish and watch for passing ships. It was your mother, Derdriu, who taught us how to fish, right there, on that stone."

A sandy beach, where we'd landed our boat, ran along the shore from the end of the stone slab to the mouth of the creek.

"And Aidan, do you remember? One summer you carved me a toy longship, and I would sail it from this beach?"

Everywhere we went, as Harald and Aidan showed me the pastures, fields, and the longhouse of the estate, Harald recalled distant memories peopled by himself and Sigrid as children, and sometimes by my mother, too. It was as though he was seeing spirits from the past that came to life for him again as we traversed their haunts. As for me, I saw none. I learned I had been born at this place, but no memories of it lived in my mind.

The longhouse was much simpler and smaller than that on the estate in the south. On Harald's estate, the animal byre and bathhouse were in separate wings running off from the sides of the main structure. Here there was only one long rectangular building, with the byre at one end, taking up perhaps a third of the length of the structure, separated from the main living area by a timber wall. It was a simple, efficient design, though the living area smelled more strongly of beasts than in

Harald's longhouse.

This longhouse had been built overlooking the cove, and its main door, near the middle of one of the long sides of the building, faced the beach. A second door, at the end of the longhouse, opened from the animals' byre. Well-worn paths led from it to the privy located near the edge of the woods, and to the farm's two pastures.

In addition to Aidan and his wife—a plump, friendly woman named Tove, who had grown up in the nearby village—eight carls, five with families, and six thralls lived on the estate. They seemed sturdy, hardworking folk, but farmers and nothing more. Clearly I had not inherited a war band; Hrorik had kept his warriors with him at his estate to the south. The longhouse walls were hung with the shields of the carls, but the only weapons visible were a few short hand-axes, and some bows and spears that I suspected had for many years been used solely for hunting.

I hoped the lack of war gear—and of men with an inclination to use it—was evidence that the Limfjord was a safe and peaceful district. I was not yet a warrior, and certainly not fit to lead a war band. But even more, I found myself thinking that perhaps I, too, was not the stuff warriors are made of. The quiet peacefulness of the little estate led my mind to dream of living there, leading the simple life of a farmer, in rhythm with the seasons. If this farm was mine, if I was not a thrall who labored only for someone else's benefit, it could be a good life.

After we'd walked the fields and pastures and I'd met all the folk of the farm, Aidan excused himself and returned to the longhouse to supervise the preparation of a feast to celebrate our arrival. Ulf and Rolf also retired to the longhouse, to the corner used for bathing, while Lodver and Odd busied themselves in a wrestling match with several of the carls from the farm.

Harald took me by the arm. "There is one other place I would like you to see," he said.

We followed a cart path that, after crossing the shallow stream, ran like a border between the edge of the fields and the dark overhang of the forest. After a time, the path turned and headed into the woods. We'd traveled but a short distance down it, away from the open fields, when we came upon a low, wooded hill rising beside the narrow roadway.

"Here," Harald said, stepping off the road, and he led the way through the trees and up the side of the hill. Its top had been cleared, and upon it were four stone death ships, like the one we'd built for Hrorik and my mother.

"These are the graves of our ancestors," Harald

said. He pointed to the one closest to us. "Here Hrorik's father, Offa, was burned, and over there is Gorm, Hrorik's father's father. Offa died an old man in his sleep. But Gorm died when still in his prime, of a fever that grew when a wound he'd received in a duel would not heal.

"This grave to our left is the death ship of Haldar Greycloak, who came to the Limfjord from the Vestfold, up north across the water in the lands of the Norse. He was the first of our line to settle here. He married the daughter of a chieftain and was the father of Gorm. Haldar was a great warrior. He was killed by wolves one winter. Hrorik told me the tale, as it had been told to him by his father. That winter the weather was especially harsh. There were many blizzards, and large portions of the Limfjord froze solid. The cold and the frequent snowfalls drove the packs out from the depths of the forest and close to the farms and villages to scavenge for food. Haldar was out hunting alone one day, and the wolves found him and killed him. Hrorik said when the men from the estate found the savaged remains of his body, it was surrounded by the bodies of four of the wolves. He had died fighting, and cost his killers dearly."

Harald pointed to the stone-outlined death ship farthest from us.

"This last grave belongs to Harald, for whom I

am named. He was Hrorik's brother. He died as a young man defending against a raid along the Limfjord by four shiploads of Sveas and Gotars. But for his courage, none in the longhouse would have escaped."

Before me lay the graves of chieftains and great men. Some of their blood ran in my veins. I wondered if the spirits of any of these men still wandered this hilltop at night as draugr, walking dead—their spirits still bound to this world, and living in their tombs. Or were these death ships now nothing more than stone markers of the place from whence their voyages to the afterworld were launched?

That night at the feast, Harald insisted that I sit at the center of the main table. "You are the master of this household, now," he said. "The place of honor is rightfully yours."

I sat there reluctantly. It felt strange; somehow wrong. It had been a day full of foreign feelings. Certainly it was very strange to walk through fields and pastures and realize that these were lands that I, Halfdan, but recently a thrall, now owned. And now I was at a feast in a longhouse, and I was seated at the head of the main table. It had not been that many weeks ago when I would not have been eating at a table at all—I would have been eating scraps among the thralls.

Aidan and his wife, Tove, had planned a sumptuous meal. Whilst living amongst the Franks and the Irish, Aidan had learned many ways of cooking and flavoring foods besides those commonly used among the Danes. Though among our people the cooking chores were mostly the province of women, Aidan worked as hard at the hearth as any kitchen thrall. He and Tove cut the venison into small chunks and simmered them in Frankish wine flavored with herbs until the meat was so tender it scarce needed chewing to be swallowed. Aidan also cut many thin, boneless slices of flesh from the sides of the salmon, fried them in a shallow iron pan in butter, and served them over slabs of fresh bread.

"Tomorrow night," he promised, "we will cook the main body of this great, beautiful fish. I will submerge it in ale and cook it slowly in a style I learned in Dorestad. Tomorrow I also will take you to the village and introduce you to the folk there."

There were many other treats besides the venison and fish. Aidan and Tove were skilled cooks. It was, without question, the finest meal I'd ever eaten, and we washed the food down with a fine mead that Aidan had been aging for many months.

When we'd all had our fill and far beyond, and

our stomachs were groaning at our excesses, Harald stood up.

"This is a special occasion," he announced, "for on this day, Halfdan, son of Hrorik, takes possession of this estate to be his own."

All raised their cups, gave a ragged and slightly drunken cheer, "Halfdan!" then drank. The serving thralls scurried among us, refilling empty cups.

"There is another reason this day is special," Harald continued. "We are in the third new moon after the Jul feast. On this farm fifteen years ago, during the third new moon after the Jul feast, Derdriu gave birth to Halfdan. He is now fifteen years of age and has truly reached manhood."

This time I barely heard the cheers that echoed round the hall. I was stunned. As a thrall, I'd never counted my existence over a greater period than one day to the next. Unlike free men and women, slaves do not come of age. The birth months of property are not celebrated. From force of habit, I'd thought no differently since I'd been freed. Suddenly I realized Harald was speaking again.

"It has been but a short time that I have considered Halfdan to be my brother," he said, "but in that time I have come to know him well. Hrorik entrusted Halfdan and his training into my care. I have quickly learned that it has been my loss that we have not shared our lives as brothers since the day of his birth."

Tears came to my eyes. Embarrassed, I ducked my head to hide them. I hoped my mother could hear Harald's words and know the blessings she had bought me by her sacrifice.

Harald laid an object wrapped in sealskin on the table in front of me. "Accept this from me, my brother Halfdan, as a gift to celebrate the memory of your birth, your attainment of manhood, and my joy that we are brothers."

Wrapped within the sealskin was a dagger. Its hilt was a short bar of brightly polished steel, tapered to a point at either end. The handle was of some dark wood, smooth and polished and warm to the touch, and the pommel was solid silver, cast with intricate designs containing tiny ships, figures, and runes. The scabbard was wood covered with soft leather, with a band of oil-soaked fur lining the metal-rimmed throat. It was when I drew the blade from its scabbard, though, that I realized the dagger's true worth. The blade was pattern-welded, its surface swirling in mysterious designs, like the currents of a river frozen in steel. I knew as soon as I saw the blade that Harald must have purchased it to be a companion to his sword, Biter. He had done me great honor by giving this dagger to me.

We celebrated far into the night. As he had

promised, Aidan told his story of the whale that swallowed a man. Because he insisted the story was true, it provoked much discussion whether anyone could survive such an experience. Ulf was of the opinion that even if one could survive, their smell afterward would be such that no one could bear to come near. Harald recited a lengthy and stirring poem about a battle fought by a mighty warrior against great odds, and we all drank many toasts. It was a fine night that will live in my memory forever.

I was awakened in the early hours of the morning by someone shaking me. Gradually I became aware that it was Harald, but I was too groggy from the mead I'd drunk and the sleep I'd not slept, to fully wake up. Harald left, and I was almost back asleep when someone dumped a pitcher of cold water on my head. I sat up, sputtering.

"Wake up, Halfdan!" Harald was squatting beside me. "And keep quiet. We are in danger. Get your weapons and join me by the hearth."

The remnants of the evening's fire lay on the hearth, now mostly just glowing embers, but low flames flickered along one remaining log. In the dim light I could see, up and down the room, others being awakened, gathering weapons, and making their way to the center of the hall. When all had arrived, Harald addressed us in a low voice.

"There may be enemies outside, around the longhouse. Ulf, tell us what you've seen."

"I woke up and felt the need to empty my water," Ulf said, "and possibly more, besides. I walked through the byre, intending to go out to the privy, but before I stepped out of the shadows of the byre doorway I heard voices outside and stopped. After a time, I saw them—dark shapes of men hiding in the edge of the woods behind the privy. Had they not carelessly revealed their position, no doubt I would be dead now, lying in a pool of piss and blood. I watched for a while. After a time, one of them stepped out into the open and waved his arm, as if to signal to someone at the other end of the longhouse. Though there's no moon, I could see the light from the stars glinting on his helm and spearpoint, and could tell that he carried a shield. We are surrounded by armed men."

The wife of one of the farm carls uttered a low wail. Tove clapped a hand over the woman's mouth, cutting off the noise, and whispered, "Silence."

Harald and Ulf were already wearing their mail brynies. As Ulf was recounting his news, Rolf slipped on his leather jerkin and tightened the laces. The men who had helms—only two of the housecarls from the estate did—pulled them on and tied the lacing under their chins. I did the same, then strung my bow.

"Halfdan, you and Ulf and Lodver, and you three," Harald said, indicating the three housecarls from the estate who were standing closest to me, "guard the main door here in the hall. It is small enough that only one man can come through at a time. Rolf, Odd, and the rest of you, come with me. We must defend the byre. If any have bows, bring them. We will need them this night."

Harald and his men left, and headed for the byre. Ulf ordered Aidan to bank the fire so no light would show within the longhouse. Then he took the women, children, and slaves to the end of the building opposite the byre. There they turned a table on its side, propped it across one corner of the room, and huddled down behind it.

One of the carls Harald had assigned to me carried a bow and quiver. I hoped he could use it.

"What is your name?" I asked him. I'd learned it earlier, but could not recall it now.

"Fret," he replied.

"Fret, in a moment we'll open this door and see what's out there. If enemies are waiting, I'd rather that you and I keep them at a distance if we can."

To the men outside, we'd be hidden in the

shadows that cloaked the interior of the longhouse, but I hoped the dim light from the stars outside would reveal their presence to us.

I shook my head, trying to clear the last vestiges of sleep from it. My mind still felt slow from the amount I'd drunk at the feast, and I was having to work to concentrate my thoughts on what I was doing. It was probably a good thing. I was so intent on being alert to what was happening, it did not occur to me to be afraid.

The main door opened in. When I signaled we were in place, Ulf swung it open and folded it back against the wall. Fret and I stood with arrows nocked and our bows ready, a spear's-length back from the door's opening, slightly off to either side. It was good we hadn't stood directly in front of the doorway, for moments after Ulf swung the door aside, two arrows whistled in through its opening and thudded into the far wall.

I peered, straining, into the dark, but at first could see nothing. Suddenly, from the direction of the byre, I heard the strangled cry of a man in pain, then war cries and the clash of metal. A dark mass rose up from the ground in front of us—only a short spear-throw away from the door—and rushed forward. I realized that our attackers had crept close and had been lying, hidden in the shadows on the ground in front of the longhouse, waiting for the signal to attack.

I loosed an arrow, aiming at knee height toward the mass of charging men. Someone yelped in pain and fell sideways out of the pack. Fret shot, too, but I heard his arrow thud uselessly into a shield.

"Shoot low, at their legs," I called to him.

Quickly I nocked another arrow and drew. The charging men were close enough now that even in the dim light I could see details. A man wearing a shiny helm and a mail brynie was leading the attack, howling in a wordless war cry. His boldness cost him his life. My arrow skimmed across the top edge of his shield and struck him in the mouth. He fell forward, propelled by the momentum of his charge, and rolled with a thump against the wall of the longhouse.

Lodver and one of the estate's carls were crouched against the wall to the right side of the doorway, and Ulf and the other carl stood ready against the wall across from them on the other side of the door. As the first of the invaders reached the doorway, Ulf stepped out and blocked the way, far enough back that one man, but only one, could step inside.

A warrior with blond hair, in two long braids hanging out behind his helm, leapt in. He caught Ulf's sword on his shield, and stabbed forward with his spear. Ulf used his shield to deflect the thrust, then Lodver, still standing against the wall and hidden in its shadow, drove his spearpoint into the man's back and killed him.

The attackers learned quickly. No one followed their now-dead comrade through the doorway. Instead, men stood outside, against the walls and out of sight from Fret and me, stabbing their spears blindly through the doorway's opening, reaching into the darkness on either side. The carl beside Lodver to the right of the door cried out and staggered back, wounded in the shoulder.

Outside, a man stepped suddenly in front of the door and drew back his spear to throw.

"Ulf, down!" I cried. Ulf dropped and rolled to the side, and the spear flew harmlessly over him. I launched an arrow in return and struck the spear thrower in the face. He flopped backward without a sound. Fret shot and dropped another, who'd lunged low across the doorway opening, trying to gut Lodver with his thrust. He'd crouched behind his shield as he attacked, but left his neck and shoulders exposed.

Suddenly they turned and ran. Fret and I continued shooting as they fled. I brought one man down with an arrow through his back, and heard another cry out after Fret's shot, before all escaped from view.

Ulf scrambled on his hands and knees back to cover, on the left side of the doorway. The carl who'd been standing with Ulf on that side stepped forward to check his wounded comrade on the other side of the door, now leaning back against the wall and being examined by Lodver. As he crossed the open doorway, an arrow flew out of the dark and struck him in the side, toppling him to the ground. Ulf grabbed the man's legs and pulled him back into the shadows. By the time I reached them, Ulf had propped him against the wall of the longhouse. The man was groaning and clutching at the arrow embedded in his side. Only half of the arrow's shaft, and its feather fletching, was showing. Aidan joined us.

"I have some skill at healing," he said. "I will attend to him."

Ulf stopped him. "There's another of your men who took a spear in his shoulder. Tend to him first. He can still aid us in this fight. This one is finished in this fight for certain, and probably for good."

Ulf turned to me and clapped his hand on my shoulder.

"You shoot your bow fast and true," he said. "If we had several more like you, I'd feel more confident that we will see the morning."

Ulf seemed calm. If the danger we were in

frightened him, he hid it well. His words awakened my fear, though. Ulf was one of Harald's most seasoned warriors. If he felt concerned, our danger must be dire indeed. A wave of nausea churned the contents of my stomach. I prayed I would not vomit and embarrass myself. Beads of sweat sprang out on my forehead. I mopped them off with the sleeve of my tunic, and was thankful that the darkness in the longhouse hid the signs of my fearfulness from the others.

The carl who'd been hit by the arrow groaned softly. One of the women was at his side now, trying to give him water. He coughed, choked on it, and shook his head, indicating she should cease.

Harald entered from the byre. He was panting and paused to catch his breath before he spoke.

"It was hard going in there. They reached the door of the byre almost the same time we did, and several forced their way inside. They've withdrawn for now, though."

"Have you losses among your men?" Ulf asked.

Harald nodded. "Aye. Two dead, one wounded. One of the carls from here was our first to reach the byre door. He was caught by surprise when the attackers burst in. He took a spear through the throat. Another's head was split by an axe as we fought in the dark inside the doorway, and Odd has a wound in his leg, though he can still fight. But six of the enemy lie dead on the floor of the byre."

Ulf nodded. "They're paying a price, but I fear they have more men to pay with than we. One of our carls from the farm is dying, and one is wounded."

Ulf gestured at me. "Halfdan is a good man to have by your side in a fight," he said. "We killed four of their men for certain, at the door, and wounded or killed several others, during their charge and retreat. Most fell to Halfdan's bow."

Harald reached out and put his hand on my shoulder.

"That's high praise indeed, my brother, coming from Ulf. He has seen much battle. I am proud of you."

I felt too rattled to be pleased, though later I would remember Harald's words and take some comfort from them.

"What do you think they'll do next?" I asked.

"They will try to burn us out," Harald answered. "I do not think they'll try an assault again, after taking so many losses."

"Are they raiders?" I asked.

Harald shook his head. "I think not. There've been no foreign raiders on the Limfjord since the time when Hrorik's brother was killed many years ago. A hue and cry was raised along the fjord then, and all four shiploads of Gotars and Sveas were wiped out. No one has dared since. I fear this is the work of Ragnvald." He sighed. "If it is a matter of personal vengeance against me, at least we may be able to negotiate safe passage for the women, children, and thralls before the next attack. He may not agree, but I must try."

Harald stepped to the edge of the doorway and called out in a loud voice, "I would speak with your leader."

After a time, a voice answered from the darkness, "Who is it that wishes to speak with me?"

"I am Harald Hroriksson. Are you the leader of this war band?"

"I speak for him," came the reply. I wondered why their leader did not speak for himself.

Harald grunted. "I do not recognize the voice. Perhaps Ragnvald hopes to keep his role in this secret." He called out again. "There are women and children and thralls in the longhouse. They have no part in this fight. Will you let them pass in safety?"

"Send them out," the voice replied.

"I must have the oath of your leader," Harald insisted. "I must have his oath that they will be unharmed and that you will not take them into captivity."

A long silence followed. Harald broke it by calling out again. "Whatever your quarrel is with us, the women and children have not harmed you. There is no honor in harming them."

Finally a muffled voice, different from the first, responded, "I am the leader of these men. I give you my oath. Send them out now if they're coming at all. I will not delay my attack for long."

There was much weeping among the women-folk as they prepared to leave. Harald urged Aidan to accompany them, for he was not a warrior, but he responded, "I am not a thrall. My place is with you and Halfdan and the rest of the men."

Harald gathered the children before him and asked, "Which of you is the fastest runner?"

A boy who looked to be about ten glanced from side to side at his fellows, then spoke up. "I am, sir."

Harald knelt beside him. "Good lad. What is your name?"

"Cummian," the boy answered.

"He is my son," Aidan volunteered.

"Have you ever been to the village, Cummian?" Harald asked. "Down the cart path that runs beside the fields, and leads through the forest?" The boy nodded. "I need you to be very brave, Cummian, and very, very fast. The attackers outside are going to let the women and children and thralls leave the longhouse unharmed. As soon as you can, slip away in the dark and run to the village. Tell them raiders have landed and are attacking. Your father will be here with me and the rest of the men waiting for you to bring help back to us."

The women, their children, and the six thralls left the doorway of the longhouse in a frightened huddle. As they did so, four torches flared, one after the other, off to the right where the work-sheds were located.

"This way," a voice called. "Come this way, to the light and safety."

Peering from behind a corner of the first work-shed, a hulking giant of a warrior stood, holding a torch. In the torch's glare, I could see that he was wearing a dark cloth wrapped around his head and helm to form a hood, masking all of his face except his eyes. As I watched, he called out. "Come this way," he shouted in a hoarse voice. I recognized from its sound, muffled though it was by the cloth, that he was the leader who'd spoken his oath out from the darkness.

The last of our women, children, and thralls passed from sight beyond the edge of the work-shed, into the welcoming circle of light from the torches. The leader of the attackers stepped back behind the shed, totally hidden now from my view.

Suddenly his voice roared out, "Kill them all! There can be none alive to tell the tale."

It lasted only moments. We could hear the screams, but could see almost nothing. I saw a woman—it looked like Tove—stagger into view, clutching at a spreading bloodstain on the front of her dress. A warrior stepped into view behind her swinging a sword, and cut her down.

Aidan rushed past me out the door clutching a broadaxe in his hand. "Oath breakers!" he screamed. "Oath breakers!" Ulf grabbed at his sleeve to stop him, but he pulled free. As he neared the worksheds, an arrow flew out of the dark and pierced his chest. Even from the longhouse I could hear it strike home. Aidan gave a choking cough and fell facedown. In the flickering light from the torches, the arrow's bloody head, protruding from his back, glistened wetly.

Suddenly Cummian burst into view. He must have bolted away when the slaughter started, for he was running up from the beach, darting this way and that to avoid a burly warrior who chased him, waving a bloody sword. His pursuer tripped and stumbled, and Cummian turned and headed straight for the longhouse.

"Run, boy, run," Ulf yelled, cheering him on.

The leader of the attackers stepped into view at the corner of the workshed, a spear poised over his

241

shoulder. As we watched in horror, he drew back his arm and threw. The spear struck the boy square in the back, and its bloody spearhead and a foot-long length of the shaft jutted suddenly into view from the center of his chest. The impact lifted Cummian off his feet and carried him through the air, his arms and legs flailing, till finally he fell face-down onto the ground and the shaft embedded its point in the earth.

Impossibly, the boy still lived. We could hear him crying and moaning where he lay pinned to the ground.

I pulled an arrow from my quiver. It was a hunting arrow, its head broad and sharp. With it, I could end Cummian's suffering. I started to nock it on my string, then stopped, and stabbed it into the ground in front of me.

The attackers' leader was moving toward Cummian in a low crouch, carefully covering himself with his shield. Fret put an arrow to his bow and started to draw.

"No," I said. "Let him come closer."

I pulled out another arrow, one of Hrorik's that I'd brought to fill out my quiver. It was one I'd made for him long ago, to his specifications. It was an arrow designed specifically for war, not hunting, and its head was narrow, long, and sharply pointed, to pierce armor or shields.

The villain reached Cummian. With one hand, he held his torch high, surveying his handiwork. With the other, he grasped the spear shaft. Placing a foot on the boy's back, he wrenched it free. When he did, Cummian gave one last scream, then lay still.

I'd hoped my chance would come when he retrieved his spear, and it did. With the torch in one hand and the spear in the other, Cummian's killer had to release his grip on his shield's handle and let it hang from his shoulders by its strap. The shield still covered him from just below his chin to midway down his thighs, but it lay flat against his chest now, no longer held away from his body.

The distance was too great in the poor light to shoot for his face. I pulled the arrow back to full draw, aimed at his chest, and released.

The man must have realized what a target he'd made of himself, despite the darkness and distance from the longhouse. He couldn't have reacted to the twang of my bowstring, for he moved at the same moment I released my arrow. He hurled his torch to one side and stepped sideways in the opposite direction. He saved his life by his actions, but was too late to avoid my shot altogether. I heard the thunk of my arrow hitting the wooden planks of his shield, and knew by his roar of pain that it had pierced it and his mail.

"*Now*, Fret," I said. He launched his arrow and I my second shot at the hulking shape scuttling for cover in the dark. I knew we both missed, for I heard no further cry.

For a brief time nothing happened. Then the voice of the attackers' leader, even hoarser now from anger and pain, rang out through the night. "You in there! I'll roast you like rats on a spit." To his own men he called, "Fire the longhouse!"

Four men stepped briefly into view near the worksheds. Each was holding a bow with a small bundle of flame blazing in front. They drew and released, and fire arrows streaked through the night, streaming sparks behind them like falling stars. I heard them smack into the thatched roof overhead.

"I know that voice," Harald said. "But who . . . ?"

"Harald, there's no time!" Ulf shouted. He swung the front door shut and barred it. "The woods are closer to the byre door than to here. We must try to break out that way."

Already tendrils of smoke were beginning to seep through the thatch.

"What about him?" I asked, pointing to the wounded carl—now barely conscious—leaning against the longhouse wall past the door.

"We cannot carry him," Ulf said. "It would slow us too much. All we can do is keep him from being burned alive."

He drew his knife, knelt beside the wounded man, and cut his throat with a quick swipe of his blade.

The animals in the byre were squealing and moaning with fear. Rolf appeared at the entrance between the byre and the main house and shouted, "The roof overhead is burning. Sparks are beginning to fall. If the straw in the stalls catches fire, the beasts will go mad."

"To the byre," Harald said. "We'll use the animals to shield us for as long as we can control them."

In the byre, the horses were rearing and kicking in their stalls. Hens flew about wildly, crashing into men, beasts, and walls. Above us, a hole opened in the roof, fire eating at its edges, and flaming thatch dropped into the straw of the sheep pen. Rolf threw his cloak over it and stamped the flames out.

The byre was rapidly filling with smoke. My eyes were burning and I coughed every time I drew breath. I feared that if we stayed much longer in the smoke and flames, I would be as overcome with terror as the beasts.

"Halfdan," Harald called. "The horses are too fear-crazed to be of use to us. Open the door and we'll send them out. Our attackers may think they bear riders, and run out from the cover of the trees to stop them. If they do, you and Fret kill as many as you can."

Ulf and I lifted the heavy timber used to bar the broad byre door, and Ulf carried it back to where Harald and the others were standing by the oxen. As soon as I swung the door open, arrows whirred in from the night. One of the horses was hit and it screamed in pain and fear.

Rolf opened the gates to the horses' stalls. They needed no urging. Bucking and kicking, they charged out through the byre's door.

As Harald had predicted, four or five men ran out from the cover of the trees toward the fleeing horses. Fret slew one, who was moving from the tree line with a bow half drawn. Another, running hard toward the horses, threw a spear, striking the lead horse behind its shoulder. My arrow hit this man in his side as the horse staggered and fell. The rest of the warriors turned and ran back into cover, but I brought one more down with an arrow that caught him low in his back just as he reached the edge of the trees.

The byre was now filled with smoke, and more and more blazing thatch was dropping around us from the edges of the ever-widening hole in the roof above. I stayed close to the doorway, trying to find air to breathe. A rooster, its feathers on fire, flew past me and slammed into the wall.

"Halfdan, to me!" Harald called.

He and Ulf had lashed the crossbar from the byre door across the necks of the two oxen like a widely spaced yoke. Between the two great beasts was enough space for us to stand.

"We'll use the oxen as our shield-wall, for as long as they last," Harald said. "If we can get within a spear's throw of the trees, every man should run for himself. Perhaps in the darkness of the forest some can escape."

We crowded into the space between the two beasts. I twisted my cloak in a long, loose roll, and draped it over one shoulder, so it hung across my chest and back. Then I loosed my belt and cinched it again around the ends of the rolled cloak, holding it tight to my body. Perhaps its folds would provide a little protection. My sword, which I'd not yet drawn from its scabbard, hung from my belt on my left side. My quiver, too, hung on that side, by its strap over my right shoulder. At my right hip was the dagger Harald had given me just hours before. I slung my shield across my back and pulled its strap tight, then took my position between the oxen, bow in hand, with an arrow ready on the string.

"Let us go now!" Harald shouted.

Rolf, at the rear of our hooved fortress, slapped

the oxen across their flanks with the flat of his sword, and the stolid beasts moved forward into the open as our little force crouched between them. Rolf and one of the carls from the farm positioned themselves beside each ox's hind leg and walked backward, their shields overlapping to protect our rear from missile fire.

Once outside, we gulped hungrily at the fresh air. The entire roof of the longhouse was now ablaze. The towering flames lit the area we were moving through as brightly as day, and roared like an enraged beast. Behind us, the sheep, still trapped in their pen, bleated piteously.

We'd scarcely left the byre when arrows began arcing out of the trees and thudding into the side of the ox closest to the forest. The poor beast grunted at each impact, but trudged on.

I couldn't see the archers shooting at us, but I could tell the general area of the tree line their arrows were coming from. Calling to Fret to follow my lead, I bobbed up, launched an arrow over the ox's back toward the trees, and ducked down into cover before the answering arrows could find me. On my third such shot, I was rewarded by a yell of pain from the trees.

Fret, who'd stayed low and hidden between the two oxen, seemed encouraged by my success, and he straightened and drew his bow. When he did, an arrow skimmed over the ox's back and ripped through his throat. Fret staggered a step then fell, choking on his blood and clawing at the arrow. I stepped over his writhing body as our slowly moving huddle moved on.

Rolf called a warning from behind me. "They are coming from the rear!"

I looked back over my shoulder and saw warriors rounding the corner of the longhouse at a run. They must have been the attackers from the front of the building.

"Down, Rolf," I shouted. When he crouched, I shot over him and dropped the one in the lead with an arrow in his chest. The two warriors closest behind him hurled their spears, then dropped down low behind their shields. As they threw, I sped an arrow toward them, quickly drawn and released without aiming. It skimmed harmlessly between them.

Both of the spears had been aimed at the ox on the side farther from the woods, which till now had not been wounded. One spear fell at its haunches, and would have pierced it up the center had Rolf not reached out and caught the speeding missile on his shield. It had been thrown hard, and its spearhead splintered the thin wooden planks and jutted almost a foot out the back. The other spear arced high and dropped from above into the ox's back, just behind its shoulders. The ox bellowed at the pain, and from behind us I heard cheers.

I nocked another arrow, but something fell heavily against me from behind and knocked it off my bowstring. I looked angrily over my shoulder, and was staring into the face of a dead man. One of the carls from the estate, an arrow protruding from the back of his head, had slumped against my back. His eyes were wide open and his mouth gaped as if in surprise. I shrugged his body aside, and it slid past me to the ground.

The speared ox sank moaning to its knees, blood pumping from its nostrils and mouth. Its fellow stopped, anchored to the dying ox by the timber lashed across their necks. It too was gravely wounded: By now more than a dozen arrows pierced its side. As it stood there, four more arrows flew from the trees into its body. The hapless beast gave a great sigh, and its legs collapsed from under it.

In the light from the burning longhouse I could see that the woods closest to us were filled with enemy warriors. Their faces showed white among the dark trees and foliage, and their helms glinted in the flickering light. For now they did not attack, but arrows continued to arc toward us from the tree line. We squatted down, pressed close together between the oxen's bodies, and huddled under our shields, so the arrows had no effect.

We were protected for the moment, but we were trapped and hopelessly outnumbered. None of our party who'd traveled up from the south had fallen yet, though Odd was wounded in one leg. Of the carls from the estate—less experienced warriors than Harald's men—only three still lived. As soon as our attackers reorganized sufficiently to launch a coordinated charge, we were doomed.

Behind us, the warriors who'd come from the front of the longhouse began massing together. Our doom seemed imminent.

"They will charge soon, Harald," Ulf said. "From both directions. And there are but nine of us left."

Harald had been turning his head this way and that, surveying the area. "There, to the right," he said, pointing. "See that low stone wall, between the pasture and the fields? We'll try to reach it. They will expect us to head for the woods because they are closer. The wall is in the opposite direction, but if we can get to it, we'll have cover to fight behind as we retreat, and at its end the wall runs to the forest."

Harald leaned close to me and whispered in my ear, "I do not think we will reach the wall. If the time comes that I tell you to run, you must do what I say. Run as fast as you can and do not look back."

"No!" I protested. "You are my brother. I will stay and fight with you. If we die, we die together."

"Someone must survive to avenge us," Harald said. "If you can reach the forest, they will never take you. None can match you there. You must do this thing for me. For all of us. Survive and avenge us."

Ulf, who had overheard this exchange, nodded. "There is no shame, Halfdan, in what Harald asks of you. I will die easier knowing someone survives to pay blood for blood. Now lay your bow aside and ready your sword and shield. It will be close work from here on out."

Despite Ulf's urging, I did not abandon my bow. If I could reach the forest I would need it. Instead I unslung my shield from my back, grasped its handle and my bow in my left hand, and drew my sword with my right.

We stood up as one and began running for the wall, staying as close together as we could. The leg-wounded Odd had taken earlier slowed him, though, and after a short distance, he fell behind. Archers from both groups of the enemy's warriors concentrated their shots on him. He was hit twice, in the leg and in the back, knocking him to the ground. I glanced back as I ran. He was trying to rise when the first of our pursuers reached him and swung a great two-handed axe full into his back.

Had we only the attackers from the woods to deal with, we might have succeeded. We were running directly away from them, and they probably could not have caught us in time. The attackers who'd come from the front of the house were closer, though. The five fleetest of their warriors cut across the front of our path at an angle and turned to block our way, only a short spear's throw from the protection of the wall.

We smashed into them on the run. Rolf, who'd wrenched free the spear that had pierced his shield, hurled it at the warrior closest to him as we closed. The man swung his shield up, catching the missile, but when he did, Harald swung Biter low, cutting the warrior's legs clean through above the knees. Without pausing, Harald whipped Biter up again in a backhand swing and chopped through the sword arm of the warrior standing beside his toppling comrade.

A tall warrior, with helm but no mail brynie, swung his sword in an overhand chop at me. Letting my bow fall, I dropped down on one knee and raised my shield overhead, catching the blow, then stabbed my sword upward, under the edge of his shield and into his groin. He doubled over, screaming, and fell backward to the ground clutching at the wound as I scrambled back to my feet.

Ulf, too, killed a man, but by their deaths the

men we'd fought had bought time for the rest of our pursuers to catch up. Like a pack of wolves they threw themselves at us, hacking and stabbing from all sides. Within moments, Lodver and the three remaining carls from the estate were down.

"Halfdan, stay near me!" Harald shouted.

Rolf fell, a spear through his throat and one leg nearly severed by a sword cut. Harald seemed everywhere at once, whirling and turning. He lunged to the right, thrusting Biter before him, then swung his sword at a warrior behind him, and two more of our attackers were down. His shield moved as though with a life of its own, blocking, parrying, deflecting, and always Biter darted out from behind it, chopping at hands, slashing at legs and arms, keeping our enemies at bay. Its blade whistled through the air as Harald whipped the deadly steel, now bright red with blood, back and forth.

"Ulf, my back," he cried, and spun again toward the stone wall, trying to cut a way clear.

Three more pursuers had circled around and now stood before us, arrayed side by side, blocking our way. Harald feinted to the left, then struck at the warrior in the center. The man blocked and swung a return cut, but Harald was already gone, ducking low and scuttling back as the warrior on the right jabbed out at him with a spear.

As the warrior on his left lunged forward aiming a cut at Harald, I thrust my sword at his chest, but his mail brynie deflected my blow and the point skidded aside. He swung his shield and its edge struck my wrist, sending my sword flying from my grasp. The warrior lifted his own sword overhead and hammered down at me with it. I raised my shield in a clumsy block that saved my head from being split, but the blade chopped through the rim of my shield and knocked me off balance. My feet slipped in the now blood-slicked grass and I stumbled back and sat down hard. I threw my hand behind me to keep from falling fully on my back and found my bow, lying on the ground where I'd dropped it. I swung it up and stabbed the sharpened tip into the warrior's eye as he wrenched his sword free of my shield and raised it to strike again.

The man screamed and staggered back, bumping into the villain beside him. As he did, Harald spun forward again, swinging a cut low at the feet of the uninjured man, then jerked Biter up and stabbed him in the mouth as he thrust his shield down to block the low attack. The man staggered back, spitting blood and teeth. Harald lunged to the right, punching his shield forward to block another spear thrust from the warrior there. Then, spinning completely around, he whipped Biter in an arc that ended in the neck of the man I had wounded.

"Go!" he shouted and pulled me to my feet.

Behind us, men with spears rushed Ulf from three sides. He blocked one, but the other two impaled him on their spear points and continued charging forward, bearing him to the ground, flailing at them in vain with his sword as he fell. As I started to run, the remaining fighter between us and the wall swung his sword at Harald's head. The blow glanced off his helm. Harald dropped to his knees as though stunned, but swung Biter in a sweeping arc that cut the man's legs from under him.

As Harald balanced there on his knees, swaying, I stopped and turned back to face him. Our eyes met for an instant. Again he said, though this time in little more than a whisper, "Go."

As I turned and fled a wave of attackers charged at Harald from behind, knocking him face forward on the ground. Three continued on past him in pursuit of me.

It was my good fortune that none who chased me carried spears. As I ran, I flung my shield back at my nearest pursuer. He swerved aside and it missed him, but it gained me a few precious strides.

I was younger and faster than the men who chased me, and unburdened by armor or shield.

Fear gave extra speed to my feet. Two of my pursuers quickly fell behind. The third, the one I'd thrown my shield at, kept pace behind me, neither gaining nor losing ground. As we neared the stone wall, I clawed an arrow from the quiver slapping against my hip. I cleared the low wall in a leap. As I struck ground on the far side, I spun around and fitted the arrow to my bowstring. There was no time to aim, for my pursuer was upon me. I barely had time to draw and release, but my shot struck home, the arrow darting from my bow into his stomach as he leapt the wall, sword raised to cut me down. I threw myself sideways and he sailed past me, a startled look on his face, then crumpled into a heap, groaning, when he hit the ground.

More of the enemy had joined in the chase, but were still some distance away. The remaining two of my original pursuers were nearing the wall now, though, and began sprinting toward me when they saw their comrade go down. I crouched behind the wall and, as quickly as I could, pulled arrows from my quiver and launched three, one after another. Two found their marks, dropping the two closest men. The third streaked toward the running warriors further back. The man I shot it at caught it with his shield, but he and the men around him skidded to a halt and dropped low, squatting behind their shields. They were close enough by now for me to see their eyes shining over the rims of their shields, even in the dark.

I nocked another arrow and shouted, "Who dies next?" Apparently none wished to, for the man I'd shot at began scuttling backwards behind the cover of his shield, putting more distance between himself and my bow. After a moment, the others followed his lead.

The man I'd shot as he'd leapt the wall lay on the ground behind me, moaning and cursing. I stabbed him with the sharpened horn tip of my bow in the side of his neck, where the big stream of lifeblood flows close beneath the skin. As his life left him in red spurts, I pulled my arrow from his body, then began running, crouched low behind the cover of the wall, toward the dark mass of the sheltering forest that lay at its end.

10

HALFDAN'S RUN

The men who still pursued me followed my progress at a distance, but made no serious attempt to catch me. They'd learned to fear the reach of my bow. When I came to the end of the wall and disappeared into the forest, they turned back and rejoined their fellows.

I stood a few feet back inside the tree line, hidden among the shadows, and watched the hellish scene before me. The wooden frame and timber walls of the longhouse were now burning, and the light given off by the blaze lit the cleared lands of the estate. Where Harald's and Ulf's bodies lay in the grass, and elsewhere across the fields where men had fallen, clusters of the enemy stood, pulling and tugging at the dead like dogs fighting over bones, stripping their bodies of armor, weapons, and even clothing.

Their leader appeared from behind the blazing longhouse, shouting at his men and waving his arms. Though he was a considerable distance from where I watched, I understood why his voice had sounded familiar to Harald. The helm and mask that earlier had covered his face were gone now, exposing a wild mane of long black hair and beard. The leader of the attackers was Toke.

At first my heart and mind had felt numb as I'd stood there, catching my breath after my run and trying to comprehend what had happened. Now though, the numbness faded away. I could feel my heart—my whole being—filling with hatred. *Toke!* At that instant, I would have killed him with my bare hands and teeth if I could have, and reveled at the taste of his blood. But there was nothing I could do. The distance was much too great for a bowshot. And if I ran back out of the woods now and tried to attack him, I could never fight my way through his men. I would only be cut down, and Harald's death would go unavenged. I was power-less in my anger. But at least now I knew who I had to kill.

I believed in the Gods of the Danes. I believed that they existed, though never before had I prayed to them. Gods seemed all too willing to ignore the wishes of men—even of great men. I'd always doubted they would even hear the pleas of slaves. Since becoming free, I'd never bothered to learn how to address the Gods. Few men think to thank them while good fortune is smiling on them, though many beseech the heavens for aid when all seems lost. But though I did not know how, I prayed that night. I turned my thoughts and my heart to Odin and sought his help, for he, I knew, was the God of vengeance and death.

Oak trees are sacred to Odin, that much I knew. He had been pinned with a spear to a great oak once, and had hung there for nine days, but had survived. By his suffering, he'd won for the Gods and for men the knowledge of poetry and of the runes. I knew that it is in memory of his suffering on the tree for the sake of men that sacrifices to Odin are hung on the branches of oaks.

At the forest's edge a great oak grew, its trunk bigger around than three grown men could span with their arms extended. I embraced the tree, my face against its rough bark, and spoke into it, willing the slumbering forest giant to awake and hear me and carry my prayers to Odin.

"Father Odin," I said, "hear this oath, and give me the strength and will to fulfill it." I spoke each word slowly and clearly, in case the speech of men was difficult for trees to understand. "I swear to avenge my brother Harald, and Ulf, and Rolf, and Aidan, and all of the others who died with them this night. I swear to slay Toke and all who aided him. Help me in this, All-Father. Give me this vengeance. Let my heart not feel peace until my oath is fulfilled."

I had no sacrifice to hang upon the tree. I took the dagger Harald had given me, and cut into the heel of my palm. As the blood welled up out of the wound, I pressed my hand against the tree and let my blood soak into its bark.

I felt a cool breath on my cheek as a sudden passing breeze, heralding the coming dawn, whispered through the trees. Above me, the leaves of the great oak rustled, and its branches creaked and swayed. The tree had heard—I was sure of it—and it would tell Odin of my oath.

Out in the fields, Toke's men began dragging bodies to the burning longhouse and throwing them inside. While they were occupied with their gruesome task, I crept back out of the forest and across the pasture, moving at a low crouch through the scattered strips of low mist that were forming on the ground as dawn approached. Once among the trees again on the far side, I worked my way through the woods down to where, behind the privy, the trees came closest to the longhouse. It was from that same patch of trees that the enemy's archers had launched so many deadly shafts at us when we'd tried to escape from the byre.

In the dark, I tripped over a body. He was one of Toke's archers, for a bow lay beside him and a quiver of arrows was slung by a strap from his shoulder. In the dark and confusion, he must have been forgotten by his comrades. By now I was running low on arrows—I had only eight left—so I took the arrows from his quiver, plus the arrow— it was one of mine—that had pierced his chest.

Just inside the edge of the woods, I lay prone beside a fallen log, spread my cloak over my body, and covered it with the dry, dead leaves that carpeted the ground under the trees. I would not be hidden from a close inspection, for the ground was obviously disturbed where I'd gathered the leaves. But I was concealed from anyone who merely scanned the tree line from a distance. Hopefully when daylight came, Toke would give me a chance for a killing shot.

Fatigue must have overwhelmed me, for I was startled awake by the sound of horses. It was still the gray hours of early morn. I peered from under the edge of my cloak and saw a large group of armed men on horseback approaching down the cart path. In front of me, the longhouse had burned until nothing remained but rows of stumps, low flames still flickering upon them, marking the boundaries of the walls. They were all that remained of the great timbers that had formed the frame of the structure and supported its roof. Smoking mounds of ash and charred wood filled the area within. Looking out across the smoldering ruin, I saw that the *Sea Steed*, Toke's ship, was now moored in the cove.

I watched as thin trails of smoke rose from a half-dozen points in the wreckage of the longhouse, only to be scattered by the morning breeze that was blowing in off the water. So, too, my life now lay in ruins, and my dreams were scattered and blown away. For a brief time I'd been a free man, a carl and warrior—the dream I'd cherished as a slave. I had even been raised up and acknowledged as the son of a chieftain. For a brief time I'd known the warmth and joy of a loving family. For one night only, I'd owned this estate and longhouse, and had walked on lands where I was lord. Now I was nothing, only a shadow hiding among the trees like a wild creature, hoping for vengeance.

The leader of the horsemen held up his hand, and the party of riders stopped. Toke, ringed by a group of his men, approached from the ship. Neither Toke nor any of his men now wore armor or bore shields, and they were armed with only their personal weapons, sheathed in their scabbards or stuck through their belts. As Toke came closer he held up both hands, palms outward, to show he was unarmed and came in peace.

I watched closely for a clear shot, thinking to kill Toke now. I watched in vain. Whether intentionally or not, Toke kept himself surrounded by his men.

The leader of the party of riders wore no helm. His head was shiny and bare of hair on top, but long gray hair from the back and sides of his head hung down his back in two thick braids, and his gray beard was thick and long. He wore a short, sleeveless brynie of mail and bore a shield, and was armed with a long spear and a sword that hung in a scabbard from his belt. Though he appeared aged, his bearing left no doubt he could use both.

"I am Hrodgar, headman of the village that lies down yonder road. Who are you? What happened here?" he asked.

"Bandits attacked," Toke replied. "They burned the longhouse and killed the folk of the farm. We saw the light in the sky from the flames, but arrived after their foul work was done. We were in time to gain some measure of vengeance, though."

The villagers' leader nodded to a warrior beside him. The man spurred his horse forward and rode slowly around the longhouse, in an ever widening circle, leaning over in the saddle and staring intently at the ground.

"Bandits, you say?" the old man asked. "There have been no reports of bandits in this area. Why should we believe that tale, rather than that you and your men have done this thing?"

"Hrodgar, do you not recognize me?" Toke asked. "I am Toke, Hrorik's son. This farm belongs to my father."

Hrodgar leaned forward and stared hard at Toke, then sat back in his saddle with a grunt.

"Thor's hammer, but you've grown as large as a bear. Still, I do recognize you. How go things with Hrorik and your brother Harald?"

Toke gave a loud sigh. "So the news has not reached here. Hrorik was mortally wounded in battle during a raid on England earlier this year. Harald brought him back for burial here in the land of the Danes."

There was murmuring among the horsemen and Hrodgar said, "This is grave news indeed. Hrorik was a great chieftain and well-liked among the folk along the Limfjord."

"I fear there is more grave news," Toke said. "My men and I are but recently returned from the same raid in England, and had hoped to rest here from our travels. We made camp for the evening some distance down the Limfjord, but during the night we saw the glow of the fire in the night sky and came to investigate. We found the longhouse already ablaze, and none but the bandits in sight."

Toke turned and signaled to a group of men who'd been standing back a ways, beside the work-sheds. They came forward, dragging between them a struggling man whose hands were tied behind his back. He began shouting in an accent that sounded strange to me. One of Toke's men quickly clubbed him into silence.

"What was he trying to say?" Hrodgar asked. "I could not understand his words."

"It is because he is an English Saxon," Toke replied, and I knew the man must be one of the prisoners Toke had captured in England. "Their tongue is very similar to ours, though it sounds different because of how they speak it.

"We captured this man in the fight with the bandits," Toke continued, "He seemed to be their leader. It is my thinking that he's an escaped slave."

"And those?" Hrodgar asked, pointing with his spear. For the first time I noticed a row of bodies lying in the grass beyond the remains of the long-house near the worksheds. I knew Toke's men had thrown the bodies of our dead into the burning longhouse. These bodies, I guessed, must be some of Toke's men that we'd killed.

"They are the rest of the bandits that we

killed," Toke answered. "It was a stiff fight. Three of my own men were slain, and several wounded."

Hrodgar stared at the *Sea Steed*, then at the men standing now around Toke. "Only three of your own men were killed?" he asked. "Then you travel with a small crew."

"We took losses in England," Toke replied, shrugging his shoulders.

The rider Hrodgar had dispatched returned at a canter. "The ground has drunk blood heavily in several places," he said. "It appears that those inside the house tried to break out from the byre using yon oxen to shield themselves. When the oxen fell, there was a moving battle in the direction of the wall that lies between the pasture and the fields. The heaviest fighting occurred a spear's throw from the wall. I judge that many men died there, although from blood on the ground, at least one died on the far side of the wall."

Hrodgar looked at Toke suspiciously. Toke shrugged his shoulders again. "I cannot say what happened," he said. "I was not here when it occurred. When my men and I arrived, the bodies had been moved by the bandits and had already been thrown into the fire."

"There was one other area where much blood was spilled," the scout added. "There, by the worksheds, there is much blood on the ground."

"That I can speak to," Toke offered. "It was there that we fought the bandits and slew those whom you see."

"You spoke of other grave news," Hrodgar prompted.

Toke pointed to the Englishman held by two of his men. "Note you the brynie he wears, how it has fine leather trim at the neck and sleeves? I recognize it as my brother Harald's brynie. And this," he added, taking a sword that one of his men had been holding in his hand. He drew the blade partially from its scabbard and showed it to Hrodgar. "This is Harald's sword, there can be no doubt. He called it Biter. This scum was wielding it when we clubbed him to the ground."

Hrodgar looked shaken. "We had no word that Harald had come. He would have come to the village to pay his respects if he was here. And how could he have traveled so far from the estate in the south? I see no ship other than yours."

Toke pointed to the shore. "See the small-boat on the beach? I recognize it. It is the small-boat from the *Red Eagle*. It must be how Harald traveled here. Perhaps he arrived but yesterday evening and planned to visit you this day, but fate did not allow it."

Hrodgar shook his head sadly. "This is truly dark news. With Harald died the last of his line, and they were all great men indeed. I offer no offense to you, Toke," Hrodgar added, "For you appear well on the way to becoming a great man yourself. But the blood of Hrorik's line does not flow in your veins."

Toke nodded his head slightly. "I take no offense, and I thank you for your words that give me honor. It is indeed a dark doom that the line of Hrorik, son of Offa, son of Gorm, has ended here this day with Harald's death."

Lies flowed so easily from Toke's lips. I wanted to cry out that Hrorik's line was not ended—that I lived and was a son of Hrorik. I could not. To do so now would mean instant death at the hands of Toke's men, and I doubted not that Toke would find some new lie to explain away my claim and my killing. But someday I would say the words. Someday I would say them to Toke—and I would kill him.

Hrodgar turned in his saddle toward his men and raised his voice. "We will raise a mound over the ashes of this longhouse, to honor Harald Hroriksson and those who fell here with him. Tomorrow, in the afternoon after the task is done, we'll hold the funeral feast on this site."

He turned back to Toke. "With your permission, at the funeral I will offer your captive in blood-sacrifice to the Gods and to the dead."

Toke nodded his head again. "There is one other matter," he said. "One of the bandits escaped. We saw him flee into the forest. We've caught three of the horses from the farm, and I intend to send three of my men, good archers all, to hunt him down. Your men know these parts. I would be indebted for any assistance you can give."

Hrodgar turned to the man who had scouted the ground around the longhouse. He appeared to be about forty winters of age, and had a long, thin face with a pointed nose and piercing eyes. His beard, which was a medium brown color, was trimmed close to his face, and his hair, a few shades lighter, was pulled back and tied at his neck with a leather thong.

"This is Einar," Hrodgar said. "He is the best tracker in our village. He can read a trail on the ground more clearly than most men read the runes. I'll also send Kar," he added, indicating another rider among his followers. "He is the most skilled archer among us. Einar, you will take my two hounds. What your eyes miss, their noses will find."

"This man is very dangerous," Toke said. "He's very skilled with a bow. Two of my three dead, and several of my wounded, fell to his arrows."

"We hunt him with dogs and five men armed

271

with bows," Hrodgar responded. "For one man it should be enough." He raised his voice and addressed his men. "We return now to the village. We must make known the death of Harald Hroriksson, and tell the womenfolk to begin preparations for the funeral feast."

The villagers turned and began to ride away. Hrodgar, too, wheeled his horse, but before he spurred it, he spoke again to Toke.

"I will return later this morning with men to begin work on the grave-mound. Your crew can help us. Many hands will make the work go quickly. Einar and Kar will come with the hounds. Tell your men to be ready. The sooner the hunt is begun, the closer shall be their prey." He kicked his horse and rode after his men, the last of whom were already crossing the stream.

Confident that Hrodgar was out of earshot, Toke turned to one of the men standing near him. "When the funeral feast is over, we'll sail south to the estate. If you've not caught the boy and killed him before then, ride south and rejoin us there when you've finished your task."

With the villagers' departure, I'd abandoned all thoughts of trying to kill Toke now. Even if I'd succeeded, moments later I'd be hacked to death by his men. Toke had not done this deed alone. Every member of his crew had participated. I wanted them all to pay. Only by keeping myself alive could I fully avenge Harald and those who'd died with him. It would require a long hunt, but I vowed that in the end I would kill them all.

The problem that faced me now was surviving the next few days. Five men armed with bows, and aided by dogs, would be hunting me. They were on horseback. I was afoot. They would be carrying provisions. I had none, and would have to find what sustenance I could in the forest while on the move. Those were the odds against me. In my favor were only my skills as a woodsman and with my bow. I felt fear, great fear. I wondered if the deer or the boar, when pursued through the forest by hunters and hounds, felt the kind of fear that I felt now.

I told myself that I was not a beast and must not act like one. Blind flight, driven by fear, would kill me. I must conquer my fear or I would not survive. I must depend on the few resources I had, and make them suffice. That, and hope that Odin had heard my prayer and oath, and would not turn his back on my quest to avenge Harald and the others.

The sun was well past its midday height when I first heard, in the far distance, the baying of hounds on my trail. I'd been wondering, as I trotted along narrow-game trails through the shadows under the trees, how Toke's men would give the dogs my scent. It would not agree with the tale Toke had spun to show the villagers where I'd actually entered the forest. He'd told Hrodgar that the fighting out in the fields had occurred before he and his men had arrived, and that he and his men had fought the bandits down between the work-sheds and the shore.

Perhaps Toke's men had found the empty scabbard I'd cast aside, or my helm. I'd discarded both last night when I'd first reached the shelter of the trees at the end of the stone wall. The scabbard I had no need for, without the sword, and I'd feared the helm would reflect a glint of light and betray my position when I sneaked back close to the burning longhouse. Those things would bear my scent and would be enough to allow the hounds to start casting back and forth in the woods behind the longhouse in search of me. I wondered whether the hounds or the eagle-eyed tracker, Einar, would discover where I'd lain in hiding, listening to Toke's lies to Hrodgar. I wondered whether Toke, realizing how close I'd been, would feel any fear. Did a man like Toke feel fear? I wanted him to. I wanted him to know that death stalked him. I wanted him to feel unease every time he passed close to a patch of forest, wondering if I lurked in the shadows waiting for a shot.

Using the sun as my guide, I headed south and west. I knew from our voyage up the coast that several rivers drained into the sea from the lands south of the Limfjord. I needed to stay inland, well away from the coast, so any waterways I encountered would hopefully be early in their course, and as narrow as possible, at the point I needed to cross them. I could not afford to be trapped by my pursuers against the banks of a river too broad to cross.

As I made my way through the forest, whenever I came upon a stream, however small, I made my path for a considerable distance through its waters, even if to do so took me temporarily off course. Every time the hounds lost my scent I would gain time and distance on my pursuers, while they searched to find my trail again.

Darkness fell with my pursuers still far behind me, judging by the occasional barks or baying of the hounds. I hadn't eaten since the feast. To my empty stomach, it seemed much longer than just one night ago. I felt grateful now that I'd stuffed myself so on the fine dishes Aidan and Tove had prepared. I regretted the scraps I'd left on my platter because I'd felt too gorged to eat them.

I didn't think the searchers would continue

their hunt in the dark. Under the canopy of the trees, the blackness was intense, almost palpable. They'd need torches to make any speed at all, but torches would light them up as targets if I was lying in ambush.

The darkness hindered my progress, too. After the third time I tripped over an unseen root and fell sprawling, I gave up. I needed rest anyway. I had fought a battle the night before—the first I'd ever been in—then had been pushing hard all day in my flight from my pursuers, alternately trotting and walking, a pace that ate up the miles but conserved wind and strength. I was exhausted now. My labors had drained the strength from my body, and my grief at Harald's death had sapped my spirit. If I did not rest, I risked becoming too weary to think clearly. And I could not afford to make mistakes.

That night I slept wrapped in my cloak, burrowed for warmth and concealment in a drift of leaves that had blown against the trunk of a fallen forest giant. The ground was cold and hard. Every time a breath of breeze blew, the leaves that covered me rustled and I started awake, fearing that my pursuers were upon me.

I was awakened in the middle of the night by a snuffling noise nearby. Cautiously, and as quietly as I could, I pulled back the edge of my cloak and cleared the leaves from in front of my face.

A deep, throaty growl answered my movement. In front of me—not six paces away—was a great gray wolf. He'd been investigating my scent trail leading into the leaves. Beyond him, ringed in a half circle facing my hiding place, was his pack.

I remembered Harald had told me, when showing me the graves of our ancestors, that wolves had killed the first of Hrorik's line to settle along the Limfjord. I wondered if wolves would end our line now, here in this dark forest. It seemed the sort of perverse twist of fate the Norns might like to spin.

I'd unstrung my bow when I'd lain down to sleep, so its limbs might rest also. If the pack decided to attack now, I had only my dagger to defend myself with.

Their leader hadn't moved. He continued to stand before me, head lowered, fur along his spine raised and bristling, growling and watching warily. My body was still hidden under my cloak and the drift of leaves I'd burrowed into, but my scent told him that a hated man was hiding in front of him.

The wolf's fur was sleek and he looked well fed. The winter had been mild and the deer abundant. I knew wolves did not normally feed on men, except in times of famine. On the other hand, men did not normally sleep alone in the forest without a fire.

I reared up suddenly on my knees, scattering the leaves in a great flurry, and shouted at the wolf in a wordless growl. As I did, I swung my bow out and jabbed in his direction with the sharpened horn tip. He was out of reach. In truth, I wanted only to startle him, not strike him, for the latter might provoke an attack.

The big wolf was quick—he leapt back several paces then stayed crouched there, growling louder. I growled back at him in a voice I hoped sounded menacing. As we faced each other, both watching for some sign of weakness or imminent attack, I pulled my bow slowly in front of me, braced it against my knee, and strung it.

I slid an arrow from my quiver, nocked it on the string, and felt my confidence begin to return. Though still outnumbered, I was a man again. I had the power to kill from afar. I stood up slowly, so I was looking down at the wolf, a man facing a beast. When I did, he backed up another step, and growled louder. I stopped my wordless growl and spoke to the wolf leader.

"You are a chieftain among your kind," I told him. "You possess the wisdom needed to lead them. Lead them now away from danger." I held the bow out before me. "You know of men. You know this is the power of death that strikes quick and sure from afar. If you and your followers attack, I may die, but I will kill you first. I promise it. Look in my eyes and know that I speak true. You and I have no quarrel. Take your pack and go."

The wolf leader stayed crouched before me, growling, his long teeth bared. I wondered if wolves could understand the speech of men. Behind him, a female was pacing back and forth anxiously in front of the rest of the pack, who were now sitting motionless on their haunches, watching. I wished he would make up his mind. I needed to concentrate, to keep my thoughts focused to shoot quickly enough to kill him if he leapt. But random thoughts and distractions kept sneaking into my mind. I needed to make water. And my hunger was asserting itself. I was beginning to wonder how wolf would taste.

Suddenly he turned and disappeared silently into the darkness with his pack.

When they left, the trembling began. I sat back down and leaned against the log, trying to collect my thoughts and my courage. Perhaps, I told myself, this was an omen, a sign from Odin. Perhaps I should take heart from it. Was Odin not called the wolf-feeder? As the God of war, did he not litter fields of battle with feasts for wolves, and foxes, and ravens? Perhaps he'd sent the wolves to me tonight, to signal that he'd heard my oath and would support me in it. I found some comfort in these thoughts, even though I did not fully believe them.

I knew I'd sleep no more that night. Gathering my few possessions, I continued on through the forest. My hunger was becoming a problem that required attention.

Shortly before dawn, I reached a river, and with an arrow at ready on my bow, I ranged along its banks searching for game.

In the last of the gray hours before morn, I came to a bend in the river. Sometime in the past, a great oak, its roots undercut by the river's flow, had fallen across the river from the other side. Beginning in the middle of the river and reaching over close to the bank on which I stood, an island had formed along the upstream side of the trunk, from silt trapped by the great tree's branches. The tree's fall had happened sufficiently long ago that grasses, low shrubs, and even a few small saplings grew on the island.

As I watched from behind a thicket on the river's bank, two ducks, which had spent the night huddled together in the tall grasses on the shore of the little island, stretched their wings and waddled over to the water's edge. One fell to my bow while the other escaped, flying low over the water, squawking in alarm.

The top of the great tree rested on the bank

near where I stood. Like ribs on an old skeleton that the flesh has long ago vanished from, the remains of its branches jutted out randomly from the trunk. Only the thickest part of the branches remained attached; the outer ends of the branches—all of the smaller forks, twigs, and dead foliage—had long ago rotted away.

Using the trunk as a bridge, I crossed to the island and broke my fast. I skinned the duck's breast, and over a tiny fire, burning just two or three twigs at a time so as to make no column of smoke, I seared the meat in the flames until it was cooked through. The duck's legs I saved for a later meal.

After I'd eaten, I explored the little island and its surrounds. As I did, a plan began to form itself in my mind.

On the side of the river I'd come from, where the top of the great oak had landed, the tree's branches and some boulders along the shore they'd fallen on had combined to raise the trunk far enough above the river's surface so the water's flow was not blocked. Although the center of the river was dammed by the trunk and the silt that had been trapped by its branches, a deep and swift-flowing channel coursed between the island and the bank on that side of the river.

On the far side of the river, a giant tangle of

roots and earth had fallen with the tree into the water. For a long time, the river must have been almost totally blocked on that side, for from the edge of the island out to the end of the tree's roots, the bottom had filled with silt, leaving the water at times just ankle-deep, and never higher than my knees. I waded out and looked beyond the roots. Eventually the swirling waters had cut a narrow channel around the end of the tangled mass of roots, and the river flowed there past them steadily now again, though not so deep, wide, nor swiftly as the channel under the head of the tree on the other side of the island.

The span from the last solid footing among the roots to the bank on this side was no more than five feet. The tree provided a natural bridge across the river for a man on foot, though it would be of no use to a man on horseback. As I looked up, I saw something else. Whether from rain or river's flood, over time the earth packed about the roots deep up underneath the base of the trunk had been eroded away. I realized that what at first appeared to be just shadow from the mass of roots and earth above was actually an opening. I crawled up and found a hollow large enough for a man to lay curled in, invisible to any, save one who found the entrance directly below.

In an instant I could see the entire plan in my

mind. I had been given an opportunity by the forest or Odin—or both. If I was clever and acted boldly, I might be able to reduce the odds against me. For a brief time, I might become the hunter, instead of the prey. But I knew I must move quickly if I was to set my trap, for I had much trail to lay.

I dropped down from the hollow under the roots, and waded through the shallow water back to the island. For my plan to work, it was essential that no scent trail lead to my hiding place.

Climbing up on the fallen trunk, I returned to the bank from whence I'd first come. I ran as fast as my legs and lungs could take me, back to the point where I'd first come upon the river. From there I continued on downstream. When the hounds and trackers following my trail found where I'd reached the river, they would discover that my path led in both directions along the river's edge. I hoped the two trails would make them think I'd had to search in both directions, looking for a place to cross. I needed to split the hunting party, to make them divide and follow both trails. I knew I could not take them all on at once.

The spirit of the river must have been aiding me. Not far downstream, I came upon shallows where the river was moving slower, never more than waist-deep, and could be forded. I left clear footprints on the bank for those behind to read, took off my clothing, and, holding it and my weapons overhead, waded across the river.

Once ashore, I dressed and began running through the woods, a short distance in from and parallel to the river, heading back upstream. Looking through the gaps between the trees I reached a point where I could see where the great tree had fallen across the river, deeper into the forest. There I turned and laid a trail heading away from the river, deeper into the forest. I was running short of time now, for I could hear the dogs barking and howling in the distance. I did not journey far into the woods, perhaps two or three bowshots, when I found a trickle of running water. Judging I could risk no more time on my false trail, I ended it at the tiny stream's edge. Being careful to walk backward wherever the soil was soft, and keeping my steps in my earlier footprints, I backtracked, retracing the path I'd just made.

As I neared the spot where my false trail had turned away from the river and headed into the forest, I knew I'd reached a critical point in my plan. I had to abandon my false trail now and cut over to the island, but I needed to be certain that when the dogs came this way they would lead the hunters with them into the forest, away from the river. A short distance from where I'd made the turn and headed into the woods, I made water against the base of a tree. Hopefully the strength of that scent would pull the dogs to it, and away from my true path. Then I backtracked the rest of the way along my false trail to the point where I'd turned and headed toward the depths of the forest.

Bracing my foot on a stone so it would leave no telltale mark in the earth, I leapt as far off my trail as I could. My new trail, the true one, commenced perhaps five feet from the old. It was the best I could do with so little time. I knew the trackers would eventually find this second trail. The most I could hope for when that happened was that they would misread it and not realize what I had truly done. To help confuse them, at the river's edge I turned with my back to the water and stomped my feet hard into the soft soil, creating a deep and obvious sign. To anyone who found the imprints, I hoped it would look as though I'd jumped from the tree to the bank, across the narrow span of river beyond the root end of the tree.

Standing on a stone again so as not to leave evidence that would show my true path, I leapt across the gap from the bank out onto the root mass, climbed over its tangled arms down to the trunk, and hurriedly ran along its length to where I could drop down onto the island.

The dogs were much louder now. From their

sound, I guessed they must be close to the point where my trail had first reached the river and divided. I murmured a prayer to Odin, requesting victory over my enemies.

I suddenly realized that the baying of one of the hounds was gradually fading, while the other was growing louder, and I knew my pursuers had split up. So far, my plan was working.

Moving quickly, I tied one end of my spare bowstring to the top of a small sapling growing in the sandy soil of the island. Crouching behind some bushes a few feet away, I pulled the string until the sapling was bent partly over, then pinned the end of the bowstring to the ground under my foot. I took five arrows from my quiver and stuck them point-first in the sand in front of me and readied a sixth arrow on my bow.

The hound appeared from behind the thicket where, at dawn, I'd hidden and spotted the ducks. His sudden appearance startled me, for he was tracking silently now, except for occasional whines as he zigged and zagged, nose to the ground, following my scent. He ran back and forth along the bank, sniffing the ground. Then he stood, his front paws up on the trunk of the tree, and bayed loudly. He'd found where I'd first climbed up onto the fallen trunk to cross over to the island early that morning.

Moments later, two riders appeared. One was a member of Toke's crew, the other the villager named Kar. Both had arrows nocked on their bows and at the ready. I stared at Toke's man and let the focus of my gaze tighten until I saw only the point on his breast under which his evil heart beat.

I let the bowstring slip from under my foot, and the sapling whipped upright. Both men were skilled. Their arrows passed through the sapling's branches. Had the little tree concealed an enemy, he would have been dead.

I stood. My first arrow hit Toke's man full in the chest. Kar snatched a second arrow from his quiver and was laying it on his string, but my arrows were at the ready in front of me and I was faster. My second shot skimmed past the front of his leg and buried itself almost up to its feathers in the side of his horse's chest.

Kar's horse reared and he dropped his bow as he grabbed wildly for the reins, trying to keep from falling. The hound, who'd spied me when I stood, bounded up onto the fallen trunk of the tree and charged along it in my direction.

I hadn't anticipated his attack. I snatched a third arrow and pivoted toward him, snapping off a quick shot as he leapt. My arrow almost missed, striking him far back in the side a split second before he crashed into me and knocked me flat on my back. He stood astride my body, his snarling face above mine, his long fangs bared. Then, with a growl, he turned to snap at the arrow jutting from his side. It was all that saved me from losing my throat to his fangs. I seized his neck with both hands and forced his head back and held it there, my left hand buried in the thick fur under his jaws, while I snatched my dagger free with my right hand and plunged its blade into his chest, over and over, until he died.

I'd lost sight of Kar when I'd fallen under the hound's attack. Was he waiting now, bow at ready, in case I reappeared? I could see nothing showing above the edge of the riverbank. Staying low, I eased myself from under the dead hound's body, found my bow, and fitted an arrow to its string. I picked up a stone, and tossed it into the brush a few feet away, then stood up, drawing my bow as I did, searching for any sign of my enemies.

Toke's man lay on the ground, dead. His horse was gone. Farther back from the edge of the river, Kar's horse had fallen, and had pinned Kar's leg beneath it. I could see him kicking and pushing at the dead horse with his arms and other leg, trying to shift its weight aside.

I remembered my prayer to Odin. He had heard and had granted me victory. A God who listens to men and answers their prayers deserves thanks. I took my dagger and slit open the dead hound's belly. Reaching inside, I felt until I found its heart, and ripped and cut it free. I hung the heart as a blood-offering in the branches of the little sapling I'd used as a decoy. Hopefully the ravens, Odin's messengers, would find it there.

Up on the bank, Kar was calling loudly for help. I gathered my weapons, rinsed the blood from my hand in the river's waters, then crossed the tree-bridge and approached where he lay, trapped by the body of his horse. I intended to kill him. He'd hunted me and would have killed me without mercy. I had an arrow nocked and ready across my bow.

He'd propped himself up on one elbow and held a small axe in his other hand. As I approached, he cocked his arm back as if ready to throw. It was a brave gesture, but he had no chance of beating my arrow. He knew it. I could see the knowledge of his death, and fear, in his eyes.

For some reason, his fear moved me and cooled the anger in my blood. He wasn't part of Toke's crew. He was not a murderer. He was from the village, folk who had long been friends with Harald and Aidan. He thought he was hunting one of their killers.

"Toss your axe this way," I told him. "Gently, but quickly, and I'll let you live. There are things I need to do, and I do not wish to have an axe thrown at me while I'm doing them. Do not make me kill you. I have no wish to."

"Why should I trust you?" Kar asked, his voice quavering from his fear. "You are a bandit and a murderer."

"I am neither," I answered, "but I do not have time to argue the matter with you. Think on this: If it was my wish to kill you, I could easily do so now, without trying to persuade you to lay down your weapon. Think you of my shot from ambush. Do you think it was an accident where my arrow struck? I could have killed you instead of your horse. I have no quarrel with men of the village. Only with Toke and his crew."

I lied when I told him I'd hit his horse on purpose, but he did not need to know that. The man stared at me, as if trying to read my soul through my eyes. I wondered what he looked for and what he saw. Whatever it was, it must have been enough.

Kar tossed his axe at my feet. It was a handy size, both as a tool and a weapon, and I decided to keep it. I gathered Kar's bow and the bow belonging to Toke's man, and chopped them both through with the axe. I saved their bowstrings, and added the better arrows from both of their quivers to my own. The rest I destroyed.

On the body of Toke's man I found a leather

pouch filled with bread and salted pork, and a leather skin filled with water. I found more food in a saddlebag on Kar's horse and added it to the pouch, then slung it and the waterskin over my shoulder.

Kar had been watching me silently.

"Was your leg injured when the horse fell on it?" I asked.

"Aye. It feels as though it's broken."

"Good," I said. "When they capture the dead man's horse, use it to return to the village. This is not your fight. Tell that to Einar, also."

Kar started. "How do you know his name?" he asked.

I didn't answer. "And when you get back to the village," I told him, "remember these words and tell them to Hrodgar: The honeyed tongue conceals a black heart. Toke is not to be trusted. The line of Hrorik is not ended."

I realized I couldn't let Kar tell the others where I went. I walked over to him with the axe in my hand. Fear filled his eyes again.

"You said you would not kill me," he protested.

I turned the axe so the back of the blade, where it joined the shaft, was facing forward.

"I will not," I answered, "but you must sleep for a time," and I swung the axe against his head.

I could hear the thundering of hooves in the distance. I wanted to leave a message for Toke's other men. I'd never learned how to read the runes or write with them, but I knew a few of the characters. I knew the rune "haegl," because Harald had carved his name in runes on the doors of his bed-closet at home, and I recalled the shape of the first letter of his name. I knelt now over the body of Toke's dead warrior and carved ✳ in his forehead with the point of my dagger. My vengeance was for Harald, and I wanted Toke's men to know that—and to feel fear.

Sheathing my dagger, I turned and ran across the tree-bridge, dropped down onto the island, and headed for my hiding place under the great tree's roots.

From where I lay hidden in the dark womb of earth, deep in the heart of the roots, I tried to picture the progress of the hunters from the sounds I could hear. Horses approached on the near bank, the root side of the river, coming out of the woods from where they'd finally found where I'd leapt from my false trail and headed for the island. I'd known it wouldn't fool them forever, but it had kept them away long enough. They were following the dog, which barked occasionally as it ran. I heard shouts of alarm and knew they must have spotted the bodies of their comrades on the ground across the river.

I could hear the voice of Einar, the tracker from the village, as he studied the ground and explained what he read there to the others.

"See the deep footprints here. He must have leapt from the tree's end across the river's channel here."

"But the trail in the forest led nowhere," another voice said.

"Maybe. Maybe not. There were several trails to follow. At least one of them was a false trail, laid to set a trap," Einar replied. "Maybe all the trails we've found were false, and we've yet to find the true one. This is not an unthinking beast we're following. It's a man, and a clever one at that. If we're not careful, we'll become the hunted, and not he."

They galloped off along the riverbank, no doubt headed back to the ford, to cross back over the river and reach the ground where their comrades had fallen.

Several times during the afternoon I heard the crunch of footsteps on the sand of the island. Once I heard the whining of a hound on the trunk of the tree somewhere above my head, and a voice calling it to heel. I wondered how skilled a tracker Einar was. No true trail led away from the ambush site, showing the way I'd left. Would he realize I was still hiding somewhere nearby?

They camped that night on the shore near

where Kar and Toke's man had fallen. Once I thought I heard angry voices, but could not distinguish the words. The smell of roasting meat drifted across the river to where I lay, burrowed deep within the roots at the base of the tree, and made my mouth water. Kar's dead horse had provided them an impromptu feast. I dined instead on salted pork, stale bread, and sips of water. It was food, and I was grateful for it, for I was hungry.

While I lay cramped and uncomfortable in my little burrow, I marveled at how readily I'd become a killer. When Harald had taught me how to use weapons, I'd sometimes wondered whether, in real combat, I would have the will to use them against another. When the time had come, I'd crossed that bridge without thinking. It was only now I realized that I was changed. I had faced the test and passed it. I was blooded. I didn't even know for certain how many men I'd killed, for during the attack on the estate I'd fired many arrows at dim shapes or sounds in the dark. I did know that no matter how many I had slain, I regretted none of their deaths. I knew, also, that I was eager to kill again. Many men must die before Harald and the others would be avenged.

My pursuers did not make an early start in the morning, waiting instead until full daylight. I smiled a grim smile at that. After yesterday, they feared an ambush. Even after they left, I stayed hidden up under the roots of the fallen tree. I'd laid a trap for them. I needed to beware, now, that they might try a ruse or trap in return to catch me.

A while after they rode away from their camp-site, I heard the hoofbeats of their horses clattering along the bank opposite the root end of the tree, coming up from the ford downstream. Opposite the tree, they turned and headed into the forest.

It was a short trail they were following, but the only one that led away from the ambush site. As I'd hoped, Einar must have concluded that I'd crossed the river on the tree-bridge and run into the forest after the ambush, then entered the bed of the tiny stream, wading for a time through its waters, caus-ing the dog to lose my scent. They knew it was a tactic I'd used before, to try and throw the dogs off my trail. Einar, Toke's two men, and the hound would range up and down the banks of the little brook, looking for signs that I'd left the streambed, and for a new scent trail. I had no way of knowing how long they'd search before Einar would suspect he'd guessed wrong. But eventually, when they found no trail leaving the stream, he would. I had no time to waste.

I'd been ready since dawn. I climbed stiffly out of my hideaway, dropped into the shallow water, and waded toward the shore of the island. I had almost stepped from the river's waters onto the sandy shore when something gave me pause. I stood there in the water for several long moments, studying the scene before me, trying to understand what had stayed me, before I understood. Something had protected me from what my eyes at first had missed. Perhaps the spirit of Harald, or my mother, was watching over me.

Someone, probably Einar, had taken a branch and swept the sandy soil on the island clean of all footprints. The ground on either bank of the river was confused now with crisscrossed trails, but new footprints in the sand of the island would be clear evidence of recent passage.

I returned through the water to where the roots hung down and, using them as a rough ladder, climbed up onto the trunk and crossed to the far bank. I left wet footprints for the first few yards along the tree's trunk, but hopefully they'd dry before Einar and the others returned. As I passed above the island, I saw that no one had taken down the hound's heart I'd hung in sacrifice. It takes a brave man or a fool to interfere with a gift made to the Gods.

I looked longingly at the carcass of the dead horse when I passed the site where my pursuers had camped the night before. The thought of fresh meat made my mouth water, and I could use the strength it would give me, but I feared that if I cut meat from the carcass, the sharp eyes of Einar would detect it. He would doubtless find my trail soon enough, but the longer he had to search, the greater lead I would gain. I moved back into the forest far enough from the river to be invisible from anyone watching from the far bank, but still close enough to follow the course of the river, and set off at a trot.

During the day, I passed two shallows where the river could be forded. At each, I ran my trail down to the water's edge and stepped out into the river. At each, I waded a short distance upstream before I climbed back onto the bank and continued my journey on the same side of the river. I hoped that each false trail would cause my pursuers to lose time searching in vain on the far bank, trying to pick up my spoor again. My ambush had bettered the odds I was facing, but also had put my pursuers much closer on my trail. I wanted to lengthen my lead on them again.

It was not until the third shallows I came to, late in the afternoon, that I actually crossed. Holding my clothes and weapons over my head, I waded across the river through waist-deep water. Once close to the far bank, I raised my feet and floated, letting the current carry me downstream, till I came to where the mouth of a small stream emptied its waters into the river's flow. Holding my clothes and weapons aloft with one hand and paddling with the other, I swam to shore at the stream's mouth.

Standing in the shallow streambed, I dressed, and over a twig fire, roasted my two duck legs and ate them. By now it was late in the afternoon. I was tired and needed a place to rest the night. I'd managed to strike a good blow, yet I was still the prey, running before hunters on horseback who had a hound to speed their search. It was wearing me down. I had to stay well ahead of them. If they caught up with me, they could surround me and pick me off with their bows when I moved from cover, or charge me from different directions like wolves move in for the kill on a deer. Either way, I would surely die.

I waded along the shallow bed of the stream until dusk. In the last light of the day I saw a hill, steep and round like a young woman's breast, rising from the forest floor. Climbing out of the stream, I trudged toward it. Its sides were rocky, but wooded with scattered trees and brush. The crown of the hill was bare except for low underbrush and the stump of a great ash tree that had been shattered by lightning at a point twice as high up its trunk as my height. The tall stump stood above the hilltop like a solitary sentinel, watching over the forest below. The rest of the tree lay, like the body of a fallen giant, stretched down the far side of the hill.

I wondered what could have caused the mighty God Thor such anger, that he would summon the fury of the storm and hurl a thunderbolt to destroy this tree. Had the Gods quarreled among themselves, and Thor had vented his anger on the forest? It must have happened last summer, when foliage was full on the tree, for numerous dead leaves still clung to its branches. Along the top side of the fallen trunk, the branches were still whole, but on the sides and underneath they'd been broken and crushed by the fall, forming a dense tangle around the fallen trunk.

I slept that night with my back against the giant stump, wrapped tightly in my cloak. I was concealed from spying eyes by the low brush on the hilltop, but had a good view of the approach along the stream—the direction from which my pursuers would come.

When I awoke the following morning, I knew what I must do. The plan must have been whispered in my ear by some benevolent spirit while I slept, for it was fully formed in my mind when sleep left me.

I stood and studied the ground and woods

around me. The peak of the hill was high enough that I could look out across the roof of the forest. I noticed in the distance what appeared to be a break in the woods, running in a line as far as I could see. That way must lie another river or perhaps a road. For now, my problem, and hopefully its solution, lay closer at hand.

If they hadn't yet done so, eventually my hunters would find where I'd crossed the river. After the two false crossings I'd created, they'd doubtless have learned to search the bank upstream on the same side to see if my trail resumed there. Finding nothing on that side, they would cross the river and search anew.

By staying in the streambed on this side of the river, I'd bought myself time. Einar was a woodsman, though, and a skilled and tenacious tracker. I'd not been able to lose him yet, and didn't expect to. I was certain that when they found no trail on this side of the river, either, he'd realize I'd used the stream to mask my scent and passage, and they would turn their hunt up along its banks. There was no other route I could have followed.

When the hunters searched far enough along the sides of the stream, their hound would come upon the point where I'd left the water and climbed to this hilltop, and he would follow my scent trail here. That could not be undone. What I must do now was build upon it.

Laying new trail for the hound to follow, I moved down the hill's side, along the trunk of the fallen ash. I stayed on the side closest to the stream until I came to the point where the great tree's branches were thickest. Though many had been broken in the fall, the shattered stumps and stubs still jutting from the trunk held the great tree's trunk a few hand-spans above the ground.

I dropped to my stomach on the ground. Pushing with my legs and pulling with my arms and elbows, I wormed my way through the tangle of broken branches and pulled myself under the trunk. When I crawled from beneath the great tree's body on the far side, I used the hand-axe I'd taken from Kar and cleared a small space close to the trunk. Kneeling low to the ground, I found that from there I couldn't see through the tangle of branches to the open ground beyond. If I could not see out, the hunters would not be able to see in.

Just above the point where I'd crawled from beneath the trunk, an unbroken limb, as large around as my leg, jutted straight out from the trunk. Its outer end was buried in a crisscrossed thicket of branches, broken and tangled in the crushing fall.

I cut this branch through with the axe, just beyond where it joined the trunk. It fell heavily, squarely onto the space where my scent-trail emerged from under the tree. It would be the hammer, and the ground below would be the anvil. I cut two sections from a smaller branch, each almost as long as my arm. They would form the supports for my deadfall.

Straining, I lifted the thick limb up and propped it with the two supports over the low opening where I'd crawled from beneath the trunk. Using the spare bowstring I'd taken from the man I'd killed, I wound it around the two supports, up high, near where the heavy branch balanced on them, then fashioned the remainder of the cord into a noose. I draped the noose so it hung over the gap under the tree trunk, and concealed the cord with leaves and small twigs. Any being—man or dog—following my trail would have to pass their head through the noose as they pulled themselves from under the tree.

With my other spare bowstring, I lashed three arrows to the deadfall log, their shafts and sharpened-iron heads pointing down and extending a handspan below it. I could not risk my trap only injuring its victim.

When I finished, I turned and crawled and wormed my way through the broken, tangled branches until I was clear of the tree.

I hadn't planned to remain and see the results

of my handiwork. I'd planned to let my trap reduce the numbers of those who hunted me, while I moved on. But the hound and the three hunters following it had been moving silently while they'd ranged along the streambed searching for my trail. I'd barely cleared the tree's branches when the silence was shattered by baying, just a short distance away, at the point where I'd left the stream the night before. The baying continued as the hound moved rapidly toward the hill. Behind it I could hear the excited shouts of the hunters and the thudding of their horses' hooves.

I had to find a place to hide, and quickly. I spotted a cedar a short distance away, its lowest branches hanging down almost to the ground, like the skirts of a woman. An image flashed through my mind: Once as a young child, when frightened by Toke's anger and threats, I'd hidden under my mother's skirts. I ran now and dove underneath the sheltering branch-skirts of the cedar and pulled my cloak over my head. I hoped that huddled under the cloak's gray covering in the shadows under the tree, I could pass for a large stone. If the dog survived, of course, my ruse would not fool its sharp nose.

There was a narrow gap where I held the folds of my cloak pinched together in front of my face. I peered through it and tried to still my breathing.

A moment later, three men on horseback appeared on the hilltop. One of them, a crewman of Toke's, shouted orders. "Tord, go down that side of the tree. I'll go down this. Perhaps he's gone to ground in its branches. Einar, you watch from up here and warn us if you see anything."

The man who'd spoken spurred his horse down the hill on the side I was on. The hound they followed was already burrowing into the tangle of branches around the tree. Suddenly it gave one loud yelp, then was silent.

The man who hunted on my side wore a helm and a heavy, leather jerkin studded with small metal plates. A sword hung at his side, a shield was slung across his back, and he had an arrow nocked and at the ready across his bow.

"Tord, Einar," he called nervously. "Do you see anything?"

"I see nothing," Einar called out from the hill-top.

"Did you not hear the dog cry out?" the man called Tord answered, shouting unseen from the far side of the trunk. "He must be in there if he killed the dog. Beware the range of his bow. We should set fire to the tree."

Toke's man on my side of the tree was now but thirty paces from me. Had he been Einar, he would have seen the earth was disturbed where I'd scrambled under the branches and gone to ground.

I recognized the leather jerkin he was wearing. It was the jerkin that had belonged to Rolf. An image of Rolf, trailing his fishing line behind the boat on our voyage north, flashed in my mind. I wondered if there were fish to catch in the after-world. I eased my bow around in front of me and slid an arrow from my quiver.

"Einar," Tord cried. "You're supposed to be the great hunter. What do you think? Is he hiding within the branches of this tree?"

"I think," Einar called, "that I see two men who have gone from being hunters to being prey."

"Shut up, old fool," the man near me shouted angrily.

I let my cloak slide from my shoulders and, still on my knees beneath the cedar's overhanging branches, brought my bow to full draw. Toke's man was staring at the tangle of branches around the fallen ash, but he must have seen my movement from the corner of his eye. He wheeled his horse, turning toward me. I saw, down the front of Rolf's jerkin, a dark stain where his life had bled out from the wound in his throat. Toke's man started to raise his bow. Before he could bring it to bear, I shot.

It was a short distance and an easy target. When I first drew back my arrow, I intended to place it in the center of the man's chest, a killing shot. Seeing Rolf's blood changed my mind. Just before I released, I lowered my aim and let my arrow rip through his belly. He dropped his bow and screamed with pain, clutching at the feathered shaft that had suddenly sprouted from his body.

"That was for you, Rolf," I whispered, "and for all the fish you'll never catch."

The man's horse bolted, but somehow he stayed on it, hunched over and still screaming, as it dashed off through the forest.

Tord, on the far side of the great oak, called out, "Alf, Alf! What happened?"

I fitted another arrow to my bow, expecting Einar and Tord to circle and attack. To my surprise, Einar sat motionless on his horse atop the hill. I noticed that his bow was still slung across his back. He called to Tord. "It was an ambush," he said. "The bandit. He has fled now into the forest. Alf was wounded. His horse carried him that way." He pointed in the direction the horse had run. "Quickly, you must catch him. He is badly hurt."

I heard the hoofbeats of Tord's horse fading as he pursued the man I'd shot. Einar still sat motionless on his horse, watching me. I replaced my arrow in my quiver and trotted into the woods.

11

EINAR

I knew the man I'd shot was gravely wounded, and would probably die, but a wound through the belly would not kill him quickly. His death would be lingering and painful. I was glad of it. I wanted Toke and his men to suffer for their crimes.

Unless his fellows sped his passage, the wounded man's dying would delay them. I could have used the time to gain distance from my pursuers. I didn't. Einar's actions at the ambush had aroused my curiosity. His actions could have been due to cowardice, but I did not believe so. From what I'd seen of him, he seemed a dependable, competent man, and I knew Hrodgar had respected him enough to entrust the hunt for Harald's killer to him. It was unlikely that such a man was a coward.

Though the party that hunted me still outnumbered me two to one, I suspected only one of those men was now my enemy. If that was true, there was no need to continue my flight. It was time to end this hunt and kill Toke's other man.

As the sun began to drop toward the horizon in the late afternoon, filling the forest with long shadows, I crept back through the woods to the scene of my ambush.

Watching from a distance, I could see that all three horses were tethered at the top of the hill. Einar was down by the hill's base, cutting limbs from the fallen tree with an axe. After a time I saw Toke's man, the one called Tord, on the top of the hill. He was crouched beside the tall stump of the great ash. Periodically he would raise his head up above the brush that covered the hilltop and scan the hillside and woods below, searching for me. He searched in vain. I was the hunter now, stalking my prey. I moved through the forest as invisible and silent as a wolf.

All afternoon I watched Einar cut branches and drag them to the top of the hill. Once night fell, they kept a large fire blazing. The sight of it made me smile. The fire's bright light might comfort Tord, and bolster his courage, but it would illuminate him for my bow, too.

✦ ✦ ✦

When the hour was long past midnight, the time when the darkness seems blackest and sleep tugs at a man's eyelids, I began creeping up the hill toward the fire, slithering along the ground on my belly like some great serpent. I'd left my cloak, the leather bag of food, and my quiver hidden beside a tree at the base of the hill. I carried my bow and four arrows in one hand, and my dagger and small axe were at my belt. It was time to finish it.

Tord had positioned himself with his back against the stump. He'd built a brush barricade close around himself with some of the branches Einar had dragged to the hilltop. He'd arranged the saddles and gear from the three horses, plus his own shield and that of the wounded man, across the front of the low, brush wall to provide additional protection. Only his head, protected by a steel helm, showed occasionally above the wall of his little fortress when he'd raise up and look around. It would be enough. Once I got close enough, I would pin that head to the stump with one of my arrows.

The man I'd shot lay in front of Tord's barricade, covered by a cloak, near the fire. Mostly he moaned quietly, but at intervals he let out piercing shrieks. Einar was sitting on his shield at the opposite side of the fire from Tord's fortress.

As I neared the hilltop, the wounded man screamed again.

"I wish he would shut up," Tord snapped. "Why can't he go ahead and die? Why don't you end his misery for him?"

"He's your comrade," Einar replied. "He is your responsibility. You kill him, if that's what you want."

Tord raised his bow. "Kill him now. Kill him now . . . or I'll shoot you."

Einar gave a harsh chuckle and spit on the ground. "Without me, alone in this forest," he said, "how far do you think you'd get on your own?"

"The old military road cannot be far from here," Tord retorted. "When I find it, I can head south. I'll be safe then . . ." But he lowered his bow and said nothing more.

Einar was whittling at a piece of wood with his knife. After a time, he stood up and stuck the knife in its scabbard at his belt.

"I need to add wood to the fire," he said. He walked to Tord's barricade and pulled a branch from it, thick as a man's wrist and as long as an arm. He started to turn back to the fire. Then, without warning, he swung the limb hard and fast into the side of Tord's head. Tord's helm clanged and flew off his head as he slumped sideways onto the ground.

Working quickly, Einar knelt and fumbled at one of the saddles, then stood up holding a coil of rope. He pulled and kicked the brush barricade aside, knelt beside Tord's unconscious form, and tied one end of the rope to Tord's right wrist.

Still carrying the loose end of the rope, Einar stood, walked around the stump, and grabbed Tord's other wrist. He pulled hard on the wrist and the rope, dragging Tord up to a sitting position, his back against the stump, and wrenched his arms backward so they stretched behind him. Einar looped the rope around Tord's other wrist, then pulled it tight across the back side of the tree trunk and knotted it there.

Einar walked around the fire collecting all of the weapons, both his own and those of Toke's men, and placed them in a heap on one side of the fire. Walking to the opposite side of the fire, across from the weapons, he turned toward the darkness, raised both hands to show they were empty, and called out, "Come out now, that we may speak. It is as you said to Kar. There is no fight between you and me."

I pondered his words and actions, searching for a trap or sign of deception. Finding none, I stood up and walked forward into the light. As I did, though, I slipped my small axe from my belt and carried it ready in my hand.

"Gods," Einar said, when I rose from the ground. "I could feel your presence, like one feels wolves in the forest at night, circling beyond the reach of the fire's light. But I did not know you were so close. I've been curious to see the one Kar described as a beardless lad."

He stared long at my face, as though he could read it like he read tracks on the ground. I stared back, still looking for signs of trickery. It was Einar who broke the silence.

"Beardless you may be, but you're no lad—regardless of your youth. Only a man, and a rare one at that, deals death the way you do. I've seen it in your actions, and I can see it now in your eyes, as well. You're a rare killer, for certain."

Later, when I recalled Einar's words, they would trouble me. It had been only days since I'd first killed a man. In truth, I'd found it easy; far too easy. Killing another should be difficult, and should trouble your heart afterward. It had troubled me less than killing a deer or even a hare. Such beasts were innocent. The men I'd killed were not. But this man Einar, clearly a seasoned warrior, thought me unusual—a "rare killer." What kind of creature was I? What had I become? Did I truly possess some kind of horrible talent—a gift for slaying? Surely I did not. Surely Einar was wrong.

That night, as I stepped into the firelight and

faced Einar, no such thoughts burdened my mind.

"Why do you help me?" I asked him.

"You told Kar the line of Hrorik is not ended," Einar replied. "My name is Einar, whom men call Sharp-Eye. My past is tied to the line of Hrorik. I owe a blood-debt to Hrorik's line."

"What do you mean?" I asked, puzzled.

"Many, many years ago, when Hrorik was a young man," Einar said, "four shiploads of Gotars and Sveas sailed into the Limfjord. In the night, two ships landed at the farm of Offa, and two at the estate of another chieftain farther down the fjord. At the other estate, all of the men were killed, and the women and children stolen. At Offa's farm, though, Harald, the older brother of Hrorik and the namesake of Hrorik's son, walked the fields that night, unable to sleep. He saw the ships pulling into shore, oars muffled, and roused the household. With his father, brother, and their carls, he fought the raiders at the shore until the folk of the farm could flee into the safety of the forest.

"Because the numbers of the invaders were so great, once their families were safe, the fighting men of the household also retreated to the safety of the forest. All save Harald. Dodging the arrows of the invaders, he ran to the byre, took the swiftest horse, and rode to the village to warn the folk there."

I interrupted him impatiently. "I did not ask for a tale. I wanted an answer."

Einar was unperturbed by my words or my impatience. "Some answers cannot be found in a few words," he replied. "They cannot be understood without a full telling. Do not let your haste rob you of knowledge.

"As I was saying," he continued, "Harald rode to warn the village. It was well he did so. Ere long, all four ships of the raiders, their taste for blood and plunder whetted by their earlier attacks, appeared off our village and their warriors waded ashore. I was but a child at the time, seven years of age. All of the women, children, and thralls had fled to safety in the forest at Harald's warning. All but me. I was long on curiosity then, and short on good sense. I was beaten thoroughly for it the next morning, but I stayed, hidden on the rooftop of my father's house, and watched the battle.

"The men of our village arrayed themselves in a shield-wall across the road that runs through the center of our village. My father was among them, and Harald fought at his side. The Gotars and Sveas greatly outnumbered our men. The battle looked to go badly indeed, until Harald, my father, and Hrodgar, who was then a warrior in his prime, cut their way through the enemy's ranks to where their leader stood. He was a tall Svear with a long blond mustache hanging down onto his chest. Up till that point in the battle, he'd stood behind the enemy shield-wall, surrounded by his housecarls, bellowing encouragement to his men. Some leaders choose to lead the battle from the front, others to direct it from behind.

"My father reached him first. The warrior in front of the enemy leader died under Father's spear, trying to stop him. But while they fought, the big Svear lunged forward, swinging his sword with such might that it split my father's shield and cut into his shoulder, driving him to his knees. I thought then that I would see my father die before my eyes, but Hrodgar lunged forward and stabbed his spear with such force that it pierced the chieftain's brynie front and back, and the spear point stuck out between his shoulder blades. At the same time Harald swung his sword and struck a blow that nearly severed the Svear chieftain's head from his neck.

"Most of the Sveas, especially those who were fighting close to their chieftain, turned and ran for their ships when they saw their leader fall, but the Gotars were made of sterner stuff, and continued to press the fight hard against the men of our village. Harald stood astride my father, who lay wounded on the ground, and refused to retreat, though he took many wounds. Had he done otherwise, I would have grown up fatherless. That is the blood-debt I owe to the line of Hrorik. That is why I have done what you see here this night."

I studied Einar curiously. He did not know me—or even know who I was. Yet he'd attacked and disarmed Toke's man, laid down his own arms, and called on me to enter his camp, putting his own life in my hands. All this because a stranger had told Kar that Hrorik's line still lived, and because years ago Hrorik's brother had saved his father. He was either a man who greatly prized honor, or a great fool. I would not have done as he had. I had lived most of my life as a thrall, and thralls do not worry themselves about honor.

"How did the battle end?" I asked, wondering as I did if it was a mistake to encourage him to speak more.

"Back at Offa's estate," Einar continued, "after they made certain their families were safely hidden in the forest, Offa, Hrorik, and their men traveled at quick-march down the road toward our village. They arrived not long after the Svear chieftain was slain, and fell upon the rear of the enemy's lines. Then the warriors of the village, together with Offa and his men, made a great slaughter, crushing the Gotars between them. None were spared. Even those raiders who made it to their ships did not in the end escape. The Limfjord filled with ships bristling with armed men, hungry for revenge against the raiders. None of the enemy ships reached the sea."

"And Harald?"

"It was after Offa and his men had attacked. The remaining Sveas and Gotars were fleeing, and the battle on land was all but over. Harald was weak and weary from his many wounds, and let his shield hang low, for no enemy was near. An arrow flew back at our lines from among the routed invaders and struck him in the throat."

I said nothing, mulling the tale Einar had told me. Harald my brother, and Harald the brother of Hrorik, had both died young. I decided that if ever the day came that I had a son, though I loved my brother Harald dearly and would honor him, I would not risk giving his ill-fated name to another of our line.

"As I stated," Einar said, "I have been pondering the words you spoke to Kar, and told him to tell Hrodgar. 'The line of Hrorik is not ended,' you said. And I have been thinking of the events that have occurred since this hunt began. There is more for me to read here than just footprints on the floor of the forest. I think the rune you carved upon the head of the man you killed in your first ambush can only be for Harald, son of Hrorik, who died in the fight at the estate. I think you marked the dead man to show his death was a blood-debt.

"If you were the murderous bandit that Toke claimed, you would have killed Kar, too. Instead you spared him, but killed Toke's man as an act of vengeance for Harald. Who are you?"

I did not answer. Einar was not deterred. I began to suspect he must actually be known by his comrades as the Long-Winded, not Sharp-Eye, for again he began to speak.

"'The line of Hrorik is not ended,'" he repeated. "I was long confused by that, for all in the village know that Harald was Hrorik's only son. But then I remembered the Irish woman, the thrall, whom Hrorik was so taken with. You are her son, aren't you?"

He was a clever man in many ways. I nodded. "I am," I answered. "Harald was my brother, and I have sworn to avenge his murder. Halfdan is my name."

Einar's eyes traveled over me.

"Your clothes are soiled and bloodstained now," he said, "but clearly of fine make, and fit you well. They're not the clothes of a thrall."

I nodded again. "I was raised up by Hrorik before his death."

"Let us sit and rest our legs," Einar said. "I have food and drink, and you must be hungry. Feed yourself, and while you do, tell me of the attack on the farm and how you alone escaped. I know Toke's tale must have been a lie, and he was somehow involved. I would know what truly happened."

Einar's fare was simple—just salted pork, stale bread, hard cheese, and water—but after my sparse rations on my flight it was welcome. I wolfed down all he offered me. Between bites, I told him of the quarrel between Harald and Toke, and how Toke had repaid Harald's insults to him with the treacherous attack in the night.

"What happened beside the worksheds?" Einar asked, interrupting me. "I could tell a great spilling of blood occurred there."

I was speechless for a moment as in my mind I saw again the slaughter of the women and children I'd witnessed that night, lit by flickering torchlight.

"Harald mistakenly believed the attack was led by Ragnvald, a chieftain whose son he'd killed," I answered. "He negotiated for the women, children, and thralls to leave the longhouse in safety. The leader of the attackers—Toke, though we did not realize it at the time—gave Harald his oath granting them safe passage, but his word was false. The women, children, and thralls were all killed when they were beyond our protection."

"That was Niddingsvaark indeed," Einar said, a disgusted look on his face. "Toke is a man without honor."

319

"Afterward, they shot fire arrows and set the roof above our heads ablaze," I continued. "We tried to break out and escape to the woods, using the animals from the byre as cover, but there were too many of Toke's men and too few of us."

"How did you escape?" Einar asked.

"Harald had told me, before we made our final run, that if he ordered me to leave him and the others and flee, I must do it. He said I alone among us would be likely to escape if I reached the forest, and someone must survive to avenge all who fell. When Toke's men swarmed upon us in the final attack Harald cut a way clear for me to escape. In the final moments of the fight, only Harald and Ulf were left, fighting back to back, and Harald killed many of Toke's warriors before they fell."

Einar stiffened as I spoke my last sentence. "What was the name you spoke?" he asked. "The name of the warrior who fell at Harald's side?"

"Ulf," I replied.

"Describe him for me," Einar demanded. When I did, he put his face in his hands, for a moment. When he removed his hands, I saw he was weeping. "He was my kinsman," he said. "My sister's son. I loved him greatly. He left the village eight years ago after his wife died, to join Hrorik's household. I have raised his son."

320

By now Tord was fully awake and listening to us. I drew my dagger and pointed it at him.

"I have sworn to kill every man who took part in the attack," I said to Einar. "It is my intention to kill this man and the wounded man, too, but you have suffered a loss also. You can kill them if you wish, to avenge Ulf."

"Do not be so hasty," Einar said. "These men possess something you need."

I frowned. "Only their lives," I answered.

"Do you know the names of every man in Toke's crew?" Einar asked.

I shook my head. Einar walked over to where he'd been sitting when I'd first crept close to the hilltop, and picked up two sticks that were lying on the ground. Each was twice as long as a hand, and as big around as two fingers together. Both were stripped clean of bark, and whittled flat to make four sides. There were runes carved on each of the sticks.

"Ship's crews change," Einar said. "Men join, men leave. A crew like Toke's, which has taken heavy losses, will add many new men to its crew. How will you know who to kill?"

It was a problem I hadn't thought of.

"I've listened much to the talk of Toke's men while we've been on this hunt," Einar continued, "and it is my practice to remember what I've heard. His men spoke carelessly of having more than forty men in their crew when the *Sea Steed* left England. Yet when I was with Hrodgar when we met Toke there at the farm, the crew we saw could not have numbered even thirty. More than ten men, perhaps close to twenty, must have died in the battle that took Harald's life. Many of the *Sea Steed*'s crew have already paid the price for their and Toke's treachery. It is those who remain of his crew, including these who hunted you, whom you must kill to complete your vengeance. It is certain that Toke will recruit more men to fill out his crew, but they will be innocent of the murders you seek to avenge."

When I'd sworn to kill all who'd slain Harald and the others, I hadn't thought through the consequences of my oath. Einar was right. Toke was certain to recruit more men to fill his crew. And some of those now serving with him, who had participated in the murders, might leave. How was I to identify those I'd sworn to kill? How was I to track them all down? It could take a long time to fulfill my oath. A long time, and a lot of killing.

Einar continued. "Tonight, while Tord sat awake, afraid to sleep, I drew him into conversation about his fellows. Who is the strongest on your ship? Who can drink the most ale? That sort of thing. As we talked, I was carving on these

322

sticks. I told him I was just whittling to pass the time and stay alert, but the truth was I was carving the runes for the names he told me. At the time, I thought to give these to Hrodgar. It would be on him, I believed, to bring a charge against Toke at the Thing if the truth could be uncovered. Now perhaps it will be you who does so. I have fifteen names so far. I figure we have close to fifteen others to learn, or somewhat less, since by the morrow's sunrise three will not have survived this hunt."

We both turned and looked at Tord, who'd been listening intently.

"I will tell you nothing," Tord spat. He thought for a moment, then added, "Unless you agree to let me go."

Einar walked over and squatted beside Tord. He pointed back at me.

"My new comrade here tends to be a hasty man," he said, "but I am not. Here is the only bargain I'll offer you: If you tell me what I need to know, I will kill you quickly and painlessly. If you do not, I'll slice your belly open—carefully, just deep enough to cut through the skin and muscle— and I'll pull your guts out into your lap. And if that is not enough to loosen your tongue, I'll build a fire upon them and cook your entrails while you watch. Is this how you wish to die? Think carefully. . . . No one but us will know if you tell us the names of your comrades, and you will save yourself much pain."

I wondered if Einar would carry through with his threat. It was a very creative torture he'd planned. And he thought I was a rare killer? I told myself I would never have thought of such a thing, and felt better for it.

Tord cursed Einar and refused to talk. Einar knelt before him and began cutting his tunic off. Once he'd exposed the skin of Tord's belly, he placed his knife's edge against it and began to press it into the skin.

I never found out if Einar would have carried his threat through to its gruesome end. Before his skin split open under the knife, Tord reconsidered and told us the names of all of Toke's crewmen. Einar carved the runes to name each man in Toke's crew who still lived into the wood of the tally sticks with his knife. Then he used his knife to cut Tord's and Alf's throats.

"For you, Ulf," he said, as he spilled their blood.

Einar handed me the two sticks he'd carved. "You should keep these," he said. "It's you who've sworn the oath."

I looked at the two sticks, carved with strange figures. It was good, I supposed, to have a record of the names of the guilty. There was a problem, though. I could not read runes. My mother had taught me to read and write the Latin tongue. But she herself had never learned to write the language of the north, and no one else had taught the runes to me. Reading and writing were not skills a thrall needed. It was a problem I'd deal with later. I stowed the two sticks in my quiver.

"What is your plan now?" Einar asked.

I realized I had not thought beyond merely surviving the pursuit, beyond escaping my hunters and finding a chance to turn on them. I hadn't thought how I might find Toke and kill him and his men. Now that I did think about it, I felt daunted. Killing three men in the forest had been difficult enough. Killing a chieftain and his entire crew seemed impossible.

"I do not have a plan," I answered truthfully.

"Let me offer you advice," Einar said. "It is one thing to take vengeance against carls by killing them from ambush. But Toke is a chieftain and the grandson of a great jarl. He's considered by many to be a great man in his own right.

"Toke is a great man who has committed a great wrong. To truly achieve vengeance, you must do more than just kill him. You must destroy his name and blacken his memory, for those are what live on after a man is dead. You must destroy his honor by making all see him for what he truly is—

not a chieftain, not a great man, but a Nithing, an oath-breaking murderer, a treacherous slayer of his own foster brother."

"Only by a suit brought against him in a Thing can Toke be declared a Nithing," I protested. Even *I* knew that from hearing tales told during the long winter nights. "How can I ever hope to win such a case? On my oath alone? Not long ago I was just a thrall, whereas Toke is, as you yourself have pointed out, a chieftain. And his crew will surely give their oaths and testimony to support his. They'll not admit their own crimes."

"You must take time to win your revenge," Einar explained. "Beware of being hasty. It is a weakness I see in you that you must guard against. Ale drunk before the brewing's finished is weak and sour. So, too, your vengeance will not be nearly as sweet, if you do not dishonor Toke to all men before you kill him. An arrow in the back from ambush is far too gentle an end for a villain like Toke."

Before I'd met Einar, merely spilling Toke's blood had seemed quite satisfactory. A part of me was wishing I'd never realized Einar might be an ally. Had I killed him in ignorance, the task that lay before me would seem much simpler.

"What do you propose?" I asked him.

"You must gain stature among honorable men,

and gain allies," Einar said. "You will need them to win a case at a Thing. Already you have found one ally in me. If need be, I can testify that I heard Tord confess the attack and murders before he died. The vengeance you seek is an important one. It must be properly done. Toke is still a young man himself. He will give you time."

I wanted Toke's life. I wanted to see his blood stain the ground, as Harald's had. I was not at all sure that killing his honor, too, was worth the trouble.

Einar had told me what I must accomplish, but he'd not revealed how. He was not an easy man to pull a straight answer from.

"What are you proposing?" I asked again. "How shall I win stature and gain these powerful allies? I am but fifteen years of age. Most of my life I was a thrall. I've lost my family. I have nothing, and am nobody."

"Go south to Hedeby," Einar replied. "You'll find longships there, loading provisions and looking to round out their crews. The summer raiding season is almost upon us. Join a ship's crew and go i-viking. Though young, you're bold and true, and have already killed more men than many who are years older than you. Become a respected warrior. Gain a high-ranking chieftain as your ally if you can. Above all, develop patience. When the time for your vengeance is ripe, you will know it. The Gods will give you a chance to bring justice to Toke. The Gods hate a Nithing as much as all men of honor do."

Though my heart protested, in my mind I knew Einar's counsel was wise. It was ironic. I'd often dreamed, as a thrall, of crossing the seas as a Viking raider. I'd dreamed of it as a path to adventure and glory. Now, it seemed, it was to be my path to vengeance. I wondered how long a journey it would be.

12

THE ROAD
TO THE SEA

The next morning, I began my preparations to travel south to Hedeby. Einar, ever loquacious, admonished me with many suggestions and warnings. "A traveler cannot carry better gear than good sense and caution," he told me. I thought that advice seemed obvious and not worth the breath it took to speak it. But Einar, I was learning, greatly enjoyed the sound of his own voice. He also urged me to more fully equip myself from the gear of the two dead men, Tord and Alf. That, I thought, was a sound suggestion.

Tord's helm was simple—a conical construction with a heavy nasal bar of flattened iron hanging down the center in front to protect the face. But examining it closely, I could see that all the welds and rivets had been skillfully done, and I was able to adjust the leather suspension system inside so it fit my head well. His woolen cloak was long and heavy, similar to mine in size, though not as nicely made. I took it, too, for extra warmth on cold or rainy nights, and to wrap my belongings in.

The only other armor possessed by either man was the metal-studded leather jerkin Alf had worn, which before had belonged to Rolf. Though it did not turn weapons aside as well as a mail brynie, it provided more protection than no armor at all, and it was well made. Other than bloodstains, it was in good condition. Despite the deaths of its two previous owners, it had only one small cut in it, in the front where my arrow had entered.

Alf's shield was unusual. It was almost a hand's span smaller than most, and where most shields are made of a single layer of planks of linden wood, riveted together at the rim and center boss, his was made of thin slats of oak in two layers, laid crosswise to each other and riveted. As an archer, I would frequently have to carry my shield slung, even in battle. The smaller size would be more comfortable when it hung across my back, though it would give less protection in a fight. The idea of combining the toughness of oak with alternating layers of thin slats, their grain running across each other, I liked greatly. Such a shield should be difficult to split or pierce.

Only Alf had possessed a sword. I thought it balanced poorly and didn't take it. For now, I would rely on my dagger and the small axe I'd taken from the villager Kar. I took Alf's quiver and stuffed it with all of the arrows both men had possessed. If I was to offer my services as an archer to a chieftain going raiding or to war, I would need many arrows. Two quivers full did not seem too many.

Between the two dead men, they'd been carrying twenty-three small English silver coins. I tried to share the silver with Einar, but he insisted I would need it more than he. I gave him three coins, though, to take to Hrodgar.

"Tell him I regret I had to kill his hounds," I said, "but I had no choice. I know a man can become greatly attached to hounds. My father Hrorik was to his. Silver will not compensate for the loss I've caused, but I offer it to show Hrodgar my regret."

Einar grinned at my words. "Why do you smile?" I asked.

"Hrodgar sent his hounds to hunt a murderer and bandit. It's a rare bandit indeed who asks pardon and pays recompense for killing the hounds that hunt him."

❖ ❖ ❖

I spent a chilly day wrapped in naught but the extra cloak I'd taken from Tord's gear, washing my clothing in the stream. I weighted them with rocks to hold them underwater and let them soak all morning, then scrubbed them with sand. While they dried, spread out on boulders in the sun, I stitched the rips and tears, using a coarse needle I whittled from a twig and thread I unraveled from the dead men's clothes. My tunic, trousers, and cloak would never again resemble the fine garments Sigrid had made for me, but many of the stains of soil and blood washed out, and those that remained were reduced to faded shadows on the cloth. At least now I no longer looked as though I'd spent several days slaughtering pigs.

Einar left me to return to his village at midday. Before he departed, he draped the bodies of Toke's two dead warriors over the back of one of the horses and told me he would take them into the forest, and leave them there. "You're not planning to leave here until tomorrow morn," he said, "after your clothes have dried and you've rested. It is best not to sleep with the bodies nearby. It is certain they'll attract wolves, and it may be that the spirits of these dead men will linger near their bodies in the night, angry at their deaths, for the spirits of these men will not be welcome among the heroes and Gods in Valhalla."

I wondered if Einar was right about the dead men's spirits. Would they wander the earth forever as draugr, restless dead, or would they find their way to Hel and spend the afterlife in the realm of the dead? Harald had told me that when an evil man died, often his spirit was doomed to wander the earth, trapped near where his bones lie. The sudden chill you sometimes feel for no reason when traveling through a forest, or along a road, was the breath of the invisible, watching dead, he'd said.

Einar walked with me to the top of the hill and pointed to the line visible in the distant treetops that I'd noticed the day before. "That marks the great road, which many call the old military road," he said. "It's ancient and runs the length of Jutland, from the Limfjord in the north down to the Danevirke, the great earthen wall in the south that King Godfred built across the southern border of the kingdom of the Danes many years ago, when the Franks threatened to invade our land. My father, who at the time was a young man not yet married, and his father both responded to the summons of the king and helped build the great wall.

"The old military road has been there since before the memory of any living man. It will take you to Hedeby, which is on the Sliefjord, on the east coast of Jutland down by the Danevirke. The journey from Limfjord to Hedeby can be made in five days at a hard ride. From here, at an easy pace, it should take you no more than seven, or at most eight."

Einar mounted his own horse, and took the reins of the horse that bore the bodies. The third horse, a brown mare, I would keep, that my long journey south would be eased.

"Safe journey," I said to him.

"And to you," he replied. "Be wary of all you meet, for you have undertaken a dangerous task and know not who may be your ally or your enemy as you pursue it." He smiled. "And take special care as you travel in these parts, for I've heard rumor that a dangerous bandit is abroad."

I traveled south at a leisurely pace, set in part by the pain that developed in my seat and back from spending long hours astride a horse. Though I knew the rudiments of riding, my actual time on horseback had until now been very limited, and I found it soon became an uncomfortable experience. Many hours the mare and I both walked, me leading her by the reins instead of riding.

By the third day, my aching legs and back tempted me to abandon her altogether, but I knew that at journey's end I could trade the mare for provisions or silver, so I did not.

Several times along the journey, in the early morning or late afternoon, my progress was further delayed while I paused to hunt, for I thought it wise to save my small supply of salted, dried meat for a time when haste was critical and taste was not.

It was a haunted trip. Now that my mind was not filled with concerns for survival, my thoughts by day and my dreams by night were constantly visited by memories of Ulf, Rolf, Aidan, and the others who'd died, and especially of Harald. Harald came to me often in the night, as I slept. His face was pale and his eyes were sad, but he never spoke. How I longed to hear his voice and his laughter again. Whenever I called out to him, though, he disappeared. Whenever my own voice calling Harald's name awakened me in the night after a dream-world visit from him, I wept—for the dead and for myself. Never in my life had I felt so alone as I did on that journey south.

There came a morning when, as I prepared to mount my horse and embark upon the day's journey, I was struck by the realization that the sun's position as it rose above the trees looked the same as it had at Hrorik's estate, in the same hour of the morn. I was overcome with a longing to ride east, to find our fjord and see Sigrid and Ubbe again, even all of the other carls and thralls who lived on the estate. Though there were few I knew truly well, and fewer still I counted as comrades, they were at least familiar, for I'd known them all since childhood. I mounted my horse and turned her away from the road, toward the coast and the rising sun.

We traveled through the forest but a few paces when I pulled up against the reins and stopped. Ahead of me, somewhere to the east, lay the world I'd grown up in; the world where I'd been transformed from thrall to free, and from a boy to a man. It was the world where my sister Sigrid still lived, the only family that remained to me; the only person still alive who loved me, and whom I loved. Behind me lay the road that led south to Hedeby and a new and unknown life.

I knew I could not go east. I could not return to my home. In my mind, I saw again the night of the attack and heard Toke's voice shouting, "Kill them all! There can be no witnesses." The morning after the attack, I'd heard Toke tell the men he'd sent to hunt me that he would meet them at the estate. If he was not already there, he would be soon.

Even if I somehow managed to meet secretly with Sigrid and Ubbe, I would place their lives in danger merely by giving them knowledge of Toke's treachery, and by letting them know I still lived. They could not possess such knowledge and act unchanged around Toke. Toke was a villain, but he was no fool.

By killing his own brother and murdering the women and children after giving his oath that they'd be safe, Toke had committed terrible crimes. For now, as far as he was aware, only his own men knew the truth, and their own guilt ensured their silence. If Toke ever suspected that Sigrid or Ubbe had discovered what he'd done, I feared he'd have them killed, too. Reluctantly, I turned the mare back to the road, and spurred her toward the unknown.

During the last days of my journey south, the road passed in and out of forested lands. For long stretches it crossed open heaths, and twice in the distance I saw great mounds, the tombs of ancient kings. Toward the evening of the seventh day, the road reentered woodlands, though these were far more open than the wild, trackless forests I'd traversed farther north. Often I saw stumps where trees and brush had been cut, and many side tracks ran into the woods off of the main road.

On the final day, the road turned and headed due east. At times I glimpsed to the south a low ridge which I knew must be the Danevirke—the great earthen wall that marked the southern boundary of the lands of the Danes.

I rounded a bend in the road and found myself at the edge of the woods. The land fell gently away below me to the shore of a great fjord, shimmering in the afternoon sun. At the water's edge was a walled town.

I was unprepared for the size of Hedeby. I'd expected it to be larger than anything I'd seen, for even I knew it was the largest town in all of Denmark. But that foreknowledge left me unprepared for what I saw when the town first came into view.

Hedeby was located on a shallow inlet off the southern side of the Schleifjord, a long, narrow fjord that cut deep into the land on the east coast of Jutland. A wide ditch had been dug in a great half circle from shore to shore around the entire town. Inside the ditch, the town was defended by an earthen wall topped with a wooden palisade. Outside the wall, the land was open and there were pastures where scattered sheep and cattle grazed, interspersed with fields that were still bare due to the earliness of the season. Anchored at a breakwater just offshore from the town were four longships and several smaller boats. A fifth longship was approaching up the fjord, its sail furled and its oars churning the water.

From the point where I sat astride my horse, where the roadway exited the forest and led down into the town, I could see, visible over the top of the wall, more rooftops than I'd ever imagined existed in one place. The roofs seemed jammed together, as if the buildings there had been built so close they must be almost touching each other. I could not understand how so many people could live so close together. How could so many be fed? Could the land here provide honest work for so many? How was there enough air for all to breathe?

I'd arrived in the late afternoon, just before the change of tide. For a brief period there was no breeze blowing off the water. Trails of smoke rose into the sky above many of the roofs, forming a sooty, gray cloud that hovered like the threat of a storm. It struck me as a fearful thing that so many men living together in one place possessed the ability to create such a cloud, soiling the sky itself. I wondered if it was an omen, a sign to warn me that this way lay darkness and doom.

I had fought shoulder to shoulder with Harald and his men against attackers in the night. In my flight through the forest, I had not lost myself to fear, but had managed to outwit my pursuers and defeat them. But the sight of Hedeby unmanned me now. What was I doing here? I was no warrior. I did not belong in a place like this, filled with wily town folk, and men who lived the Viking life.

They'd all see me for what I was: a lost boy, without a home.

I lost my nerve then and turned my horse to ride back into the woods. There, at least, I felt at home. The forest held no unknown terrors for me. There I knew I could provide food and shelter for myself. I could make my home in the forest. It would be a spare and lonely life for certain, but one I knew I could master.

The harsh cawing of a bird startled me from my thoughts. I looked up and saw a raven perched above me in a tree just off the road. It cocked its head and stared at me with one gleaming, black eye, then cawed again. Its cry sounded like hard, mocking laughter. It shamed me.

My mother had died because she'd believed in me. She'd seen the promise of the man I might become and had given her own life to bring that promise into being. Harald, too, had died believing in me. He'd trusted that I could, and would, avenge him and the others Toke had murdered. Harald had died believing in my skills as a warrior and in my honor as a man. What right had I to doubt my mother and Harald now, and betray their trust?

I had sworn an oath to Odin to avenge my brother, Harald. Was I so weak that I would abandon it now? Was my heart so empty of courage that

I would let my mother and Harald die in vain? Ravens were Odin's messengers. If I abandoned my quest and dishonored my oath, the God would know.

A breeze sprang up, marking the change of the tide. It caught the smoke above the town and blew it away.

I turned my horse back toward the town. I did not know what I would find in Hedeby, and beyond. I knew, though, that that way lay my destiny, the fate the Norns were weaving for me. I kicked the mare into a trot and rode on to greet it.

LIST OF CHARACTERS

Aidan
The abbot of an Irish monastery who was captured by the Danish chieftain Hrorik, became a thrall, and later became foreman on one of Hrorik's estates.

Alf
A member of Toke's crew who hunts Halfdan.

Ase
The wife of Ubbe and a priestess of the goddesses Freyja and Frigg.

Caidoc
An Irish king under the High King of Ulster, and the father of Derdriu.

Cummian
The young son of Aidan and Tove.

Derdriu
Daughter of King Caidoc captured by the chieftain Hrorik in a raid on Ireland, who became Hrorik's concubine and the mother of Halfdan.

Einar
A skilled tracker from the village on the Limfjord in northern Denmark where Hrodgar is the headman.

Eanwulf	The ealdorman, or king's representative, who governs Somersetshire in the West Saxon Kingdom in England.
Fasti	A thrall, or slave, on Hrorik's southern estate.
Fret	A carl, or free man, who lives on Hrorik's estate on the Limfjord in northern Denmark.
Frial	An Irish king.
Gudrod	A carl skilled in carpentry who lives on Hrorik's southern estate.
Gunhild	The current wife of the Danish chieftain Hrorik, and the mother of Toke by a previous marriage.
Gunnar	A carl and blacksmith who lives on Hrorik's southern estate.
Halfdan	The son of Hrorik, a Danish chieftain, and Derdriu, an Irish noblewoman who became Hrorik's slave.
Harald	The son of the Danish chieftain Hrorik by his first wife Helge, and Sigrid's twin brother.
Helge	Hrorik's first wife, now deceased, who was the mother of Harald and Sigrid.
Horik	The King of the Danes during the ninth century from A.D. 813 to 854.
Hrodgar	The headman of the village on the Limfjord in northern Denmark near Hrorik's northern estate.
Hrorik	A Danish chieftain, and the father of Halfdan, Harald, and Sigrid.
Hrut	A thrall, or slave, on Hrorik's southern estate.

Ing	A thrall, or slave, on Hrorik's southern estate.
Kar	A skilled archer from the village on the Limfjord in northern Denmark where Hrodgar is the headman.
Kilian	The oldest son of King Frial of Ireland, and Derdriu's betrothed.
Odd	A carl in Hrorik's household, and one of Harald's men.
Osric	The ealdorman, or king's representative, who governs Dorsetshire in the West Saxon Kingdom in England.
Rolf	A carl in Hrorik's household, and one of Harald's men.
Sigrid	The daughter of the Danish chieftain Hrorik by his first wife Helge, and Harald's twin sister.
Snorre	The helmsman and second-in-command on Toke's ship, the *Sea Steed*.
Toke	Gunhild's son by her first marriage, and Hrorik's stepson.
Tord	A member of Toke's crew who hunts Halfdan.
Tove	The wife of Aidan, the foreman on Hrorik's northern estate.
Ubbe	The foreman of Hrorik's southern estate in central Denmark.
Ulf	A carl in Hrorik's household, and one of Harald's men.

GLOSSARY

berserks: Warriors in Scandinavian society who were noted for their exceptional fierceness and fearlessness in battle, and for their moody, difficult dispositions in periods of peace. Ancient Scandinavian sagas sometimes describe berserks as possessing the supernatural ability to take on the forms of bears or wolves or assume their powers in battle. Some modern scholars have suggested that the barely controllable warriors known as berserks may have suffered from mental illness, possibly manic depression or schizophrenia.

Birka: A coastal town in Sweden that served as one of the main Viking-age trading centers. Birka formed the northern end of a long trade route running down several rivers through the lands of modern Russia, eventually reaching the Black Sea. Using the Eastern Road, as the route was called, the Vikings traded with the Byzantine Empire and with the Moorish kingdoms of the Middle East that lay beyond.

broadaxe: An axe whose broad, heavy blade is ground flat on one side. A broadaxe—a tool, not a weapon like the much lighter Danish great-axe— was used to square and smooth timbers.

brynie: A shirt of mail armor.

byre: A barn or animal shed.

carl: A free man in Scandinavian society.

chape: The tip of a sword scabbard, frequently made of metal and, among the Vikings, often highly decorated, designed to protect the scabbard from abrasion and wear.

Danevirke: A great earthen wall built across the base of the Jutland peninsula of Denmark, from coast to coast, to protect the Danish lands from invasion by the Franks.

Dorestad: A Frankish port and trading center located near the convergence of the Rhine and Lek Rivers, in the area now forming part of the Netherlands. Dorestad was one of the largest trade centers of early medieval Europe.

draugr: Walking dead; a dead person who was not at rest and roamed in the night.

Freyja: The Scandinavian Goddess of love, fertility, and healing.

Freyr: The Scandinavian God of fertility.

Frigg: The Scandinavian goddess of marriage and the hearth; the wife of the chieftain of the Gods, Odin.

Hedeby: The largest town in ninth-century Denmark, and a major Viking-age trading center. Hedeby was located at the base of the Jutland peninsula, on the eastern side, on a fjord jutting inland from the coast.

housecarl: A warrior in the service of a nobleman.

hnefatafl: A popular Viking board game, the name of which roughly translates as "King's Table." The game was played on a board divided into regular squares, somewhat like a chess board. One player set his pieces up in the center of the board and attempted to move his king to the board's outer rim. The other player started with his pieces surrounding the "king's" pieces, and attempted to capture the king before it could escape.

i-viking: To go raiding.

jarl: A very high-ranking chieftain in Scandinavian society who ruled over a large area of land on behalf of the king.

Jutland: The peninsula that forms the mainland of modern and ancient Denmark, named after the Jutes, one of the ancient Danish tribes.

Limfjord: A huge, protected fjord that runs completely across the northern tip of the Jutland peninsula, providing a protected passage between the Baltic and North Seas.

longship: The long, narrow ship used for war by the peoples of Viking-age Scandinavia. Longships had shallow drafts, allowing them to be beached or to travel up rivers, and were designed to be propelled swiftly by either sail or rowing. They were sometimes also called dragonships, because many longships had carved heads of dragons decorating the stempost of the bow.

Niddingsvaark: Work of infamy; the dishonorable acts of a Nithing.

Nithing: One who was not considered a person because he has no honor.

Norns: Three ancient sisters who, the pagan Scandinavians believed, sat together at the base of the world-tree and wove the fates of all men on their looms.

Norse: The Scandinavians who lived in the area of modern Norway. During the mid-ninth century, large portions of the Norse lands were at least nominally ruled by the Danish king. Non-Scandinavians sometimes used the term Norsemen, or Northmen, to describe any Viking raiders from the Scandinavian lands.

Odin: The Scandinavian God of death, war, wisdom, vengeance, and poetry; the chieftain of the Gods.

runes: The alphabet used for writing in the ancient Scandinavian and Germanic languages.

seax: A large, single-edged knife, somewhat similar in appearance to an American Bowie knife, used as both a weapon and tool by the Vikings and Anglo-Saxons.

Schleifjord: A long fjord on the east coast of the Jutland peninsula, near its base, on which the town of Hedeby was located.

skald: A poet.

small axe: A hand weapon, similar in size to a hatchet or tomahawk.

stemposts: The timbers at either end of a longship forming the curved vertical extensions of the keel to which the planks of the ship's hull were attached

Svear: A member of the Sveas tribe.

Sveas: One of the Scandinavian tribes who inhabited the area of modern Sweden.

thegn: A minor noble in Anglo-Saxon society; the warrior class that formed the backbone of English armies during the Viking period.

Thing: An assembly held periodically in Scandinavian cultures where men would present suits to be decided by vote according to law. Things were the forerunner and origin of what became, centuries later in English culture, the concept of trial by jury.

Thor: The Scandinavian god of thunder and fertile harvests.

thrall: A slave in Scandinavian society.

Valhalla: The "Hall of the Slain," the great feast-hall of the God Odin, which was the home in the afterworld of brave warriors in Scandinavian mythology.

Valkyries: Warrior maidens who served the God Odin and carried fallen warriors to his feast-hall, Valhalla, where they spent their days fighting and their nights feasting.

wergild: The amount that must be paid to make recompense for killing a man.

White Christ: The Vikings' name for the Christian God, believed to be a derogatory term implying cowardice, because he allowed himself to be captured and killed without fighting back against his captors.

ACKNOWLEDGMENTS

Telling this tale has long been a dream and passion of mine. I would not have been able to, though, without the enthusiasm and support of my agent, Laura Rennert, and my editors, Susan Rich and Kristin Marang, for whose assistance I am very grateful.

HISTORICAL NOTES

Modern historians generally consider the Viking Age to have begun in the latter part of the eighth century A.D. and ended in the eleventh century, though those dates are somewhat arbitrary, and are tied to the modern perception that Viking-Age Scandinavians were primarily crude, barbarian pirates. Some historians, in fact, tie the beginning and end of the Viking Age to specific Viking raids: the small Viking attack on the English monastery of Lindisfarne in A.D. 793, and the failed invasion of England by Norwegian King Harald Hardrada, ended by his death at the battle of Stamford Bridge in A.D. 1066. That same year the Normans, descendants of Vikings who had settled in France in the area around the mouth of the Seine River, crossed

355

the English Channel and conquered England, bringing an end to the Anglo-Saxon rule of that island.

Viking-Age Scandinavians were not barbarians, though, and were far more than merely very organized and successful pirates. They were adventurers, explorers, and merchants, a people with a vibrant culture with its own highly developed artistic aesthetic, tradition of oral literature, and a strong code of ethics and honor. Though many today picture Vikings as typically clothed in crude, rough garments of fur, wealthy Vikings were far more likely to be clothed in fine garments of richly patterned wool, linen, or even silk from China. Vikings from Norway settled Iceland, discovered and settled Greenland, and even discovered the North American continent. Vikings founded the town of Dublin in Ireland, and turned the northern English town of York, which the Vikings called Jorvik, into one of the busiest trading centers of northern Europe. Swedish Vikings founded the early medieval kingdom of Russia, and created trade routes down its rivers that allowed them to trade regularly with the Eastern Roman Empire in Constantinople and the Arab kingdoms beyond. Much of England was conquered and settled by primarily Danish Vikings during the late ninth and early tenth centuries. Many aspects and concepts that now are considered "English" in origin, such as the idea of an individual's freedom as outweighing the rights of the state, or the right to trial by a jury of one's peers, were brought to England by the Vikings and became custom there in the heavily Viking-settled area known as the Danelaw. From the late ninth century through the mid-tenth century, a Viking kingdom existed in the north of England, and Danish kings ruled all of England from A.D. 1016 through 1042.

There is truth, of course, behind the popular image of Vikings as violent pirates who preyed upon the peoples of early medieval Europe. A truly dark side of the Viking culture is that they were heavily involved in the slave trade, for prisoners—particularly women and children—were often part of the plunder captured by the Vikings in their raids, for later return in exchange for ransom or for sale as slaves in other lands if ransom could not be paid.

This side of the Vikings must be viewed in the context of the times, though. Plundering the possessions of defeated enemies was a standard practice among all peoples long before and after the Viking Age. All of the cultures of Europe, and indeed most, if not all of the rest of the world, possessed and traded in slaves during this period. For example, the Frankish King Charles the Great, or

Charlemagne, generally considered to be a paragon of culture and Christianity during the early Middle Ages, waged a brutal thirty-year war against the Saxon peoples who lived on the European continent just to the south of Denmark so he could take their lands for his own people. Charlemagne's war against the Saxons, which almost amounted to a campaign of genocide, included such acts as the massacre of more than four thousand unarmed Saxon captives and the sale into slavery of thousands of the Saxon people, once they were militarily defeated. Compared with such acts by their contemporaries, the ravages of Vikings were merely typical of their time.

I have chosen to set the tale of Halfdan during the middle of the ninth century, before Christianity began to spread through the pagan north, and while most Viking raids were still the exploits of private adventurers, rather than ambitious Viking kings. Though I am sure I have made mistakes, I have tried to the best of my ability to create for the reader a vivid and accurate picture of the ninth-century Viking world. Though the character of Halfdan and his personal exploits are entirely works of fiction, some events described actually occurred. The battle in England which proved to be Hrorik's doom, for example, is based on an entry in the *Saxon Chronicle*, a running account of the history of early England recorded by generations of English monks, which reads, for the year 845:

> *This year ealdorman Eanwulf, with the men of Somersetshire, and Bishop Ealstan, and ealdorman Osric, with the men of Dorsetshire, fought at the mouth of the Parret [River] with the Danish army; and there, after making a great slaughter, obtained the victory.*

Additionally, in this first installment of Halfdan's tale, there are rumblings of a plan by the Danish King to strike at the Franks, while their three kings are fighting among themselves. During A.D. 845, the Danes did in fact launch a massive two-pronged attack on the Franks, one part of which was led by legendary Viking leader Ragnar Logbrod up the Seine River. But that is a tale to be told another day.

One final note about Halfdan and his bow. As I have described it, the bow used by Halfdan is similar to the powerful and deadly longbows which the English used to dominate warfare during the late Middle Ages. Though the origin of the English longbow is a matter of great speculation, it is a fact that a few Viking Age bows have been found in Scandinavia that precisely match in design and size the later English longbow. Several accounts exist in Viking sagas of exceptionally skilled archers who were highly valued for their ability to kill at long range, and several major battles during the Viking Age were decided when the king or leader of one of the armies was slain by a well-aimed arrow. Though Halfdan and his bow are works of fiction, such archers did exist during the Viking Age.

I have created a website, at

www.strongbowsaga.com

to provide my readers with additional historical background, including photos and other illustrations, about the real Viking world as it existed during the middle and late ninth century, when Halfdan's tale is set. I encourage those interested in learning more to visit.